KU-241-553

Working-class Stories of the 1890s

Edited with an introduction by

P. J. Keating

THE POLYTECHNIC OF WALES
LIBRARY
TREFOREST

Routledge & Kegan Paul
London

STORE
823.809355 820-32
WOR   "189"
          WOR

89886

First published 1971
by Routledge & Kegan Paul Ltd
Broadway House, 68–74 Carter Lane
London, EC4V 5EL
First published as a paperback 1975
Printed in Great Britain
by Cox & Wyman Ltd,
London, Reading and Fakenham.
Set in Monotype Plantin
© introduction and selection P. J. Keating 1971
No part of this book may be reproduced
in any form without permission from
the publisher, except for the quotation
of brief passages in criticism

ISBN 0 7100 6987 1 (c)
ISBN 0 7100 8257 6 (p)

(7.8.92)

Contents

Acknowledgments

The author and publishers wish to thank the following for permission to reprint extracts from the sources listed below:

The literary executors of Arthur Morrison for 'Introduction' and 'Lizerunt' from *Tales of Mean Streets*, by Arthur Morrison.

Mrs George Bambridge, Macmillan & Co. Ltd and Doubleday & Co. Inc. for 'The Record of Badalia Herodsfoot' by Rudyard Kipling, from *Many Inventions*.

The author and publishers have attempted to locate the owners of the copyright of certain material in this book.

Introduction

Reviewing Arthur Morrison's *A Child of the Jago*, H. G. Wells noted a new concern in English fiction: 'The son of the alcoholic proletarian, the apparently exhausted topic of Dr Barnardo, has suddenly replaced the woman with the past in the current novel ... It is indisputable that the rediscovery of Oliver Twist is upon us.'[1] Together with Morrison's novel Wells had in mind James Barrie's *Sentimental Tommy* and S. R. Crockett's *Cleg Kelly: Arab of the City*, all three of which were published in 1896; and beyond these specific works he was pointing out that not since the 1840s had there been such a widespread desire to write fiction centred upon working-class life. The young Dickens was a more natural point of comparison than Mrs Gaskell or Disraeli. Like Dickens the novelists of the nineties wrote primarily about London: their work dealt with the poor of a great metropolis rather than the industrial workers of northern manufacturing cities, with slums and streets rather than factories. The slum novelists were themselves aware of this affinity with Dickens, though while they usually expressed great admiration for his work, they also felt that one of their tasks was to bring him up to date. The ambiguous position this placed them in was well understood by George Gissing, one of Dickens's most enthusiastic late-Victorian admirers:

It is a thankless task to write of such a man as Dickens in disparaging phrase. I am impatient to reach that point of my essay where I shall be at liberty to speak with admiration unstinted, to dwell upon the strength of the master's work, and exalt him where he is unsurpassed. But it is necessary to clear the way. So great a change has come over the theory and practice of fiction in the England of our times that we must needs treat of Dickens as, in many respects, antiquated.[2]

The case against Dickens was that in order to preserve a close relationship with his readers he had glossed over painful subjects; smothering reality with humour and surrendering objectivity in favour of moral purpose. The genuineness of his sympathy for the poor and his genius as a humorist were never doubted. What made many late-Victorian writers uneasy about him was his apparent lack of artistic seriousness, especially on the question of realism, for, as Gissing goes on to point out: 'Novelists of today desire above everything to be recognized as sincere in their picturing of life.'[3] Jane Findlater, an admirer of Dickens but also an enthusiast for the slum literature of the nineties, combined the views of Wells and Gissing. 'Have you read *Oliver* lately?' she asked her readers, 'Or do you remember him distinctly enough to establish comparisons between him and his grandchildren of the "nineties"? Such comparisons are laughable enough. How the whole presentation of low life has been turned round about since the publication of *Oliver Twist*!'[4]

In this respect at least the slum novelists were reacting against Dickens, but it is misleading to assume automatically that they were therefore imitators of Zola's particular brand of French Naturalism. They imbibed the theory of artistic objectivity which was widespread in late-Victorian criticism, and they took advantage of the freer atmosphere of the nineties—largely pioneered by Zola—to treat more frankly than their mid-Victorian predecessors of swearing, sex and violence. But whereas the early novels of George Moore and the short stories of Hubert Crackanthorpe, fine as they are, even today retain a certain feeling of having been translated from French originals, the writers represented in this anthology remained essentially English. Moral purpose, though veiled, never disappears entirely; the finer qualities of human personality are not ruthlessly and inevitably destroyed by environment or heredity; and the personal feelings of the author, if not so obvious as in Dickens, are everywhere apparent.

If a French influence is discernible it is probable that it came indirectly from Rudyard Kipling whose short stories and ballads caused a sensation in the late eighties and early nineties. Earlier Victorian novelists had regarded working-class life as simply one part of a total social pattern, taking a cross section of English society and adopting as a behavioural norm either the middle- or upper-class characters of their novels, or a similar point of view imposed by themselves. This is true of Mrs Gaskell, Disraeli and Charles Kingsley, as well as of Dickens and the two most important novelists of working-class life writing in the eighties, Walter Besant and George Gissing. Kipling's approach was entirely different. By employing the short story and ballad rather than the full-length novel he succeeded in focusing attention completely on working-class life; and by dispensing with the traditional kind of class comparison he could allow his working-class characters (Ortheris, Mulvaney, Learoyd and Tommy Atkins) to establish their own pattern of behaviour. The reader is still aware of Kipling's own attitudes occasionally breaking through, but rarely does he step forward and pronounce judgment in the manner of earlier English novelists. As the involved narrator of his early stories, however, Kipling does sometimes comment upon his characters, as in this statement about Tommy Atkins, the archetypal private soldier: 'There is nobody to speak for Thomas except people who have theories to work off on him; and nobody understands Thomas except Thomas; and he does not always know what is the matter with himself.'[5] Kipling was determined to learn how to speak for the inarticulate working man (in both his military and civilian environments) without imposing upon him attitudes and values alien to his natural way of life, and this particular sense of purpose was shared by almost all of the writers represented in this anthology. This helps explain the absence of middle- and upper-class characters, the stark brutality of many of the violent scenes, the rejection of humour based on working-class ignorance or eccentricity, and the elaborate phonetics which were employed in an attempt to capture the actual sound of London working-class voices.

For the social background to these stories it is necessary to look to the upsurge of interest in the East End of London which began in the late seventies, reached a peak about ten years later and continued far into the twentieth century. It is impossible to determine an exact starting point for a movement so diverse in aims and so varied in expression, but 1875 is as reasonable a date as any. In this year Samuel Barnett, rector of St Jude's, Whitechapel, visited Oxford University and discussed with a group of lecturers and undergraduates his plan to establish a University Settlement in the East End. Barnett's principal concern was with the stultifying class uniformity of East End life. He aimed to introduce variety and guidance by creating an educational institution run by 'settlers' —university teachers and students who would go to live and work in the East End for varying lengths of time. They were not to be regarded, or to regard themselves, as philanthropists, but rather as enlightened cultural missionaries who were willing to 'learn as much as to teach, to receive as much as to give'.[6] Barnett's settlement, named Toynbee Hall after the Oxford economist Arnold Toynbee, was opened officially in 1884, the first of a large number of similar institutions.

Journalists, social reformers and imaginative writers were not far behind Barnett in drawing attention to the neglected East End. In 1882 a novel by Walter Besant, *All Sorts and Conditions of Men*, placed the settlement idea in a fairy-tale framework and became an immense popular success. The 'Palace of Delight' which Besant's wealthy slum visitors built to transform East End working-class life bore little resemblance to reality, but it did serve to establish in the public mind an image of the East End as somewhere bleak and monotonous, and it also helped raise the money for a real-life People's Palace which was built on the Mile End Road and opened by Queen Victoria in 1887. In 1883 two publications of a more serious nature than Besant's romance gave further publicity to the condition of the London poor: *The Bitter Cry of Outcast London* by Andrew Mearns and W. C. Preston, and George Sims's *How the Poor Live*. Finally in 1886 Charles Booth began work on his great survey *Life and Labour of the People in London* (17 vols., 1902–3), the first volume of which, *East London*, appeared in 1889.

It would be difficult to exaggerate the degree of interest in the East End shown by settlers, philanthropists, religious missionaries, journalists, salvationists and sociologists during the eighties. But writers of fiction did not show the same kind of interest until the social groundwork, as it were, had been prepared for them. This had been achieved by 1890, and in the same year, as we have seen, Kipling's stories and ballads began to be published in England.

The stories in this anthology need to be considered in relation to these two dominant influences.

(II)

The chronology of the pieces reprinted here has been slightly altered to allow Morrison's 'A Street' to act as an introduction. It was published originally as a separate sketch in October 1891, and later employed by Morrison to introduce his first collection of working-class stories, *Tales of Mean Streets* (1894). Kipling's 'Badalia Herodsfoot' preceded 'A Street' by almost a year, but this was the only one of his stories to deal specifically with the East End, and it was Morrison's interpretation rather than Kipling's which established the predominant tone of slum fiction in the nineties.

'Many and misty are people's notions of the East End,' Morrison writes, 'and each is commonly but the distorted shadow of a minor feature.' It was to correct this habit of treating 'minor features' of East End life as though they represented the norm that Morrison first wrote this sketch. While acknowledging the poverty and misery in the East End, he regards its most characteristic quality as being an oppressive, all-pervading, monotony; and the street he chooses as representative is inhabited by 'decent' respectable working-class families, far removed in every sense from Hyde Park agitators and charitable cases. By means of a series of graphic vignettes, all conveyed in a flat, terse style expressive of the monotony he is describing, Morrison succeeded in creating an interpretation of a working-class environment unlike anything earlier in Victorian fiction. He makes no real attempt to objectify his description (this is very much one man's view), and there is little reason for us to believe that the inhabitants of the street are themselves aware of 'its utter remoteness from delight', but such objections do not weaken the success and originality of Morrison's portrait. In this sketch he dispensed with the Victorian tradition of hysterically described slum environments peopled by the suffering poor, the debased and the jolly, and offered instead the ordinariness of working-class life.

Morrison is best remembered today for his portrayal of working-class violence in 'Lizerunt', *A Child of the Jago* and *The Hole in the Wall* (1920). It is, however, a mark of his considerable sociological good sense that in each of these works there is a special reason why violence should be treated so prominently. *Jago* describes life in a criminal ghetto and *The Hole in the Wall* a particularly violent period of East End history. 'Lizerunt' also needs to be related to the *Mean Streets* stories as a whole. Although Billy Chope, the debased hero, seems a rather unlikely inhabitant of 'A Street', he is always treated as an exception, and 'Lizerunt' was the only story in the collection of thirteen to feature such a person. Morrison accepted that violence was one part of working-class life (a minor, though important, feature), and was determined to portray it with the same honesty and frankness which are so characteristic of his studies of monotony and stultifying respectability.

'Lizerunt' clearly owes much to Kipling's 'Badalia Herodsfoot'. In both, the central situation is the rapid transition of a young working-class girl from a happy, carefree courtship (the 'days of fatness' in Kipling's words) to a degrading marriage which culminates in death for Badalia and enforced prostitution for Lizer. Both stories are also remarkable for the dispassionate tone of the narrators. Kipling is more successful in conveying the bustle and activity of working-class life that surrounds Badalia, and also provides an interesting, if rather jaundiced, insight into philanthropic work; but Badalia's death is sentimentalized, and the final note of pessimism—'the wail of the dying prostitute who could not die'—is hardly convincing. Morrison is more ruthless. Lizer's descent is presented as a three-act tragedy, moving swiftly from the Bank Holiday on Wanstead Flats when she is made to feel like Helen of Troy as two men fight over her, to the moment Billy Chope, the eventual victor of that particular skirmish, hurls her into the street.

Nevinson's volume of short stories *Neighbours of Ours* has always been overshadowed by Morrison's *Mean Streets*, published just a few weeks earlier. Nevinson felt that because of this unfortunate timing his book never received the publicity it deserved and this is as true today as it was in the nineties. But it is doubtful whether *Neighbours of Ours* could have achieved the huge popular success of Morrison's early work; it lacks the stark immediacy of the best *Mean Streets* stories and demands from the reader a more subtle degree of participation. As we have seen, Morrison tends to explore different aspects of working-class life in separate stories or novels which then need to be related to each other before a total picture can emerge. Nevinson reverses this technique. His successful use of a cockney narrator—who does not himself play a central role in the stories—serves to establish an inside view of working-class life, and as the narrator is describing what is natural to him, he is not in a position to classify or departmentalize. The environment is still largely monotonous and occasionally squalid, but these qualities are never transferred to the inhabitants who are simply allowed to get on with the business of living. This is one of the virtually unique characteristics of Nevinson's stories; another is that the love affairs with which they deal (one being inter-class, the other inter-race) are handled with a complete lack of condescension. They are rare in that while the events take place in a genuine working-class setting, the class of the protagonists is not the most important thing about them. It would be impossible to say this about any of the other stories reprinted here.

Edwin Pugh and Clarence Rook are more obviously present than Kipling, Morrison or Nevinson. With the exception of 'The Inevitable Thing', the fictional content of their work is slight. They observe, describe and comment upon working-class life more in the manner of amateur sociologists than novelists, and produce sketches rather than short stories. This is especially true of Rook. In the introduction to his remarkable study of Hooligan life he claimed that the stories he had to tell were completely true:

> This is neither a novel, nor in any sense a work of
> imagination. Whatever value or interest the following chapters
> possess must come from the fact that their hero has a real existence.
> I have tried to set forth, as far as possible in his own words,
> certain scenes from the life of a young criminal with whom I
> chanced to make acquaintance, a boy who has grown up
> in the midst of those who gain their living on the crooked,
> who takes life and its belongings as he finds them, and is
> not in the least ashamed of himself.

We cannot, of course, fully accept Rook's disclaimer. The principal incidents in many of the sketches are too slickly presented for them to pass as unadulterated reporting, and we are often conscious that they belong generically to the age-old literature of roguery. Where Rook breaks from this tradition is in paying less attention to the 'rogue' aspect and more to the social phenomenon of Hooliganism. His sympathy for Alf is sufficiently apparent, but is not a sympathy that depends on admiration for his smartness, skill or cunning at moments of danger. To take up the *Oliver Twist* comparison once again, Alf is the Artful Dodger modernized for the sociologically-conscious nineties: he is a product of Charles Booth's rather than Dickens's London. The Artful Dodger is seen almost entirely in relation to criminal life, a world separate from that inhabited by the poor and working classes, and it is because of this that he can be allowed his great moment of personal triumph at the close of the book when he defies—and gains a moral victory over—a corrupt court. The qualities he displays in that final scene are felt by us to be admirable simply because he is the complete criminal; the 'rogue' element is so effective that it forces us to forget that Dickens has a class point to make as well. Alf's petty criminality, on the other hand, is rooted in an exactly realized working-class environment. His world embraces not only Patrick Hooligan (a Fagin stripped of his archetypal nature), but Lambeth Walk street market, pubs, houses and shops. While he still possesses much the same kind of sharpness and wit as the Artful Dodger, his working-class background is never divorced from his criminal activities, and he can therefore never expect to enjoy any similar moral victory over the forces of law and order.

'The First and Last Meeting of the M.S.H.D.S.' and 'A Small Talk Exchange' are examples of Edwin Pugh's earliest work, and they do not show the confidence in writing about working-class life that he was later to attain. What is observable is a degree of affection for his characters more strongly Dickensian than is to be found in any other writer represented here, and a determination to write of everyday working-class life without accepting either monotony or violence as its predominant characteristic. Instead Pugh emphasizes the fundamental genuineness of his working-class characters. In the first of these two stories the tables are turned on a pretentious minister determined to 'elevate' the working man; while in the second the pretensions of the working-class characters themselves are mocked, but gently and with an affection on Pugh's part that is all too obvious. As a short story 'The Inevitable Thing' represents a considerable advance. It explores the psychology of a working-class drunkard without ever seeming to suggest that she is other than exceptional in her class. Like Alf, Moll is part of a specific community and the effectiveness of the story comes from her attempt to find a substitute for her lost respectability. Moll's relationship with Bet's parents is treated with a subtlety which is completely absent from the earlier stories. It is also worth noting that the ending of 'The Inevitable Thing' when Moll, responsible now for Bet's death, finds understanding and comfort with another social outcast, is the only concession to the 'yellow' side of nineties' literature in the whole of this anthology.

The remaining two stories—Gissing's 'Lou and Liz' and Adcock's 'At the Dock Gate'—are much less impressive. 'At the Dock Gate' is included here as an example of a new kind of sentimentalism in writing about the working classes which became very common in the late nineties, and which looked back not to Dickens but to Morrison. 'Lou and Liz' is included less for its intrinsic worth than as an acknowledgment of the important place held by Gissing in any wider study of late-Victorian fiction of working-class life. His working-class novels were all published in the eighties, and during the following decade he dealt with the subject only occasionally in short stories written for periodical publication. By this time the sympathy that Gissing once possessed for the working classes had disappeared, and it is now impossible to read 'Lou and Liz' without being made aware of the author's condescension.

It would be a mistake to make extravagant critical claims for these stories, but there can be no doubt that the best of them were in their day genuinely experimental. They indicate a willingness to break from past models and an eagerness to claim for the working man a central place in English fiction. In this—as in the uncertainty of attitude so often apparent—they reflect late-Victorian England's concern with a new and frightening democratic age.

P. J. KEATING

University of Leicester

NOTES

[1] 'A Slum Novel', *The Saturday Review*, LXXXII (28 November 1896), p. 573.

[2] *Charles Dickens* (1898), p. 63.   [3] *Ibid.*, p. 64.

[4] 'The Slum Movement in Fiction', *Stones From a Glass House* (1904), p. 70.

[5] 'In the Matter of a Private', *Soldiers Three* (Macmillan's Uniform Edition, 1899), p. 77. The story was first published in 1888.

[6] Henrietta Barnett, *Canon Barnett* (2 vols., 1918), I, p. 302.

Arthur Morrison

A Street

This street is in the East End. There is no need to say in the East End of what. The East End is a vast city, as famous in its way as any the hand of man has made. But who knows the East End? It is down through Cornhill and out beyond Leadenhall Street and Aldgate Pump, one will say: a shocking place, where he once went with a curate; an evil plexus of slums that hide human creeping things; where filthy men and women live on penn'orths of gin, where collars and clean shirts are decencies unknown, where every citizen wears a black eye, and none ever combs his hair. The East End is a place, says another, which is given over to the Unemployed. And the Unemployed is a race whose token is a clay pipe, and whose enemy is soap: now and again it migrates bodily to Hyde Park with banners, and furnishes adjacent police courts with disorderly drunks. Still another knows the East End only as the place whence begging letters come; there are coal and blanket funds there, all perennially insolvent, and everybody always wants a day in the country. Many and misty are people's notions of the East End; and each is commonly but the distorted shadow of a minor feature. Foul slums there are in the East End, of course, as there are in the West; want and misery there are, as wherever a host is gathered together to fight for food. But they are not often spectacular in kind.

Of this street there are about one hundred and fifty yards—on the same pattern all. It is not pretty to look at. A dingy little brick house twenty feet high, with three square holes to carry the windows, and an oblong hole to carry the door, is not a pleasing object; and each side of this street is formed by two or three score of such houses in a row, with one front wall in common. And the effect is as of stables.

Round the corner there are a baker's, a chandler's and a beer-shop. They are not included in the view from any of the rectangular holes; but they are well known to every denizen, and the chandler goes to church on Sunday and pays for his seat. At the opposite end, turnings lead to streets less rigidly respectable: some where 'Mangling done here' stares from windows, and where doors are left carelessly open; others where squalid women sit on doorsteps, and girls go to factories in white aprons. Many such turnings, of as many grades of decency, are set between this and the nearest slum.

They are not a very noisy or obtrusive lot in this street. They do not go to Hyde Park with banners, and they seldom fight. It is just possible that one or two among them, at some point in a life of ups and downs, may have been indebted to a coal and blanket fund; but whosoever these may be, they would rather die than publish the disgrace, and it is probable that they very nearly did so ere submitting to it.

Some who inhabit this street are in the docks, some in the gas-works, some in one or other of the few shipbuilding yards that yet survive on the Thames. Two families in a house is the general rule, for there are six rooms behind each set of holes: this, unless 'young men lodgers' are taken in, or there are grown sons paying for bed and board. As for the grown daughters, they marry as soon as may be. Domestic service is a social descent, and little under millinery and dressmaking is compatible with self-respect. The general servant may be caught young among the turnings at the end where mangling is done; and the factory girls live still further off, in places skirting slums.

Every morning at half past five there is a curious demonstration. The street resounds with thunderous knockings, repeated upon door after door, and acknowledged ever by a muffled shout from within. These signals are the work of the night-watchman or the early policeman, or both, and they summon the sleepers to go forth to the docks, the gasworks and the ship-yards. To be awakened in this wise costs fourpence a week, and for this four-pence a fierce rivalry rages between night-watchmen and police-men. The night-watchman—a sort of by-blow of the ancient 'Charley', and himself a fast vanishing quantity—is the real pro-fessional performer; but he goes to the wall, because a large connection must be worked if the pursuit is to pay at fourpence a

2

knocker. Now, it is not easy to bang at two knockers three-quarters of a mile apart, and a hundred others lying between, all punctually at half past five. Wherefore the policeman, to whom the fourpence is but a perquisite, and who is content with a smaller round, is rapidly supplanting the night-watchman, whose cry of 'Past nine o'clock', as he collects orders in the evening, is now seldom heard.

The knocking and the shouting pass, and there comes the noise of opening and shutting of doors, and a clattering away to the docks, the gasworks and the ship-yards. Later more door-shutting is heard, and then the trotting of sorrow-laden little feet along the grim street to the grim Board School three grim streets off. Then silence, save for a subdued sound of scrubbing here and there, and the puny squall of croupy infants. After this, a new trotting of little feet to docks, gasworks and ship-yards with father's dinner in a basin and a red handkerchief, and so to the Board School again. More muffled scrubbing and more squalling, and perhaps a feeble attempt or two at decorating the blankness of a square hole here and there by pouring water into a grimy flower-pot full of dirt. Then comes the trot of little feet toward the oblong holes, heralding the slower tread of sooty artisans; a smell of bloater up and down; nightfall; the fighting of boys in the street, perhaps of men at the corner near the beer-shop; sleep. And this is the record of a day in this street; and every day is hopelessly the same.

Every day, that is, but Sunday. On Sunday morning a smell of cooking floats round the corner from the half-shut baker's, and the little feet trot down the street under steaming burdens of beef, potatoes and batter pudding—the lucky little feet these, with Sunday boots on them, when father is in good work and has brought home all his money; not the poor little feet in worn shoes, carrying little bodies in the threadbare clothes of all the week, when father is out of work, or ill, or drunk, and the Sunday cooking may very easily be done at home—if any there be to do.

On Sunday morning one or two heads of families appear in wonderful black suits, with unnumbered creases and wrinklings at the seams. At their sides and about their heels trot the unresting little feet, and from under painful little velvet caps and straw hats stare solemn little faces towelled to a polish. Thus disposed and arrayed, they fare gravely through the grim little streets to a grim Little Bethel where are gathered together others in like garb and attendance; and for two hours they endure the frantic menace of hell-fire.

Most of the men, however, lie in shirt and trousers on their beds and read the Sunday paper; while some are driven forth—for they hinder the housework—to loaf, and await the opening of the beer-shop round the corner. Thus goes Sunday in this street, and every Sunday is the same as every other Sunday, so that one monotony is broken with another. For the women, however, Sunday is much as other days, except that there is rather more work for them. The break in their round of the week is washing day.

No event in the outer world makes any impression in this street. Nations may rise, or may totter in ruin; but here the colourless day will work through its twenty-four hours just as it did yesterday, and just as it will tomorrow. Without there may be party strife, wars and rumours of wars, public rejoicings; but the trotting of the little feet will be neither quickened nor stayed. Those quaint little women, the girl-children of this street, who use a motherly management towards all girl-things younger than themselves, and towards all boys as old or older, with 'Bless the child!' or 'Drat the the children!'—those quaint little women will still go marketing with big baskets, and will regard the price of bacon as chief among human considerations. Nothing disturbs this street—nothing but a strike.

Nobody laughs here—life is too serious a thing; nobody sings. There was once a woman who sang—a young wife from the country. But she bore children, and her voice cracked. Then her man died, and she sang no more. They took away her home, and with her children about her skirts she left this street for ever. The other women did not think much of her. She was 'helpless'.

One of the square holes in this street—one of the single, ground-floor holes—is found, on individual examination, to differ from the others. There has been an attempt to make it into a shop-window. Half a dozen candles, a few sickly sugarsticks, certain shrivelled bloaters, some bootlaces, and a bundle or two of firewood compose a stock which at night is sometimes lighted by a little paraffin lamp in a tin sconce, and sometimes by a candle. A widow lives here—a gaunt, bony widow, with sunken, red eyes. She has other sources of income than the candles and the bootlaces: she washes and chars all day, and she sews cheap shirts at night. Two 'young men lodgers', moreover, sleep upstairs, and the children sleep in the back room; she herself is supposed not to sleep at all. The police-man does not knock here in the morning—the widow wakes the lodgers herself; and nobody in the street behind ever looks out of window before going to bed, no matter how late, without seeing a light in the widow's room where she plies her needle. She is a quiet woman, who speaks little with her neighbours, having other things to do: a woman of pronounced character, to whom it would be unadvisable—even dangerous—to offer coals or blankets. Hers was the strongest contempt for the helpless woman who sang: a contempt whose added bitterness might be traced to its source. For when the singing woman was marketing, from which door of the pawnshop had she twice met the widow coming forth?

This is not a dirty street, taken as a whole. The widow's house is one of the cleanest, and the widow's children match the house. The one house cleaner than the widow's is ruled by a despotic Scotch-woman, who drives every hawker off her whitened step, and rubs her door handle if a hand have rested on it. The Scotch-woman has made several attempts to accommodate 'young men lodgers', but they have ended in shrill rows.

There is no house without children in this street, and the number of them grows ever and ever greater. Nine-tenths of the doctor's visits are on this account alone, and his appearances are the chief matter of such conversation as the women make across the fences. One after another the little strangers come, to live through lives as flat and colourless as the day's life in this street. Existence dawns, and the doctor-watchman's door-knock resounds along the row of rectangular holes. Then a muffled cry announces that a small new being has come to trudge and sweat its way in the ap-pointed groove. Later, the trotting of little feet and the school; the mid-day play hour, when love peeps even into this street; after that more trotting of little feet—strange little feet, new little feet—and the scrubbing, and the squalling, and the barren flower-pot; the end of the sooty day's work; the last home-coming; nightfall; sleep.

When love's light falls into some corner of the street, it falls at an early hour of this mean life, and is itself but a dusty ray. It falls early, because it is the sole bright thing which the street sees, and is watched for and counted on. Lads and lasses, awkwardly arm-in-arm, go pacing up and down this street, before the natural interest in marbles and doll's houses would have left them in a brighter

place. They are 'keeping company'; the manner of which pro-
ceeding is indigenous—is a custom native to the place. The young
people first 'walk out' in pairs. There is no exchange of promises,
no troth-plight, no engagement, no love-talk. They patrol the
streets side by side, usually in silence, sometimes with fatuous
chatter. There are no dances, no tennis, no water-parties, no
picnics to bring them together: so they must walk out, or be
unacquainted. If two of them grow dissatisfied with each other's
company, nothing is easier than to separate and walk out with
somebody else. When by these means each has found a fit mate (or
thinks so), a ring is bought, and the odd association becomes a
regular engagement; but this is not until the walking out has
endured for many months. The two stages of courtship are spoken
of indiscriminately as 'keeping company', but a very careful dis-
tinction is drawn between them by the parties concerned. Nevertheless, in the walking out period it would be almost as great a
breach of faith for either to walk out with more than one, as it
would be if the full engagement had been made. And love-making
in this street is a dreary thing, when one thinks of love-making in
other places. It begins—and it ends—too soon.

Nobody from this street goes to the theatre. That would mean a
long journey, and it would cost money which might buy bread and
beer and boots. For those, too, who wear black Sunday suits it
would be sinful. Nobody reads poetry or romance. The very words
are foreign. A Sunday paper in some few houses provides such
reading as this street is disposed to achieve. Now and again a penny
novel has been found among the private treasures of a growing
daughter, and has been wrathfully confiscated. For the air of this
street is unfavourable to the ideal.

Yet there are aspirations. There has lately come into the street a
young man lodger who belongs to a Mutual Improvement Society.
Membership in this society is regarded as a sort of learned degree,
and at its meetings debates are held and papers smugly read by
lamentably self-satisfied young men lodgers, whose only preparation
for debating and writing is a fathomless ignorance. For ignorance is
the inevitable portion of dwellers here: seeing nothing, reading
nothing and considering nothing.

Where in the East End lies this street? Everywhere. The
hundred-and-fifty yards is only a link in a long and a mightily
tangled chain—is only a turn in a tortuous maze. This street of the

square holes is hundreds of miles long. That it is planned in short lengths is true, but there is no other way in the world that can more properly be called a single street, because of its dismal lack of accent, its sordid uniformity, its utter remoteness from delight.

The Record of
Badalia Herodsfoot

The year's at the spring
And day's at the morn;
Morning's at seven;
The hill-side's dew-pearled;
The lark's on the wing;
The snail's on the thorn:
God's in His heaven—
All's right with the world!

Pippa Passes

This is not that Badalia whose spare names were Joanna, Pugnacious and M'Canna, as the song says, but another and a much nicer lady.

In the beginning of things she had been unregenerate; had worn the heavy fluffy fringe which is the ornament of the costermonger's girl, and there is a legend in Gunnison Street that on her wedding-day she, a flare-lamp in either hand, danced dances on a discarded lover's winkle-barrow, till a policeman interfered, and then Badalia danced with the Law amid shoutings. Those were her days of fatness, and they did not last long, for her husband after two years took himself another woman, and passed out of Badalia's life, over Badalia's senseless body; for he stifled protest with blows. While she was enjoying her widowhood the baby that the husband had not taken away died of croup, and Badalia was altogether alone. With rare fidelity she listened to no proposals for a second marriage according to the customs of Gunnison Street, which do not differ from those of the Barralong. 'My man,' she explained to her suitors, ' 'e'll come back one o' these days, an' then, like as not, 'e'd take an' kill me if I was livin' 'long o' you. You don't know Tom; I do. Now you go. I can do for myself—not 'avin' a kid.' She did for herself with a mangle, some tending of babies, and an occasional sale of flowers. This latter trade is one that needs capital, and takes the vendor very far westward, insomuch that the return journey from, let us say, the Burlington Arcade to Gunnison Street, E., is an excuse for drink, and then, as Badalia pointed out, 'You come 'ome with your shawl arf off of your back, an' your bonnick under your arm, and the price of nothing-at-all in your pocket, let alone a slop takin' care o' you'. Badalia did not drink, but she knew her sisterhood, and gave them rude counsel. Otherwise she kept herself to herself, and meditated a great deal upon Tom Herodsfoot, her husband, who would come back some day, and the baby who would never return. In what manner these thoughts wrought upon her mind will not be known.

Her entry into society dates from the night when she rose literally under the feet of the Reverend Eustace Hanna, on the landing of No. 17 Gunnison Street, and told him that he was a fool without discernment in the dispensation of his district charities.

'You give Lascar Loo custids,' said she, without the formality of introduction; 'give her pork-wine. Garn! Giver 'er blankits. Garn 'ome! 'Er mother, she eats 'em all, and drinks the blankits. Gits 'em back from the shop, she does, before you come visiting again, so as to 'ave 'em all handy an' proper; an' Lascar Loo she sez to you, "Oh, my mother's that good to me!" she do. Lascar Loo 'ad better talk so, bein' sick abed, 'r else 'er mother would kill 'er. Garn! you're a bloomin' gardener—you an' yer custids! Lascar Loo don't never smell of 'em even.'

Thereon the curate, instead of being offended, recognized in the heavy eyes under the fringe the soul of a fellow-worker, and so bade Badalia mount guard over Lascar Loo, when the next jelly or custard should arrive, to see that the invalid actually ate it. This Badalia did, to the disgust of Lascar Loo's mother, and the sharing of a black eye between the three; but Lascar Loo got her custard, and, coughing heartily, rather enjoyed the fray.

Later on, partly through the Reverend Eustace Hanna's swift recognition of her uses, and partly through certain tales poured out with moist eyes and flushed cheeks by Sister Eva, youngest and most impressionable of the Little Sisters of the Red Diamond, it

9

came to pass that Badalia, arrogant, fluffy-fringed, and perfectly
unlicensed in speech, won a recognized place among such as
labour in Gunnison Street.

These were a mixed corps, zealous or hysterical, faint-hearted or
only very wearied of battle against misery, according to their lights.
The most part were consumed with small rivalries and personal
jealousies, to be retailed confidentially to their own tiny cliques in
the pauses between wrestling with death for the body of a mori-
bund laundress, or scheming for further mission-grants to resole a
consumptive compositor's very consumptive boots. There was a
rector that lived in dread of pauperizing the poor, would fain have
held bazaars for fresh altar-cloths, and prayed in secret for a large
new brass bird, with eyes of red glass, fondly believed to be car-
buncles. There was Brother Victor, of the Order of Little Ease,
who knew a great deal about altar-cloths, but kept his knowledge
in the background while he strove to propitiate Mrs Jessel, the
Secretary of the Tea-Cup Board, who had money to dispense, but
hated Rome—even though Rome would, on its honour, do no
more than fill the stomach, leaving the dazed soul to the mercies of
Mrs Jessel. There were all the Little Sisters of the Red Diamond,
daughters of the horseleech, crying 'Give' when their own charity
was exhausted, and pitifully explaining to such as demanded an
account of their disbursements in return for one half-sovereign,
that relief-work in a bad district can hardly be systematized on the
accounts side without expensive duplication of staff. There was the
Reverend Eustace Hanna, who worked impartially with Ladies'
Committees, Androgynous Leagues and Guilds, Brother Victor,
and anybody else who could give him money, boots or blankets, or
that more precious help that allows itself to be directed by those
who know. And all these people learned, one by one, to consult
Badalia on matters of personal character, right to relief, and hope
of eventual reformation in Gunnison Street. Her answers were
seldom cheering, but she possessed special knowledge and
complete confidence in herself.

'I'm Gunnison Street,' she said to the austere Mrs Jessel. 'I
know what's what, *I* do, an' they don't want your religion, Mum,
not a single ——. Excuse me. It's all right when they comes to die,
Mum, but till they die what they wants is things to eat. The men
they'll shif' for themselves. That's why Nick Lapworth sez to you
that 'e wants to be confirmed an' all that. 'E won't never lead no

new life, nor 'is wife won't get no good out o' all the money you gives 'im. No more you can't pauperize them as 'asn't things to begin with. They're bloomin' well pauped. The women they can't shif' for themselves—'specially bein' always confined. 'Ow should they? They wants things if they can get 'em anyways. If not they dies, and a good job too, for women is cruel put upon in Gunnison Street.'

'Do you believe that—that Mrs Herodsfoot is altogether a proper person to trust funds to?' said Mrs Jessel to the curate after this conversation. 'She seems to be utterly godless in her speech at least.'

The curate agreed. She was godless according to Mrs Jessel's views, but did not Mrs Jessel think that since Badalia knew Gunnison Street and its needs, as none other knew it, she might in a humble way be, as it were, the scullion of charity from purer sources, and that if, say, the Tea-Cup Board could give a few shillings a week, and the Little Sisters of the Red Diamond a few more, and, yes, he himself could raise yet a few more, the total, not at all likely to be excessive, might be handed over to Badalia to dispense among her associates. Thus Mrs Jessel herself would be set free to attend more directly to the spiritual wants of certain large-limbed hulking men who sat picturesquely on the lower benches of her gatherings and sought for truth—which is quite as precious as silver, when you know the market for it.

'She'll favour her own friends,' said Mrs Jessel. The curate refrained from mirth, and, after wise flattery, carried his point. To her unbounded pride Badalia was appointed the dispenser of a grant—a weekly trust, to be held for the benefit of Gunnison Street.

'I don't know what we can get together each week,' said the curate to her. 'But here are seventeen shillings to start with. You do what you like with them among your people, only let me know how it goes so that we shan't get muddled in the accounts. D'you see?'

'Ho yuss! 'Taint much though, is it?' said Badalia, regarding the white coins in her palm. The sacred fever of the administrator, only known to those who have tasted power, burned in her veins. 'Boots is boots, unless they're give you, an' then they ain't fit to wear unless they're mended top an' bottom; an' jellies is jellies; an' I don't think anything o' that cheap pork-wine, but it all comes to something. It'll go quicker 'n a quartern of gin—seventeen bob. An' I'll keep a book—same as I used to do before Tom went an' took up 'long o' that pan-faced slut in Hennessy's Rents. We was the only barrer that kep' regular books, me an'—'im.'

She bought a large copy-book—her unschooled handwriting demanded room—and in it she wrote the story of her war; bodily, as befits a general, and for no other eyes than her own and those of the Reverend Eustace Hanna. Long ere the pages were full the mottled cover had been soaked in kerosene—Lascar Loo's mother, defrauded of her percentage on her daughter's custards, invaded Badalia's room in 17 Gunnison Street, and fought with her to the damage of the lamp and her own hair. It was hard, too, to carry the precious 'pork-wine' in one hand and the book in the other through an eternally thirsty land; so red stains were added to those of the oil. But the Reverend Eustace Hanna, looking at the matter of the book, never objected. The generous scrawls told their own tale, Badalia every Saturday night supplying the chorus between the written statements thus:

Mrs Hikkey, very ill brandy 3d. Cab for hospital, she had to go 1s. Mrs Poone confined. In money for tea (she took it I know, sir) 6d. Met her husband out looking for work.

'I slapped 'is face for a bone-idle beggar! 'E won't get no work becos 'e's—excuse me, sir. Won't you go on?' The curate continued—

Mrs Vincent. Confid. No linning for baby. Most untidy. In money 2s. 6d. Some cloths from Miss Evva.

'Did Sister Eva do that?' said the curate very softly. Now charity was Sister Eva's bounden duty, yet to one man's eyes each act of her daily toil was a manifestation of angelic grace and goodness—a thing to perpetually admire.

'Yes, sir. She went back to the Sisters' 'Ome an' took 'em off 'er own bed. Most beautiful marked too. Go on, sir. That makes up four and thruppence.'

Mrs Junnet to keep good fire coals is up. 7d.

Mrs Lockhart took a baby to nurse to earn a triffle but mother can't pay husband summons over and over. He won't Help. Cash 2s. 2d. Worked in a ketchin but had to leave. Fire, tea and shin of beef 1s. 7½d.

'There was a fight there, sir,' said Badalia. 'Not me, sir. 'Er 'usband, o' course 'e come in at the wrong time, was wishful to 'ave the beef, so I calls up the next floor an' down comes that mulatter man wot sells the sword-stick canes, top o' Ludgate-'ill. "Muley," sez I, "you big black beast, you, take an' kill this big white beast 'ere." I knew I couldn't stop Tom Lockhart 'alf drunk, with the beef in 'is 'ands. "I'll beef 'm," sez Muley, an' 'e did it, with that pore woman a-cryin' in the next room, an' the top banisters on that landin' is broke out, but she got 'er beef-tea, an' Tom 'e's got 'is gruel. Will you go on, sir?'

'No, I think it will be all right. I'll sign for the week,' said the curate. One gets so used to these things profanely called human documents.

'Mrs Churner's baby's got diptheery,' said Badalia, turning to go.

'Where's that? The Churners of Painter's Alley, or the other Churners in Houghton Street?'

'Houghton Street. The Painter's Alley people, they're sold up an' left.'

'Sister Eva's sitting one night a week with old Mrs Probyn in Houghton Street—isn't she?' said the curate uneasily.

'Yes; but she won't sit no longer. I've took up Mrs Probyn. I can't talk 'er no religion, but she don't want it; an' Miss Eva she don't want no diptheery, tho' she sez she does. Don't you be afraid for Miss Eva.'

'But—but you'll get it, perhaps.'

'Like as not.' She looked the curate between the eyes, and her own eyes flamed under the fringe. 'Maybe I'd like to get it, for aught you know.'

The curate thought upon these words for a little time till he began to think of Sister Eva in the grey cloak with the white bonnet-ribbons under the chin. Then he thought no more of Badalia.

What Badalia thought was never expressed in words, but it is known in Gunnison Street that Lascar Loo's mother, sitting blind drunk on her own doorstep, was that night captured and wrapped up in the war-cloud of Badalia's wrath, so that she did not know whether she stood on her head or her heels, and after being soundly bumped on every particular stair up to her room, was set down on Badalia's bed, there to whimper and quiver till the dawn, protesting that all the world was against her, and calling on the names of children long since slain by dirt and neglect. Badalia, snorting, went out to war, and since the hosts of the enemy were many, found enough work to keep her busy till the dawn.

As she had promised, she took Mrs Probyn into her own care, and began by nearly startling the old lady into a fit with the announcement that 'there ain't no God like as not, an' if there *is* it don't matter to you or me, an' any'ow you take this jelly'. Sister Eva objected to being shut off from her pious work in Houghton Street, but Badalia insisted, and by fair words and the promise of favours to come so prevailed on three or four of the more sober men of the neighbourhood that they blockaded the door whenever Sister Eva attempted to force an entry, and pleaded the diphtheria as an excuse. 'I've got to keep 'er out o' 'arm's way,' said Badalia, 'an' out she keeps. The curick won't care a —— for me, but—he wouldn't any'ow.'

The effect of that quarantine was to shift the sphere of Sister Eva's activity to other streets, and notably those most haunted by the Reverend Eustace Hanna and Brother Victor, of the Order of Little Ease. There exists, for all their human bickerings, a very close brotherhood in the ranks of those whose work lies in Gunnison Street. To begin with, they have seen pain—pain that no word or deed of theirs can alleviate—life born into Death, and Death crowded down by unhappy life. Also they understand the full significance of drink, which is a knowledge hidden from very many well-meaning people, and some of them have fought with the beasts at Ephesus. They meet at unseemly hours in unseemly places, exchange a word or two of hasty counsel, advice or suggestion, and pass on to their appointed toil, since time is precious and lives hang in the balance of five minutes. For many, the gas-lamps are their sun, and the Covent Garden wains the chariots of their twilight. They have all in their station begged for money, so that the freemasonry of the mendicant binds them together.

To all these influences there was added in the case of two workers that thing which men have agreed to call Love. The chance that Sister Eva might catch diphtheria did not enter into the curate's head till Badalia had spoken. Then it seemed a thing intolerable and monstrous that she should be exposed not only to this risk, but any accident whatever of the streets. A wain coming round a corner might kill her; the rotten staircases on which she trod daily and nightly might collapse and maim her; there was danger in the tottering coping-stones of certain crazy houses that he knew well;

danger more deadly within those houses. What if one of a thousand drunken men crushed out that precious life? A woman had once flung a chair at the curate's head. Sister Eva's arm would not be strong enough to ward off a chair. There were also knives that were quick to fly. These and other considerations cast the soul of the Reverend Eustace Hanna into torment that no leaning upon Providence could relieve. God was indubitably great and terrible—one had only to walk through Gunnison Street to see that much—but it would be better, vastly better, that Eva should have the protection of his own arm. And the world that was not too busy to watch might have seen a woman, not too young, light-haired and light-eyed, slightly assertive in her speech, and very limited in such ideas as lay beyond the immediate sphere of her duty, where the eyes of the Reverend Eustace Hanna turned to follow the footsteps of a Queen crowned in a little grey bonnet with white ribbons under the chin.

If that bonnet appeared for a moment at the bottom of a court-yard, or nodded at him on a dark staircase, then there was hope yet for Lascar Loo, living on one lung and the memory of past excesses, hope even for whining sodden Nick Lapworth, blasphem-ing, in the hope of money, over the pangs of a 'true conversion this time, s'elp me Gawd, sir'. If that bonnet did not appear for a day, the mind of the curate was filled with lively pictures of horror, visions of stretchers, a crowd at some villainous crossing, and a policeman—he could see that policeman—jerking out over his shoulder the details of the accident, and ordering the man who would have set his body against the wheels—heavy dray wheels, he could see them—to 'move on'. Then there was less hope for the salvation of Gunnison Street and all in it.

This agony Brother Victor beheld one day when he was coming from a death-bed. He saw the light in the eye, the relaxing muscles of the mouth, and heard a new ring in the voice that had told flat all that forenoon. Sister Eva had turned into Gunnison Street after a forty-eight hours' eternity of absence. She had not been run over. Brother Victor's heart must have suffered in some human fashion, or he would never have seen what he saw. But the Law of his Church made suffering easy. His duty was to go on with his work until he died, even as Badalia went on. She, magnifying her office, faced the drunken husband; coaxed the doubly shiftless, thriftless girl-wife into a little forethought, and begged clothes when and where she could for the scrofulous babes that multiplied like the green scum on the untopped water-cisterns.

The story of her deeds was written in the book that the curate signed weekly, but she never told him any more of fights and tumults in the street. 'Miss Eva does 'er work 'er way. I does mine mine. But I do more than Miss Eva ten times over, an' "Thank yer, Badalia," sez 'e, "that'll do for this week." I wonder what Tom's doin' now 'long o' that—other woman. 'Seems like as if I'd go an' look at 'im one o' these days. But I'd cut 'er liver out—couldn't 'elp myself. Better not go, p'raps.'

Hennessy's Rents lay more than two miles from Gunnison Street, and were inhabited by much the same class of people. Tom had established himself there with Jenny Wabstow, his new woman, and for weeks lived in great fear of Badalia's suddenly descending upon him. The prospect of actual fighting did not scare him; but he objected to the police-court that would follow, and the orders for maintenance and other devices of a law that cannot understand the simple rule that 'when a man's tired of a woman 'e ain't such a bloomin' fool as to live with 'er no more, an' that's the long an' short of it'. For some months his new wife wore very well, and kept Tom in a state of decent fear and consequent orderliness. Also work was plentiful. Then a baby was born, and, following the law of his kind, Tom, little interested in the children he helped to produce, sought distraction in drink. He had confined himself, as a rule, to beer, which is stupefying and comparatively innocuous: at least, it clogs the legs, and though the heart may ardently desire to kill, sleep comes swiftly, and the crime often remains undone. Spirits, being more volatile, allow both the flesh and the soul to work together—generally to the inconvenience of others. Tom discovered that there was merit in whisky—if you only took enough of it—cold. He took as much as he could purchase or get given to him, and by the time that his woman was fit to go abroad again, the two rooms of their household were stripped of many valuable articles. Then the woman spoke her mind, not once, but several times, with point, fluency and metaphor; and Tom was indignant at being deprived of peace at the end of his day's work, which included much whisky. He therefore withdrew himself from the solace and companionship of Jenny Wabstow, and she therefore pursued him with more metaphors. At the last, Tom would turn round and hit her—

sometimes across the head, and sometimes across the breast, and the bruises furnished material for discussion on door-steps among such women as had been treated in like manner by their husbands. They were not few.

But no very public scandal had occurred till Tom one day saw fit to open negotiations with a young woman for matrimony according to the laws of free selection. He was getting very tired of Jenny, and the young woman was earning enough from flower-selling to keep him in comfort, whereas Jenny was expecting another baby, and most unreasonably expected consideration on this account. The shapelessness of her figure revolted him, and he said as much in the language of his breed. Jenny cried till Mrs Hart, lineal descendant, and Irish of the 'mother to Mike of the donkey-cart', stopped her on her own staircase and whispered: 'God be good to you, Jenny, my woman, for I see how 'tis with you.' Jenny wept more than ever, and gave Mrs Hart a penny and some kisses, while Tom was conducting his own wooing at the corner of the street.

The young woman, prompted by pride, not by virtue, told Jenny of his offers, and Jenny spoke to Tom that night. The altercation began in their own rooms, but Tom tried to escape; and in the end all Hennessy's Rents gathered themselves upon the pavement and formed a court to which Jenny appealed from time to time, her hair loose on her neck, her raiment in extreme disorder, and her steps astray from drink. 'When your man drinks, you'd better drink too! It don't 'urt so much when 'e 'its you then,' says the Wisdom of the Women. And surely they ought to know.

'Look at 'im!' shrieked Jenny. 'Look at 'im, standin' there without any word to say for himself, that 'ud smitch off and leave me an' never so much as a shillin' lef' be'ind! You call yourself a man—you call yourself the bleedin' shadow of a man? I've seen better men than you made outer chewed paper and spat out arterwards. Look at 'im! 'E's been drunk since Thursday last, an' 'e'll be drunk s' long's 'e can get drink. 'E's took all I've got, an' me—an' me—as you see—'

A murmur of sympathy from the women.

'Took it all, he did, an' atop of his blasted pickin' an' stealin'—yes, you, you thief—'e goes off an' tries to take up 'long o' that'—here followed a complete and minute description of the young woman. Luckily, she was not on the spot to hear. ' 'E'll serve 'er as 'e served me! 'E'll drink every bloomin' copper she makes an' then leave 'er alone, same as 'e done me! Oh, women, look you, I've bore 'im one an' there's another on the way, an' 'e'd up an' leave me as I am now—the stinkin' dorg. An' you *may* leave me. I don't want none o' your leavin's. Go away! Get away!' The hoarseness of passion overpowered the voice. The crowd attracted a policeman as Tom began to slink away.

'Look at 'im,' said Jenny, grateful for the new listener. 'Ain't there no law for such as 'im? 'E's took all my money, 'e's beat me once, twice an' over. 'E's swine drunk when 'e ain't mad drunk, an' now, an' now 'e's trying to pick up along o' another woman. 'Im I give up a four times better man for. Ain't there no law?'

'What's the matter now? You go into your 'ouse. I'll see to the man. 'As 'e been 'itting you?' said the policeman.

''Ittin' me? 'E's cut my 'eart in two, an' 'e stands there grinnin' tho' 'twas all a play to 'im.'

'You go on into your 'ouse an' lie down a bit.'

'I'm a married woman, I tell you, an' I'll 'ave my 'usband!'

'I ain't done her no bloomin' 'arm,' said Tom from the edge of the crowd. He felt that public opinion was running against him.

'You ain't done me any bloomin' good, you dorg. I'm a married woman, I am, an' I won't 'ave my 'usband took from me.'

'Well, if you *are* a married woman, cover your breasts,' said the policeman soothingly. He was used to domestic brawls.

'Shan't—thank you for your impidence. Look 'ere!' She tore open her dishevelled bodice and showed such crescent-shaped bruises as are made by a well-applied chair-back. 'That's what 'e done to me acause my heart wouldn't break quick enough! 'E's tried to get in an' break it. Look at that, Tom, that you gave me last night; an' I made it up with you. But that was before I knew what you were tryin' to do 'long o' that woman—'

'D'you charge 'im?' said the policeman. ' 'E'll get a month for it, per'aps.'

'No,' said Jenny firmly. It was one thing to expose her man to the scorn of the street, and another to lead him to jail.

'Then you go in an' lie down, and you'—this to the crowd—'pass along the pavement, there. Pass along. 'Taint nothing to laugh at.' To Tom, who was being sympathized with by his friends, 'It's good for you she didn't charge you, but mind this now, the next time,' etc.

Tom did not at all appreciate Jenny's forbearance, nor did his friends help to compose his mind. He had whacked the woman because she was a nuisance. For precisely the same reason he had cast about for a new mate. And all his kind acts had ended in a truly painful scene in the street, a most unjustifiable exposure by and of his woman, and a certain loss of caste—this he realized dimly—among his associates. Consequently, all women were nuisances, and consequently whisky was a good thing. His friends condoled with him. Perhaps he had been more hard on his woman than she deserved, but her disgraceful conduct under provocation excused all offence.

'I wouldn't 'ave no more to do with 'er—a woman like that there,' said one comforter.

'Let 'er go an' dig for her bloomin' self. A man wears 'isself out to 'is bones shovin' meat down their mouths, while they sit at 'ome easy all day; an' the very fust time, mark you, you 'as a bit of a difference, an' very proper too for a man as *is* a man, she ups an' 'as you out into the street, callin' you Gawd knows what all. What's the good o' that, I arx you?' So spoke the second comforter.

The whisky was the third, and his suggestion struck Tom as the best of all. He would return to Badalia his wife. Probably she would have been doing something wrong while he had been away, and he could then vindicate his authority as a husband. Certainly she would have money. Single women always seemed to possess the pence that God and the Government denied to hard-working men. He refreshed himself with more whisky. It was beyond any doubt that Badalia would have done something wrong. She might even have married another man. He would wait till the new husband was out of the way, and, after kicking Badalia, get money and a long-absent sense of satisfaction. There is much virtue in a creed or a law, but when all is prayed and suffered, drink is the only thing that will make clean all a man's deeds in his own eyes. Pity it is that the effects are not permanent.

Tom parted with his friends, bidding them tell Jenny that he was going to Gunnison Street, and would return to her arms no more. Because this was the Devil's message, they remembered and severally delivered it, with drunken distinctness, in Jenny's ears. Then Tom took more drink till his drunkenness rolled back and stood off from him as a wave rolls back and stands off the wreck it will swamp. He reached the traffic-polished black asphalte of a side-street and trod warily among the reflections of the shop-lamps that burned in gulfs of pitchy darkness, fathoms beneath his boot-heels. He was very sober indeed. Looking down his past, he beheld that he was justified of all his actions so entirely and perfectly that if Badalia had in his absence dared to lead a blameless life he would smash her for not having gone wrong.

Badalia at that moment was in her own room after the regular nightly skirmish with Lascar Loo's mother. To a reproof as stinging as a Gunnison Street tongue could make it, the old woman, detected for the hundredth time in the theft of the poor delicacies meant for the invalid, could only cackle and answer—

'D'you think Loo's never bilked a man in 'er life? She's dyin' now—on'y she's so cunning long about it. Me! I'll live for twenty years yet.'

Badalia shook her, more on principle than in any hope of curing her, and thrust her into the night, where she collapsed on the pavement and called upon the Devil to slay Badalia.

He came upon the word in the shape of a man with a very pale face who asked for her by name. Lascar Loo's mother remembered. It was Badalia's husband—and the return of a husband to Gunnison Street was generally followed by beatings.

'Where's my wife?' said Tom. 'Where's my slut of a wife?'

'Upstairs an' be —— to her,' said the old woman, falling over on her side. ''Ave you come back for 'er, Tom?'

'Yes. 'Oo's she took up while I bin gone?'

'All the bloomin' curicks in the parish. She's that set up you wouldn't know 'er.'

''Strewth she is!'

'Oh, yuss. Mor'n that, she's always round an' about with them sniffin' Sisters of Charity an' the curick. Mor'n that, 'e gives 'er money—pounds an' pounds a week. Been keepin' her that way for months, 'e 'as. No wonder you wouldn't 'ave nothin' to do with 'er when you left. An' she keeps me outer the food-stuff they gets for me lyin' dyin' out 'ere like a dorg. She's been a blazin' bad un has Badalia since you lef'.'

'Got the same room still, 'as she?' said Tom, striding over Lascar Loo's mother, who was picking at the chinks between the pave-stones.

'Yes, but so fine you wouldn't know it.'

Tom went up the stairs and the old lady chuckled. Tom was

angry. Badalia would not be able to bump people for some time to come, or to interfere with the heaven-appointed distribution of custards.

Badalia, undressing to go to bed, heard feet on the stair that she knew well. Ere they stopped to kick at her door she had, in her own fashion, thought over very many things.

'Tom's back,' she said to herself. 'An' I'm glad . . . spite o' the curick an' everythink.'

She opened the door, crying his name.

The man pushed her aside.

'I don't want none o' your kissin's an' slaverin's. I'm sick of 'em,' said he.

'You ain't 'ad so many neither to make you sick these two years past.'

'I've 'ad better. Got any money?'

'On'y a little—orful little.'

'That's a —— lie, an' you know it.'

''Taint—and, oh Tom, what's the use o' talkin' money the minute you come back? Didn't you like Jenny? I knowed you wouldn't.'

'Shut your 'ead. Ain't you got enough to make a man drunk fair?'

'You don't want bein' made more drunk any. You're drunk a'ready. You come to bed, Tom.'

'To you?'

'Ay, to me. Ain't I nothin'—spite o' Jenny?'

She put out her arms as she spoke. But the drink held Tom fast.

'Not for me,' said he, steadying himself against the wall. 'Don't I know 'ow you've been goin' on while I was away, yah!'

'Arsk about!' said Badalia indignantly, drawing herself together. ''Oo sez anythink agin me 'ere?'

''Oo sez? W'y, everybody. I ain't come back more'n a minute 'fore I finds you've been with the curick Gawd knows where. Wot curick was 'e?'

'The curick that's 'ere always,' said Badalia hastily. She was thinking of anything rather than the Rev. Eustace Hanna at that moment. Tom sat down gravely in the only chair in the room. Badalia continued her arrangements for going to bed.

'Pretty thing that,' said Tom, 'to tell your own lawful married 'usband—an' I guv five bob for the weddin'-ring. Curick that's 'ere always! Cool as brass you are. Ain't you got no shame? Ain't 'e under the bed now?'

'Tom, you're bleedin' drunk. I ain't done nothin' to be 'shamed of.'

'You! You don't know wot shame is. But I ain't come 'ere to mess with you. Give me wot you've got, an' then I'll dress you down an' go to Jenny.'

'I ain't got nothin' 'cept some coppers an' a shillin' or so.'

'Wot's that about the curick keepin' you on five poun' a week?'

''Oo told you that?'

'Lascar Loo's mother, lyin' on the pavemint outside, an' more honest than you'll ever be. Give me wot you've got!'

Badalia passed over to a little shell pin-cushion on the mantel-piece, drew thence four shillings and threepence—the lawful earnings of her trade—and held them out to the man who was rocking in his chair and surveying the room with wide-opened, rolling eyes.

'That ain't five poun',' said he drowsily.

'I ain't got no more. Take it an' go—if you won't stay.'

Tom rose slowly, gripping the arms of the chair. 'Wot about the curick's money that 'e guv you?' said he. 'Lascar Loo's mother told me. You give it over to me now, or I'll make you.'

'Lascar Loo's mother don't know anything about it.'

'She do, an' more than you want her to know.'

'She don't. I've bumped the 'eart out of 'er, and I can't give you the money. Anythin' else but that, Tom, an' everythin' else but that, Tom, I'll give willin' and true. 'Tain't my money. Won't the dollar be enough? That money's my trust. There's a book along of it too.'

'Your trust? Wot are you doin' with any trust that your 'usband don't know of? You an' your trust! Take you that!'

Tom stepped towards her and delivered a blow of the clenched fist across the mouth. 'Give me wot you've got,' said he, in the thick, abstracted voice of one talking in dreams.

'I won't,' said Badalia, staggering to the wash-stand. With any other man than her husband she would have fought savagely as a wild cat; but Tom had been absent two years, and, perhaps, a little timely submission would win him back to her. None the less, the weekly trust was sacred.

The wave that had so long held back descended on Tom's brain.

He caught Badalia by the throat and forced her to her knees. It seemed just to him in that hour to punish an erring wife for two years of wilful desertion; and the more, in that she had confessed her guilt by refusing to give up the wage of sin.

Lascar Loo's mother waited on the pavement without for the sounds of lamentation, but none came. Even if Tom had released her gullet Badalia would not have screamed.

'Give it up, you slut!' said Tom. 'Is that 'ow you pay me back for all I've done?'

'I can't. 'Tain't my money. Gawd forgive you, Tom, for wot you're—.' The voice ceased as the grip tightened, and Tom heaved Badalia against the bed. Her forehead struck the bed-post, and she sank, half kneeling, on the floor. It was impossible for a self-respecting man to refrain from kicking her: so Tom kicked with the deadly intelligence born of whisky. The head drooped to the floor, and Tom kicked at that till the crisp tingle of hair striking through his nailed boot with the chill of cold water, warned him that it might be as well to desist.

'Where's the curick's money, you kep' woman?' he whispered in the blood-stained ear. But there was no answer—only a rattling at the door, and the voice of Jenny Wabstow crying ferociously, 'Come out o' that, Tom, an' come 'ome with me! An' you, Badalia, I'll tear your face off its bones!'

Tom's friends had delivered their message, and Jenny, after the first flood of passionate tears, rose up to follow Tom, and, if possible, to win him back. She was prepared even to endure an exemplary whacking for her performances in Hennessy's Rents. Lascar Loo's mother guided her to the chamber of horrors, and chuckled as she retired down the staircase. If Tom had not banged the soul out of Badalia, there would at least be a royal fight between that Badalia and Jenny. And Lascar Loo's mother knew well that Hell has no fury like a woman fighting above the life that is quick in her.

Still there was no sound audible in the street. Jenny swung back the unbolted door, to discover her man stupidly regarding a heap by the bed. An eminent murderer has remarked that if people did not die so untidily, most men, and all women, would commit at least one murder in their lives. Tom was reflecting on the present untidiness, and the whisky was fighting with the clear current of his thoughts.

'Don't make that noise,' he said. 'Come in quick.'

'My Gawd!' said Jenny, checking like a startled wild beast. 'Wot's all this 'ere? You ain't—'

'Dunno. 'S'pose I did it.'

'Did it! You done it a sight too well this time.'

'She was aggravatin',' said Tom thickly, dropping back into the chair. 'That aggravatin' you'd never believe. Livin' on the fat o' the land among these aristocratic parsons an' all. Look at them white curtings on the bed. *We* ain't got no white curtings. What I want to know is—' The voice died as Badalia's had died, but from a different cause. The whisky was tightening its grip after the accomplished deed, and Tom's eyes were beginning to close. Badalia on the floor breathed heavily.

'No, nor like to 'ave,' said Jenny. 'You've done for 'er this time. You go!'

'Not me. She won't hurt. Do 'er good. I'm goin' to sleep. Look at those there clean sheets! Ain't you comin' too?'

Jenny bent over Badalia, and there was intelligence in the battered woman's eyes—intelligence and much hate.

'I never told 'im to do such,' Jenny whispered. ''Twas Tom's own doin'—none o' mine. Shall I get 'im took, dear?'

The eyes told their own story. Tom, who was beginning to snore, must not be taken by the Law.

'Go,' said Jenny. 'Get out! Get out of 'ere.'

'You—told—me—that—this afternoon,' said the man very sleepily. 'Lemme go asleep.'

'That wasn't nothing. You'd only 'it me. This time it's murder—murder—murder! Tom, you've killed 'er now.' She shook the man from his rest, and understanding with cold terror filled his fuddled brain.

'I done it for your sake, Jenny,' he whimpered feebly, trying to take her hand.

'You killed 'er for the money, same as you would ha' killed me. Get out o' this. Lay 'er on the bed first, you brute!'

They lifted Badalia on to the bed, and crept forth silently.

'I can't be took along o' you—and if you was took you'd say I made you do it, an' try to get me 'anged. Go away—anywhere outer 'ere,' said Jenny, and she dragged him down the stairs.

'Goin' to look for the curick?' said a voice from the pavement.

Lascar Loo's mother was still waiting patiently to hear Badalia squeal.

'Wot curick?' said Jenny swiftly. There was a chance of salving her conscience yet in regard to the bundle upstairs.

''Anna—63 Roomer Terrace—close 'ere,' said the old woman. She had never been favourably regarded by the curate. Perhaps, since Badalia had not squealed, Tom preferred smashing the man to the woman. There was no accounting for tastes.

Jenny thrust her man before her till they reached the nearest main road. 'Go away, now,' she gasped. 'Go off anywheres, but don't come back to me. I'll never go with you again; an', Tom—Tom, d'you 'ear me?—clean your boots.'

Vain counsel. The desperate thrust of disgust which she bestowed upon him sent him staggering face-down into the kennel, where a policeman showed interest in his welfare.

'Took for a common drunk. Gawd send they don't look at 'is boots! 'Anna, 63 Roomer Terrace!' Jenny settled her hat and ran.

The excellent housekeeper of the Roomer Chambers still remembers how there arrived a young person, blue-lipped and gasping, who cried only: 'Badalia, 17 Gunnison Street. Tell the curick to come at once—at once—at once!' and vanished into the night. This message was borne to the Rev. Eustace Hanna, then enjoying his beauty-sleep. He saw there was urgency in the demand, and unhesitatingly knocked up Brother Victor across the landing. As a matter of etiquette, Rome and England divided their cases in the district according to the creeds of the sufferers; but Badalia was an institution, and not a case, and there was no district-relief etiquette to be considered. 'Something has happened to Badalia,' the curate said, 'and it's your affair as well as mine. Dress and come along.'

'I am ready,' was the answer. 'Is there any hint of what's wrong?'

'Nothing beyond a runaway-knock and a call.'

'Then it's a confinement or a murderous assault. Badalia wouldn't wake us up for anything less. I'm qualified for both, thank God.'

The two men raced to Gunnison Street, for there were no cabs abroad, and under any circumstances a cab-fare means two days' good firing for such as are perishing with cold. Lascar Loo's mother had gone to bed, and the door was naturally on the latch.

They found considerably more than they had expected in
Badalia's room, and the Church of Rome acquitted itself nobly
with bandages, while the Church of England could only pray to be
delivered from the sin of envy. The Order of Little Ease, recognizing that the soul is in most cases accessible through the body,
take their measures and train their men accordingly.

'She'll do now,' said Brother Victor, in a whisper. 'It's internal
bleeding, I fear, and a certain amount of injury to the brain. She
has a husband, of course?'

'They all have, more's the pity.'

'Yes, there's a domesticity about these injuries that shows their
origin.' He lowered his voice. 'It's a perfectly hopeless business,
you understand. Twelve hours at the most.'

Badalia's right hand began to beat on the counterpane, palm
down.

'I think you are wrong,' said the Church of England. 'She is
going.'

'No, that's not the picking at the counterpane,' said the Church
of Rome. 'She wants to say something; you know her better
than I.'

The curate bent very low.

'Send for Miss Eva,' said Badalia, with a cough.

'In the morning. She will come in the morning,' said the curate,
and Badalia was content. Only the Church of Rome, who knew
something of the human heart, knitted his brows and said nothing.
After all, the law of his Order was plain. His duty was to watch till
the dawn while the moon went down.

It was a little before her sinking that the Rev. Eustace Hanna
said, 'Hadn't we better send for Sister Eva? She seems to be going
fast.'

Brother Victor made no answer, but as early as decency ad-
mitted there came one to the door of the house of the Little Sisters
of the Red Diamond and demanded Sister Eva, that she might
soothe the pain of Badalia Herodsfoot. That man, saying very
little, led her to Gunnison Street, No. 17, and into the room where
Badalia lay. Then he stood on the landing, and bit the flesh of his
fingers in agony, because he was a priest trained to know, and
knew how the hearts of men and women beat back at the rebound,
so that love is born out of horror, passion declares itself when the
soul is quivering with pain.

Badalia, wise to the last, husbanded her strength till the coming of Sister Eva. It is generally maintained by the Little Sisters of the Red Diamond that she died in delirium, but since one Sister at least took a half of her dying advice, this seems uncharitable.

She tried to turn feebly on the bed, and the poor broken human machinery protested according to its nature.

Sister Eva started forward, thinking that she heard the dread forerunner of the death-rattle. Badalia lay still conscious, and spoke with startling distinctness, the irrepressible irreverence of the street-hawker, the girl who had danced on the winkle-barrow, twinkling in her one available eye.

'Sounds jest like Mrs Jessel, don't it? Before she's 'ad 'er lunch an' 'as been talkin' all the mornin' to her classes.'

Neither Sister Eva nor the curate said anything. Brother Victor stood without the door, and the breath came harshly between his teeth, for he was in pain.

'Put a cloth over my 'ead,' said Badalia. 'I've got it good, an' I don't want Miss Eva to see. I ain't pretty this time.'

'Who was it?' said the curate.

'Man from outside. Never seed 'im no more'n Adam. Drunk, I s'pose. S'elp me Gawd that's truth! Is Miss Eva 'ere? I can't see under the towel. I've got it good, Miss Eva. Excuse my not shakin' 'ands with you, but I'm not strong, an' it's fourpence for Mrs Imeny's beef-tea, an' wot you can give 'er for baby-linning. Allus 'avin' kids, these people. I 'adn't oughter talk, for *my* 'usband 'e never come a-nigh me these two years, or I'd a-bin as bad as the rest; but 'e never come a-nigh me. . . . A man come and 'it me over the 'ead, an' 'e kicked me, Miss Eva; so it was just the same's if I had ha' had a 'usband, ain't it? The book's in the drawer, Mister 'Anna, an' it's all right, an' I never guv up a copper o' the trust money—not a copper. You look under the chist o' drawers— all wot isn't spent this week is there. . . . An', Miss Eva, don't you wear that grey bonnick no more. I kep' you from the diptheery, an'—an' I didn't want to keep you so, but the curick said it 'ad to be done. I'd a sooner ha' took up with 'im than any one, only Tom 'e come, an' then—you see, Miss Eva, Tom 'e never come a-nigh me for two years, nor I 'aven't seen 'im yet. S'elp me—, I 'aven't. Do you 'ear? But you two go along, and make a match of it. I've wished otherways often, but o' course it was not for the likes o' me. If Tom 'ad come back, which 'e never did, I'd ha' been like the rest—sixpence for beef-tea for the baby, an' a shilling for layin' out the baby. You've seen it in the books, Mister 'Anna. That's what it is; an' o' course, you couldn't never 'ave nothing to do with me. But a woman she wishes as she looks, an' never you 'ave no doubt about 'im, Miss Eva. I've seen it in 'is face time an' agin—time an' agin. . . . Make it a four pound ten funeral—with a pall.'

It was a seven pound fifteen shilling funeral, and all Gunnison Street turned out to do it honour. All but two; for Lascar Loo's mother saw that a Power had departed, and that her road lay clear to the custards. Therefore, when the carriages rattled off, the cat on the doorstep heard the wail of the dying prostitute who could not die—

'Oh, mother, mother, won't you even let me lick the spoon?'

Arthur Morrison

Lizerunt

Lizer's wooing

Somewhere in the register was written the name Elizabeth Hunt; but seventeen years after the entry the spoken name was Lizerunt. Lizerunt worked at a pickle factory, and appeared abroad in an elaborate and shabby costume, usually supplemented by a white apron. Withal she was something of a beauty. That is to say, her cheeks were very red, her teeth were very large and white, her nose was small and snub, and her fringe was long and shiny; while her face, new-washed, was susceptible of a high polish. Many such girls are married at sixteen, but Lizerunt was belated, and had never a bloke at all.

Billy Chope was a year older than Lizerunt. He wore a billycock with a thin brim and a permanent dent in the crown; he had a bob-tail coat, with the collar turned up at one side and down at the other, as an expression of independence; between his meals he carried his hands in his breeches pockets; and he lived with his mother, who mangled. His conversation with Lizerunt consisted long of perfunctory nods; but great things happened this especial Thursday evening, as Lizerunt, making for home, followed the fading red beyond the furthermost end of Commercial Road. For Billy Chope, slouching in the opposite direction, lurched across the pavement as they met, and taking the nearer hand from his pocket, caught and twisted her arm, bumping her against the wall.

'Garn,' said Lizerunt, greatly pleased: 'le' go!' For she knew that this was love.

'Where yer auf to, Lizer?'

"'Ome, o' course, cheeky. Le' go'; and she snatched—in vain—
at Billy's hat.

Billy let go, and capered in front of her. She feigned to dodge by
him, careful not to be too quick, because affairs were developing.

'I say, Lizer,' said Billy, stopping his dance and becoming
business-like, 'goin' anywhere Monday?'

'Not along o' you, cheeky; you go 'long o' Beller Dawson, like
wot you did Easter.'

'Blow Beller Dawson; *she* ain't no good. I'm goin' on the Flats.
Come?'

Lizerunt, delighted but derisive, ended with a promise to 'see'.
The bloke had come at last, and she walked home with the feeling
of having taken her degree. She had half assured herself of it two
days before, when Sam Cardew threw an orange peel at her, but
went away after a little prancing on the pavement. Sam was a
smarter fellow than Billy, and earned his own living; probably his
attentions were serious; but one must prefer the bird in hand. As
for Billy Chope, he went his way, resolved himself to take home
what mangling he should find his mother had finished, and stick
to the money; also, to get all he could from her by blandishing and
bullying: that the jaunt to Wanstead Flats might be adequately
done.

There is no other fair like Whit Monday's on Wanstead Flats.
Here is a square mile and more of open land where you may howl at
large; here is no danger of losing yourself as in Epping Forest; the
public houses are always with you; shows, shies, swings, merry-go-
rounds, fried-fish stalls, donkeys are packed closer than on
Hampstead Heath; the ladies' tormentors are larger, and their
contents smell worse than at any other fair. Also, you may be
drunk and disorderly without being locked up—for the stations
won't hold everybody—and when all else has palled, you may set
fire to the turf. Hereinto Billy and Lizerunt projected themselves
from the doors of the Holly Tree on Whit Monday morning. But
through hours on hours of fried fish and half-pints both were
conscious of a deficiency. For the hat of Lizerunt was brown and
old; plush it was not, and its feather was a mere foot long and of a
very rusty black. Now, it is not decent for a factory girl from
Limehouse to go bank-holidaying under any but a hat of plush,
very high in the crown, of a wild blue or a wilder green, and carry-

ing withal an ostrich feather, pink or scarlet or what not; a feather that springs from the fore-part, climbs the crown, and drops as far down the shoulders as may be. Lizerunt knew this, and, had she had no bloke, would have stayed at home. But a chance is a chance. As it was, only another such hapless girl could measure her bitter envy of the feathers about her, or would so joyfully have given an ear for the proper splendour. Billy, too, had a vague impression, muddled by but not drowned in half-pints, that some degree of plush was condign to the occasion and to his own expenditure. Still, there was no quarrel; and the pair walked and ran with arms about each other's necks; and Lizerunt thumped her bloke on the back at proper intervals; so that the affair went regularly on the whole: although, in view of Lizerunt's shortcomings, Billy did not insist on the customary exchange of hats.

Everything, I say, went well and well enough until Billy bought a ladies' tormentor and began to squirt it at Lizerunt. For then Lizerunt went scampering madly, with piercing shrieks, until her bloke was left some little way behind, and Sam Cardew, turning up at that moment and seeing her running alone in the crowd, threw his arms about her waist and swung her round him again and again, as he floundered gallantly this way and that, among the shies and the hokey-pokey barrows.

"Ullo, Lizer! Where *are* y' a-comin' to? If I 'adn't laid 'old o' ye—!' But here Billy Chope arrived to demand what the 'ell Sam Cardew was doing with his gal. Now Sam was ever readier for a fight than Billy was; but the sum of Billy's half-pints was large: wherefore the fight began. On the skirt of an hilarious ring Lizerunt, after some small outcry, triumphed aloud. Four days before, she had no bloke; and here she stood with two, and those two fighting for her! Here in the public gaze, on the Flats! For almost five minutes she was Helen of Troy.

And in much less time Billy tasted repentance. The haze of half-pints was dispelled, and some teeth went with it. Presently, whimpering and with a bloody muzzle, he rose and made a running kick at the other. Then, being thwarted in a bolt, he flung himself down; and it was like to go hard with him at the hands of the crowd. Punch you may on Wanstead Flats, but execration and worse is your portion if you kick anybody except your wife. But, as the ring closed, the helmets of two policemen were seen to be working in over the surrounding heads, and Sam Cardew, quickly assuming his coat, turned away with such an air of blamelessness as is practicable with a damaged eye; while Billy went off unheeded in an opposite direction.

Lizerunt and her new bloke went the routine of half-pints and merry-go-rounds, and were soon on right thumping terms; and Lizerunt was as well satisfied with the issue as she was proud of the adventure. Billy was all very well; but Sam was better. She resolved to draw him for a feathered hat before next bank holiday. So the sun went down on her and her bloke hanging on each other's necks and straggling toward the Romford Road with shouts and choruses. The rest was tram-car, Bow Music Hall, half-pints and darkness.

Billy took home his wounds, and his mother, having moved his wrath by asking their origin, sought refuge with a neighbour. He accomplished his revenge in two instalments. Two nights later Lizerunt was going with a jug of beer; when somebody sprang from a dark corner, landed her under the ear, knocked her sprawling; and made off to the sound of her lamentations. She did not see who it was, but she knew; and next day Sam Cardew was swearing he'd break Billy's back. He did not, however, for that same evening a gang of seven or eight fell on him with sticks and belts. (They were Causeway chaps, while Sam was a Brady's Laner, which would have been reason enough by itself, even if Billy Chope had not been one of them.) Sam did his best for a burst through and a run, but they pulled and battered him down; and they kicked him about the head, and they kicked him about the belly; and they took to their heels when he was speechless and still.

He lay at home for near four weeks, and when he stood up again it was in many bandages. Lizerunt came often to his bedside, and twice she brought an orange. On these occasions there was much talk of vengeance. But the weeks went on. It was a month since Sam had left his bed; and Lizerunt was getting a little tired of bandages. Also, she had begun to doubt and to consider bank holiday—scarce a fortnight off. For Sam was stone broke, and a plush hat was further away than ever. And all through the later of these weeks Billy Chope was harder than ever on his mother, and she, well knowing that if he helped her by taking home he would pocket the money at the other end, had taken to finishing and delivering in his absence, and, threats failing to get at the money,

Billy Chope was impelled to punch her head and gripe her by the throat.

There was a milliner's window, with a show of nothing but fashionable plush-and-feather hats, and Lizerunt was lingering hereabouts one evening; when someone took her by the waist, and someone said, 'Which d'yer like, Lizer?—The yuller un?'

Lizerunt turned and saw that it was Billy. She pulled herself away, and backed off, sullen and distrustful. 'Garn,' she said.

'Straight,' said Billy, 'I'll sport yer one. . . . No kid, I will.'

'Garn,' said Lizerunt once more. 'Wot yer gittin' at now?'

But presently, being convinced that bashing wasn't in it, she approached less guardedly; and she went away with a paper bag and the reddest of all the plushes and the bluest of all the feathers; a hat that challenged all the Flats the next bank holiday, a hat for which no girl need have hesitated to sell her soul. As for Billy, why, he was as good as another; and you can't have everything; and Sam Cardew, with his bandages and his grunts and groans, was no great catch after all.

This was the wooing of Lizerunt: for in a few months she and Billy married under the blessing of a benignant rector, who periodically set aside a day for free weddings, and, on principle, encouraged early matrimony. And they lived with Billy's mother.

(ii)

Lizer's first

When Billy Chope married Lizerunt there was a small rejoicing. There was no wedding-party; because it was considered that what there might be to drink would be better in the family. Lizerunt's father was not, and her mother felt no interest in the affair; not having seen her daughter for a year, and happening, at the time, to have a month's engagement in respect of a drunk and disorderly. So that there were but three of them; and Billy Chope got exceedingly tipsy early in the day; and in the evening his bride bawled a continual chorus, while his mother, influenced by that unwonted quartern of gin the occasion sanctioned, wept dismally over her boy, who was much too far gone to resent it.

His was the chief reason for rejoicing. For Lizerunt had always been able to extract ten shillings a week from the pickle factory, and it was to be presumed that as Lizer Chope her earning capacity would not diminish; and the wages would make a very respectable addition to the precarious revenue, depending on the mangle, that Billy extorted from his mother. As for Lizer, she was married. That was the considerable thing; for she was but a few months short of eighteen, and that, as you know, is a little late.

Of course there were quarrels very soon; for the new Mrs Chope, less submissive at first than her mother-in-law, took a little breaking in, and a liberal renewal of the manual treatment once applied in her courting days. But the quarrels between the women were comforting to Billy: a diversion and a source of better service.

As soon as might be Lizer took the way of womankind. This circumstance brought an unexpected half-crown from the evangelical rector who had married the couple gratis; for recognizing Billy in the street by accident, and being told of Mrs Chope's prospects, as well as that Billy was out of work (a fact undeniable), he reflected that his principles did on occasion lead to discomfort of a material sort. And Billy, to whose comprehension the half-crown opened a new field of receipt, would doubtless have long remained a client of the rector, had not that zealot hastened to discover a vacancy for a warehouse porter, the offer of presentation whereunto alienated Billy Chope for ever. But there were meetings and demonstrations of the Unemployed; and it was said that shillings had been given away; and, as being at a meeting in a street was at least as amusing as being in a street where there was no meeting, Billy often went, on the off chance. But his lot was chiefly disappointment; wherefore he became more especially careful to furnish himself ere he left home.

For certain weeks cash came less freely than ever from the two women. Lizer spoke of providing for the necessities of the expected child: a manifestly absurd procedure, as Billy pointed out, since, if they were unable to clothe or feed it, the duty would fall on its grandmother. That was law, and nobody could get over it. But even with this argument, a shilling cost him many more demands and threats than it had used, and a deal more general trouble.

At last Lizer ceased from going to the pickle factory, and could not even help Billy's mother at the mangle for long. This lasted for near a week, when Billy, rising at ten with a bad mouth, resolved to stand no nonsense, and demanded two shillings.

'Two bob? Wot for?' Lizer asked.

''Cos I want it. None o' yer lip.'

'Ain't got it,' said Lizer sulkily.

'That's a bleed'n' lie.'

'Lie yerself.'

'I'll break y'in 'arves, ye blasted 'eifer!' He ran at her throat and forced her back over a chair. 'I'll pull yer face auf! If y' don't give me the money, gawblimy, I'll do for ye!'

Lizer strained and squalled. 'Le' go! You'll kill me an' the kid too!' she grunted hoarsely. Billy's mother ran in and threw her arms about him, dragging him away. 'Don't Billy,' she said, in terror. 'Don't Billy—not now! You'll get in trouble. Come away! She might go auf, an' you'd get in trouble!'

Billy Chope flung his wife over and turned to his mother. 'Take yer 'ands auf me,' he said: 'go on, or I'll gi' ye somethin' for yerself.' And he punched her in the breast by way of illustration.

'You shall 'ave what I've got, Billy, if it's money,' the mother said. 'But don't go an' git yerself in trouble, don't. Will a shillin' do?'

'No, it won't. Think I'm a bloomin' kid? I mean 'avin' two bob this mornin'.'

'I was a-keepin' it for the rent, Billy, but—'

'Yus; think o' the bleed'n' lan'lord 'fore me doncher?' And he pocketed the two shillings. 'I ain't settled with you yut, my gal,' he added to Lizer; 'mikin' about at 'ome an' 'idin' money. You wait a bit.'

Lizer had climbed into an erect position, and, gravid and slow, had got as far as the passage. Mistaking this for a safe distance, she replied with defiant railings. Billy made for her with a kick that laid her on the lower stairs, and, swinging his legs round his mother as she obstructed him, entreating him not to get in trouble, he attempted to kick again in a more telling spot. But a movement among the family upstairs and a tap at the door hinted of inter-ference, and he took himself off.

Lizer lay doubled up on the stairs, howling: but her only articu-late cry was,—'Gawd 'elp me, it's comin'!'

35

Billy went to the meeting of the Unemployed, and cheered a proposal to storm the Tower of London. But he did not join the procession following a man with a handkerchief on a stick, who promised destruction to every policeman in his path: for he knew the fate of such processions. With a few others he hung about the nearest tavern for a while, on the chance of the advent of a flush sailor from St Katharine's, disposed to treat out-o'-workers. Then he went along to a quieter beer-house and took a pint or two at his own expense. A glance down the music-hall bills hanging in the bar having given him a notion for the evening, he bethought himself of dinner, and made for home.

The front door was open, and in the first room, where the mangle stood, there were no signs of dinner. And this was at three o'clock! Billy pushed into the room behind, demanding why.

'Billy,' Lizer said faintly from her bed, 'look at the baby!'

Something was moving feebly under a flannel petticoat. Billy pulled the petticoat aside, and said,—'That? Well, it *is* a measly snipe.' It was a blind, hairless homunculus, short of a foot long, with a skinny face set in a great skull. There was a black bruise on one side from hip to armpit. Billy dropped the petticoat and said, 'Where's my dinner?'

'I dunno,' Lizer responded hazily. 'Wot's the time?'

'Time? Don't try to kid me. You git up; go on. I want my dinner.'

'Mother's gittin' it, I think,' said Lizer. 'Doctor had to slap 'im like anythink 'fore 'e'd cry. 'E don't cry now much. 'E—'

'Go on; out ye git. I do'want no more damn jaw. Git my dinner.'

'I'm a-gittin' of it, Billy,' his mother said, at the door. She had begun when he first entered. 'It won't be a minute.'

'You come 'ere; y'aint alwis s' ready to do 'er work, are ye? She ain't no call to stop there no longer, an' I owe 'er one for this mornin'. Will ye git out, or shall I kick ye?'

'She can't, Billy,' his mother said. And Lizer snivelled and said, 'You're a damn brute. Y'ought to be bleedin' well booted.'

But Billy had her by the shoulders and began to haul; and again his mother besought him to remember what he might bring upon himself. At this moment the doctor's dispenser, a fourth-year London Hospital student of many inches, who had been washing his hands in the kitchen, came in. For a moment he failed to comprehend the scene. Then he took Billy Chope by the collar, hauled him pell-mell along the passage, kicked him (hard) into the gutter, and shut the door.

When he returned to the room, Lizer, sitting up and holding on by the bed-frame, gasped hysterically: 'Ye bleedin' makeshift, I'd 'ave yer liver out if I could reach ye! You touch my 'usband, ye long pisenin' 'ound you! Ow!' And, infirm of aim, she flung a cracked teacup at his head. Billy's mother said, 'Y'ought to be ashamed of yourself, you low blaggard. If 'is father was alive 'e'd knock yer 'ead auf. Call yourself a doctor—a passel o' boys—! Git out! Go out o' my 'ouse or I'll give y'in charge!'

'But—why, hang it, he'd have killed her.' Then to Lizer—'Lie down.'

'Sha'n't lay down. Keep auf! if you come near me I'll corpse ye. You go while ye're safe!'

The dispenser appealed to Billy's mother. 'For God's sake make her lie down. She'll kill herself. I'll go. Perhaps the doctor had better come.' And he went: leaving the coast clear for Billy Chope to return and avenge his kicking.

(iii)

A change of circumstances

Lizer was some months short of twenty-one when her third child was born. The pickle factory had discarded her some time before, and since that her trade had consisted in odd jobs of charing. Odd jobs of charing have a shade the better of a pickle factory in the matter of respectability, but they are precarious, and they are worse paid at that. In the East End they are sporadic and few. Moreover, it is in the household where paid help is a rarity that the bitterness of servitude is felt. Also, the uncertainty and irregularity of the returns were a trouble to Billy Chope. He was never sure of having got them all. It might be ninepence, or a shilling, or eighteenpence. Once or twice, to his knowledge, it had been half-a-crown, from a chance job at a doctor's or a parson's, and once it was three shillings. That it might be half-a-crown or three shillings again, and that some of it was being kept back, was ever the suspicion evoked by Lizer's evening homing. Plainly, with these fluctuating and uncertain revenues, more bashing than ever was needed to ensure the extraction of the last copper; empty-handedness called for bashing on its own account; so that it was often Lizer's hap to be refused a job because of a black eye.

Lizer's self was scarcely what it had been. The red of her cheeks, once bounded only by the eyes and the mouth, had shrunk to a spot in the depth of each hollow; gaps had been driven in her big white teeth; even the snub nose had run to a point and the fringe hung dry and ragged, while the bodily outline was as a sack's. At home, the children lay in her arms or tumbled at her heels, puling and foul. Whenever she was near it, there was the mangle to be turned; for lately Billy's mother had exhibited a strange weakness, sometimes collapsing with a gasp in the act of brisk or prolonged exertion, and often leaning on whatever stood hard by and grasping at her side. This ailment she treated, when she had twopence, in such terms as made her smell of gin and peppermint; and more than once this circumstance had inflamed the breast of Billy her son, who was morally angered by this boozing away of money that was really his.

Lizer's youngest, being seven or eight months old, was mostly taking care of itself, when Billy made a welcome discovery after a hard and pinching day. The night was full of blinding wet, and the rain beat on the window as on a drum. Billy sat over a small fire in the front room smoking his pipe, while his mother folded clothes for delivery. He stamped twice on the hearth, and then, drawing off his boot, he felt inside. It was a nail. The poker head made a good anvil, and, looking about for a hammer, Billy bethought him of a brick from the mangle. He rose, and, lifting the lid of the weight-box, groped about among the clinkers and the other ballast till he came upon a small but rather heavy paper parcel. ''Ere—wot's this?' he said, and pulled it out.

His mother, whose back had been turned, hastened across the room, hand to breast (it had got to be her habit). 'What is it, Billy?' she said. 'Not that: there's nothing there. I'll get anything you want, Billy.' And she made a nervous catch at the screw of paper. But Billy fended her off, and tore the package open. It was money, arranged in little columns of farthings, halfpence, and threepenny pieces, with a few sixpences, a shilling or two, and a single half-sovereign. 'O,' said Billy, 'this is the game, is it?—

'idin' money in the mangle! Got any more?' And he hastily turned the brickbats.

'No, Billy, don't take that—don't!' implored his mother. 'There'll be some money for them things when they go 'ome—'ave that. I'm savin' it, Billy, for something partic'ler: s'elp me Gawd, I am, Billy.'

'Yes,' replied Billy, raking diligently among the clinkers, 'savin' it for a good ol' booze. An' now you won't 'ave one. Bleedin' nice thing, 'idin' money away from yer own son!'

'It ain't for that, Billy—s'elp me, it ain't; it's case anythink 'appens to me. On'y to put me away decent, Billy, that's all. We never know, an' you'll be glad of it t'elp bury me if I should go any time—'

'I'll be glad of it now,' answered Billy, who had it in his pocket; 'an' I've got it. You ain't a dyin' sort, *you* ain't; an' if you was, the parish 'ud soon tuck *you* up. P'raps you'll be straighter about money after this.'

'Let me 'ave *some*, then—you can't want it all. Give me some, an' then 'ave the money for the things. There's ten dozen and seven, and you can take 'em yerself if ye like.'

'Wot—in this 'ere rain? Not me! I bet I'd 'ave the money if I wanted it without that. 'Ere—change these 'ere fardens at the draper's wen you go out: there's two bob's worth an' a penn'orth; I don't want to bust my pockets wi' them.'

While they spoke Lizer had come in from the back room. But she said nothing: she rather busied herself with a child she had in her arms. When Billy's mother, despondent and tearful, had tramped out into the rain with a pile of clothes in an oilcloth wrapper, she said sulkily, without looking up, 'You might 'a' let 'er kep' that; you git all you want.'

At another time this remonstrance would have provoked active hostilities; but now, with the money about him, Billy was complacently disposed. 'You shutcher 'ead,' he said, 'I got this, any'ow. She can make it up out o' my rent if she likes.' This last remark was a joke, and he chuckled as he made it. For Billy's rent was a simple fiction, devised, on the suggestion of a smart canvasser, to give him a parliamentary vote.

That night Billy and Lizer slept, as usual, in the bed in the back room, where the two younger children also were. Billy's mother made a bedstead nightly with three chairs and an old trunk in the front room by the mangle, and the eldest child lay in a floor-bed near her. Early in the morning Lizer awoke at a sudden outcry of the little creature. He clawed at the handle till he opened the door, and came staggering and tumbling into the room with screams of terror. 'Wring 'is blasted neck,' his father grunted sleepily. 'Wot's the kid 'owlin' for?'

'I's 'f'aid o' g'anny—I's 'f'aid o' g'anny!' was all the child could say; and when he had said it, he fell to screaming once more.

Lizer rose and went to the next room; and straightway came a scream from her also. 'O—O—Billy! Billy! O my Gawd! Billy come 'ere!'

And Billy, fully startled, followed in Lizer's wake. He blundered in, rubbing his eyes, and saw.

Stark on her back in the huddled bed of old wrappers and shawls lay his mother. The outline of her poor face—strained in an upward stare of painful surprise—stood sharp and meagre against the black of the grate beyond. But the muddy old skin was white, and looked cleaner than its wont, and many of the wrinkles were gone.

Billy Chope, half-way across the floor, recoiled from the corpse, and glared at it pallidly from the doorway.

'Good Gawd!' he croaked faintly, 'is she dead?'

Seized by a fit of shuddering breaths, Lizer sank on the floor, and, with her head across the body, presently broke into a storm of hysterical blubbering, while Billy, white and dazed, dressed hurriedly and got out of the house.

He was at home as little as might be until the coroner's officer carried away the body two days later. When he came for his meals, he sat doubtful and querulous in the matter of the front room door's being shut. The dead once clear away, however, he resumed his faculties and clearly saw that here was a bad change for the worse. There was the mangle, but who was to work it? If Lizer did, there would be no more charing jobs—a clear loss of one third of his income. And it was not at all certain that the people who had given their mangling to his mother would give it to Lizer. Indeed, it was pretty sure that many would not, because mangling is a thing given by preference to widows, and many widows of the neighbourhood were perpetually competing for it. Widows, moreover, had the first call in most odd jobs whereunto Lizer might turn her hand: an injustice whereon Billy meditated with bitterness.

The inquest was formal and unremarked, the medical officer having no difficulty in certifying a natural death from heart disease. The bright idea of a collection among the jury, which Billy communicated, with pitiful representations, to the coroner's officer, was brutally swept aside by that functionary, made cunning by much experience. So the inquest brought him naught save disappointment and a sense of injury. . . .

The mangling orders fell away as suddenly and completely as he had feared: they were duly absorbed among the local widows. Neglect the children as Lizer might, she could no longer leave them as she had done. Things, then, were bad with Billy, and neither threats nor thumps could evoke a shilling now.

It was more than Billy could bear: so that, ''Ere,' he said one night, 'I've 'ad enough o' this. You go and get some money; go on.'

'Go an' git it?' replied Lizer. 'O yus. That's easy, ain't it? "Go an' git it," says you. 'Ow?'

'Any'ow—I don' care. Go on.'

'Why,' replied Lizer, looking up with wide eyes, 'd'ye think I can go an' pick it up in the street?'

'Course you can. Plenty others does, don't they?'

'Gawd, Billy . . . wot d'ye mean?'

'Wot I say; plenty others does it. Go on—you ain't so bleed'n' innocent as all that. Go an' see Sam Cardew. Go on—'ook it.'

Lizer, who had been kneeling at the child's floor-bed, rose to her feet, pale-faced and bright of eye.

'Stow kiddin', Billy,' she said. 'You don't mean that. I'll go round to the fact'ry in the mornin': p'raps they'll take me on temp'ry.'

'Damn the fact'ry.'

He pushed her into the passage. 'Go on—you git me some money, if ye don't want yer bleed'n' 'ead knocked auf.'

There was a scuffle in the dark passage, with certain blows, a few broken words and a sob. Then the door slammed, and Lizer Chope was in the windy street.

Henry Nevinson

The St George of Rochester

Afore that week was well out, I got took on for a job as packer in the City, and every mornin' I was up almost as soon as light, and ridin' along the Road in a Workman's Car, same as if I'd kep' a private gig. So I put in two hours work till breakfast, and mostly got 'ome again to tea by six or 'alf past, 'avin' an hour off in the middle for my dinner at a cook-shop.

One evenin' we'd all done our teas and was feelin' very comfortable, what with father 'avin' got a good job too for fittin' some chapel or ware'ouse or somethink o' that down in Bow, as 'ud keep 'im goin' pretty steady through winter in all weathers, the brickwork bein' finished off. And I was thinkin' to myself whether I'd get some fellers to come round with me and be chippin' young Duffy, or pluck up 'eart to go and pass the time of evenin' to Lina Sullivan, she bein' one o' them as likes yer best when yer 'appy. But on a sudden there comes a knockin' at the door, and little Susan Moore sticks 'er 'ead in and says, in a kind o' voice like sayin' poetry at school:

'If yer please, father's gone and 'ad another stroke, and wants to see Mr Britton very purtikler.'

'That's a bad job,' says my father; 'at that rate I reckon it's about all over with old Timmo. 'E'll snuff it, sure as I'm alive. All right, my dear, I'll come along this minute. Just set yourself down, and take a cup o' tea.'

Old Timmo 'ad fell on 'is back in ladin' a lighter the spring before, and been queer all down one side ever since, for all 'is being able to move about and carry things, but not to manage 'is lighter no more. So father tells me to come along, 'e always likin' me to see all the sights as might be, and old Timmo bein' famous as the strongest man in our parts or praps on the water anywheres, let alone 'is 'avin' won the Doggett coat and badge the very same day as 'e was twenty-one. And there's some as say 'e could 'ave beat old 'Iggins 'isself, as is called the ex-champion sculler of England, only that their ages wasn't arranged right for 'em to make a match of it through 'Iggins bein' older. And father says it's often the same way with gettin' married, seein' as there'd be a rare lot of different marriages, if only the parties 'ad started more level when they was fust born.

Timmo 'ad a 'ouse all to 'isself and family in Pennington Street close along by the Dock, 'e bein' always in good work up to the time of 'is accident, through bein' able to do as much as any two. So we knocked, and Mrs Moore came to the door, and seein' us she started cryin' and carryin' on most terrible. Stout and red she was, 'avin' a lot o' children, for all not bein' old yet. So my father pushes past 'er, tellin' 'er as praps things 'ud be better soon.

'And they couldn't be worse,' she says, 'cos if they was, we'd any'ow 'ave 'is club-money to draw and live on.'

Gettin' upstairs, we find old Timmo lyin' on 'is bed quite still, with a decent brown blanket over 'im, and a candle burnin'; and the doctor 'ad took and stuck a Bible or somethink o' that under 'is 'ead to prop it up. And one of 'is arms was layin' out over the blanket bare from the shoulder, O my soul! it was just like the front leg of a cart-'orse, barrin' the extry finish about the 'and. But 'is grey eyes seemed kind o' bigger nor usual, and 'is nose and tuft o' beard more peaky, and 'is 'ole face some'ow pale, for all its bein' dark brown as a bit o' seasoned wood—a deal darker nor what 'is 'air was, that bein' yellerish and burnt near white at the roots by the sun.

'What, Timmo!' says my father quite cheerful.

'What, George!' 'e answers, and says no more, 'e bein' always slow of speech. But that evenin' 'e'd been turnin' over what 'e 'ad to say so as to run straight on when once started, only not knowin' where to start.

'Gone aground again?' says my father.

'Not me!' 'e says, 'I ain't one to go aground, but it's like as when a barge gets run into by a steamer through no fault of 'ern. Yes, yer may 'oist the green flag over me now, same as over a wreck in the tideway.'

'Don't yer be sayin' that, Timmo,' says my father, and cops

43

THE POLYTECHNIC OF WALES
LIBRARY
TREFOREST

'old on 'is 'and, and makes as if 'e was only feelin' at 'is pulse goin'.

'Well, cheer up, mate,' says Timmo, 'that's neither 'ere nor there. What I wants is to give yer a kind of a message to take, if so be I peg out this time. Yer see it's all along of my Doggett badge, as I won fair thirty year gone, me bein' now turned of fifty.'

With that 'e looks at the badge, as was 'angin' up opposite over the fireplace, and shinin' in the candle-light, the silver 'orse on it showin' quite plain.

'I spose my missus ain't anywheres near ?' 'e whispers. 'Well, that's all right. Me and you bein' men, we understands one another; but they women understands nothink about it, bein' females, bar one as understood, and it's 'er I'm goin' to speak about—'er and my Doggett badge, them's the two ropes I've got to 'old by.

'Yer mightn't think it, mate,' 'e went on, 'but once on a time I was in love with a woman.'

'Ger on!' says my father, 'once on a time indeed! With all the females 'untin' up and down after yer all yer life, and you married three times as I 'ear say, and a fine lot o' children beside! Once in love, ger on! Men like me and you is always in love, more *or* less, just accordin'.'

'Now ye're talkin' same as any female yerself, mate,' he says. 'The kind o' love yer mean 's the common kind, as is quite right and proper in its place, but it ain't the kind as I mean. And I wasn't talkin' o' none o' my three wives neither, for all I've no word agen them, and they wasn't none of 'em bad-lookin' to start with. But it's a different kind o' woman as I'm speakin' on.'

'That's as it may be,' says my father; 'and it might so 'appen as I've been in love myself same as you, for all yer coat and badge.'

'Now keep yer 'air on, mate,' he says, 'and we'll go back to that same badge, as is the thing I was wantin' to speak about.

'Yer see,' he says, 'it came about all along of one day some thirteen or fourteen year after I'd won it. I'd worked myself up bit by bit from bein' lighterman's boy to bein' a certificated lighterman; and then, through always 'avin' a proper pride of myself, I took to the sailin' line, fust as boy, then as mate, and last of all as captain. And just about the time I'm a'goin' to tell on, I'd been captain two year gone, sailin' the barge as was then called the *Deborah Jane*, 'ailin' from Rochester, for all 'er voyage bein' from Maidstone to the West Kent Wharf close agen London Bridge, or to the 'Onduras Wharf agen Blackfriars, if so 'appen we was carryin' 'ay. And seein' as I was sailin' for a good firm and was makin' from thirty shillin' to two pound reg'lar, and at whiles five bob extry, I'd married 'er as was my fust wife, a Maidstone girl. But she died shortly before the time I'm speakin' on in her first confinement, as females will, through no fault o' mine. So I was feelin' very independent, and a bit lonesome at the same time, through 'avin' nobody waitin' for me when the *Deborah Jane* put in 'ome, as was mostly on Sunday afternoon. But I never missed 'er much on board, 'avin' the same two mates as before, and she never 'avin' made the voyage with me through females mostly not suitin' when yer urgent. And my business on the back voyage was always urgent, almost as urgent as steam, as is the urgentest thing there is.

'Well, as I was sayin', it was that Saturday afternoon, about this time or earlier in September, the flood runnin' up till 'alf after five, and the water all jumpin' about like a shoal of fish under the sun, and a draught from the west fair callin' for the sails to start. I'd just finished ladin' up with a cargo of sugar and currants and bacon and cheese and soap and that, enough to wash and fill the bellies of 'alf the villages in Kent, seein' as the *Deborah Jane*, as then was, took down eighty-five ton in 'er 'old as easy as me or you 'ud take down a quart. And we'd just drifted across to Tennant's Wharf to take on an extry sack of flour, and was puttin' the gear straight, ready to 'eave up and cast away at the turn o' the flood, and there was a line of 'eads watchin' us from the bridge, same as mostly stands watchin', no matter if there ain't nothink to watch. And on a sudden one of 'em comes down round by the steps, and stands leanin' agen a post by the Old Swan pier, close by where we was layin' along the wharf. O Christ! it's fifteen year agone or more, but there she was standin' in flesh and blood with some-think of a white dress on and a kind of bluish cloak, so as yer might almost 'ave took 'er for a 'orspital nurse. So she stands lookin' at me, and now and again I gets a sideways look at 'er in settin' up the gear. And each time as I looks, I says to myself, "She's *all* right", I says.

'Now it so 'appens I'm one o' them as can't abear to see a female by 'erself and me not speak to 'er. It's kind of unperlite not to speak, and she takes it as such. "Oh!" she says to 'erself, any female does, "so I ain't good-lookin' enough to be spoke to, ain't I?" and that makes 'er wild. So just as we'd cast off, and was swingin' slow round by the pier-end, the water bein' at the slack, I got up close agen the side, and looks up at 'er, and says quite gentle: "Eh, Miss" (I was goin' to say "My Dear", but some'ow I stuck in "Miss" instead). "Eh, Miss," I says, "it's I wish as you was comin' down the water with me, I do."

"'I *am* comin'"', she says, and steps down on the gunwale as cool as gettin' into a penny 'bus. I just put one arm round 'er to 'old 'er safe, and next moment we'd swung out into the stream, and down under the bridge. And I could 'ear the crowd on top a-laughin' and shoutin' after me, and sayin' "What chur, Timmo!" "You just bring back my old woman", and passin' undecent remarks, and singin' bits about "Nancy Lee", as was all the go in them days. But I feels 'er under this 'ere arm, she so thin and light, and I looks down on 'er and fair laughs with wonder, and she looks up at me with a kind o' look o' what a pigeon feels, as gets safe off after bein' let out o' the trap at a shootin', and is missed by the outsiders as well. But as to me bein' surprised—well, if the statue of Queen Victorier on Temple Bar 'ad walked into my barge, I couldn't 'ave been more surprised, let alone pleased. And my two mates kep' standin' and starin' at us, and they left settin' up the gear, and we just let the *Deborah Jane* drift, worse nor any common lighter, till on a sudden a big steamer as was makin' up for the Pool, started whistlin' and 'ootin' at us fit to wake a church-full of people; so I gets out the long sweep and slues 'er round just in time. And would you believe it? that lady cops 'old on the sweep alongside o' me, and pulls for 'er life. Eh, she was always a rare plucked one and no mistake, and that quick and ready! Then I gets a lot of old canvas, and 'eaps it up agen the tiller for 'er to lay on. So she lays down, and keeps lookin' sometimes at me and sometimes at the sun, as still 'ad about an hour or more to go.

'So we sets up the gear at last, and swing out the foot o' the mains'l on a pole, bein' afore the wind, and up with the spinnaker, cos the draught was almost too light to make the fores'l bulge. And I loops up a bit of a reef in the mains'l, so as to let me see what might be comin' in the way, and settles myself at the tiller, just to show the lady how the *Deborah Jane*, as then was, could move. And the draught freshenin', we fair walked past the other barges, top-s'ld as well as stumpies mind you, just the same as if they was layin' at anchor. Eh, we was urgent in my old barge, almost as urgent as what steam is. But all the time we three mates says nothink at all, we thinkin' only of one thing, and the lady was layin' in 'er blue and white, same as a patch o' sky set on the deck.

'O my soul! she was a reg'lar beauty was that woman. Some'ow from first to last she always put me in mind of my spinnaker. P'raps it was through the spinnaker being so light and kind o' dainty, it bein' made to catch any breath of draught as might be, and left clean and white, not smeared over with ochre and oil same as the other sails as is all red and brown and 'eavy. And then she'd bend and curve this way and that, for all the world like the spinnaker when the wind's 'avin' a bit of a game with it, for all 'er bein' as tough as a steel-wire stay. And mind you, it's always the spinnaker as snaps the top-mast, through bracin' it for'ard like a whip. And I've never see the man little or big but that woman could a' done just whatever she 'ad a mind to with 'im. And that's what sometimes makes me think as 'im as 'ad got 'old on 'er afore must 'ave died sudden, or somethink o' that. For she wasn't the sort as we men gets sick on, as is natural with most females, but she was always after somethink new, and all on a sudden, when nobody wasn't lookin' for it, she'd come round and say or do somethink more takin' and more sweeter nor all what she'd said or done before. No, mate; once a man 'ad got 'old on 'er 'e wasn't likely to give 'er up, unless forced to—not 'im, not me anyways. I'd as soon as 'ave give up the water, as is equally uncertain and enticin'.

'Well, as I was sayin', we travel down past Woolwich, not sayin' much, but sailin' most urgent, as is usual afore the wind, with the lee-boards 'auled up close, and the mizen swingin' with the rudder, and 'elpin' to pull us round the tacks by the Isle o' Dogs, and the iron loops and chains rattling along the 'orses, main and fore, accordin' as the sails swung over from side to side. But when we get into the long straight reach by Barkin' Level, seein' as the sun was almost down, and the evenin' closin' in cold, I give over the tiller to the mate, and went up to the lady where she was layin' starin' up at the sky, as 'ad a few stars comin' out. And I ask her if she'd fancy a drink o' tea. So she ups and comes down the bit of ladder into the cabin aft as natural as might be, me goin' fust and slidin' the shutters in front o' the berths, so as they looked same as the other cupboards all round, where I kep' the coal and eatables and cookin' things and an extry set of trouseys and guernsey agen the wet. Then I lights a bit of a fire and makes a drop of tea, and I cuts the bread, and I says:

'"I ask yer pardon, mum—"

'"Don't call me mum, please", she says, cuttin' in as quick as anythink.

'"As yer please, miss," I says, "but I thought maybe as mum showed more respeck, me not knowin' which yer might be, as 'ow should I? But, askin' yer pardon, miss, do yer take butter to yer bread?"

'"A little, please," she says.

'"I wasn't after askin' the quantity, little *or* much," I says, "but just whether or no yer takes it."

'And it's my belief it was just that little bit of extry perliteness on my part in the matter of margarine as fust made 'er start takin' o' fancy to me. But the mate always stuck out as she must 'ave 'eard from the crowd as I'd won the Doggett, and that set her lookin' at me. And I wasn't a bad-lookin' bloke in them days, nor never 'ave been. And as to them clurks and such like as was alongside of 'er lookin' at me—why, I could 'ave eat any three on 'em at once, and felt no fuller.

'Then I bring out what best I 'ad with me, laid up agen Sunday's dinner—tinned salmon, and bacon, and a bit of cold beef, and 'alf a Dutch cheese—and I give 'er the choice of just anythink she fancied, me 'aving fust set it all out nice on bits o' newspaper. So when she'd finished 'er tea, and 'ad asked me all manner of easy questions about the barge and the water and the names o' things, I says to 'er:

'"I'm not after drivin' of yer away, miss, and should dearly love for you to stop, I should. But we shan't lay up till nigh on midnight, and if yer wants to go ashore, I'll put yer out at Green'ithe or at Gravesend, askin' yer pardon all the same."

'Now, mate, you'll be thinkin' me a born fool for offerin' such a thing, me 'avin' 'er there in the cabin along of me, and no escape. And I more nor 'alf thought myself a fool too, but some'ow she'd got somethink about 'er different from other females, and it wasn't no good you thinkin' o' makin' love to 'er agen 'er will. It wasn't never no good at all. And I see smart enough as she wasn't willin' at that time.

'But when she 'eard me talk about puttin' 'er ashore, she stood up sudden, and came over to me, and for the first time—eh, mate, but it wasn't the last by no manner—she put 'er 'ands on top o' mine, and they was as sorft and light yer scarce felt 'em, same as the feelin' of water on a warm day. And she looks up into my face, as was a way she 'ad, and O Lord! when she did that, I misdoubt if even a female could 'ave said no to 'er, let alone a man of cast-iron, such as I wasn't by no means. And she begs and entreats of me to let 'er stop aboard, and not to send her back to London all alone.

'"Look," she says, kind of layin' 'old on me, "you can't refuse what a woman asks. I'll live on the deck or wherever there's room. I'll be your servant. I'll do the cookin' and washin' for you. I'll look after the ship, and make it all nice. Only don't turn me away."

'And so she went on, or words to that effeck. And it's awesome to think what that woman, bein' a lady born, must have suffered afore she could bring 'erself to speak like that to a common water-man same as me, for all me bein' captain of the barge. But bein' always terrible fond o' females, and not likin' to see none of 'em in distress, I just took on me to treat 'er same as you'd treat other females. So I smooths 'er down, and says:

'"There, there, my dear, you shall stay with me till yerself gives the word to go. I'm big enough to purtect yer, I should 'ope, and there ain't none as I knows on to say a word agen it, now as 'er as was my wife is gorne, for all this bein' no place for the likes of you."

'Then I 'eard 'er give a kind of sob, but it wasn't with cryin', she not bein' much given to the like o' that. It was just the kind of deep breath as a man gives when 'e nicks 'is boat away from under a big steamer's bows, and 'e lays easy on 'is sculls a minute, and the steamer goes swishin' past through the water.

'Then I went on deck, and settin' on the main-'orse I tell the crew as the lady wanted to stop along of us a bit, and what I reckoned was the likely reasons for that. And the mate, as always aimed at a bit of argufyin', for all not bein' over partikler 'isself—it was 'im as afterwards went off with my second wife, so as she died of 'is treatment of 'er,—'e said 'e wasn't sure if it was just the right thing to do, to keep a female on board without yer bein' married to 'er, and for 'is part 'e'd never see a lady or gen'leman as was good for much; but for the rest 'e raised no objection. And the boy says if *I* wouldn't purtect the lady, blind 'im! 'e'd purtect 'er 'isself.

'Just then the lady comes up out o' the cabin 'erself, and I tells 'er the name of Charlie and the name of Ben.

'"And might I make so bold as ask what you'd like us to call you, miss?" I says.

'"Oh, it doesn't matter," she answers. "Are we a long way from London now?"

'"Yus," I says, "we're past Erith, and makin' up to Purfleet. By daytime you'd soon see the Tilbury 'otel standin' up in the distance, and it's just past there as we'll lay up till nigh on six to-morrer mornin'."

'"Erith?" she says, "that's a pretty name. You can call me Erith."

'And that's the name she sticks in my poor 'ead under.

'By the time we laid up, me and the boy 'ad made the aft-cabin pretty tidy for 'er, clearin' out my berth and puttin' in clean beddin', as was always supplied us by the firm, same as teapots and kettles, most generous. And we'd agreed that for the time bein' I was to 'ave one o' the berths for'ard, till we see 'ow things lay. So the boy was set to sleep in front of the fire, and me and the mate in the berths on each side. But after we'd cast anchor, I couldn't 'elp but just 'ave another look down into my own cabin; and standin' still and listenin' I could 'ear by the sound of 'er breathin' as she was sleepin' better nor a corpse. And by what I could reckon, for all me never askin', no bloomin' corpse 'ad ever been through worse nor what she 'ad, nor 'ad got a better right to sleep at the end on it.

'Next day and next, and so on week after week, she still seemed best part asleep, as if she couldn't never 'ave enough of restin', for all 'er bein' always so obligin' and perlite. And from the fust start off she took on 'er to do the bit o' cookin' and washin' and such as that, same as any common female, so as she wouldn't never let us so much as light a fire or boil a kettle for ourselves, she likin' to picture 'erself as earnin' 'er own livin', for all it wasn't exackly true in the actual value of 'er work. But none on us wouldn't 'ave give 'er up for twice the cost of 'er keep, and me not if yer'd give me the command of an ironclad flagship. And that was the quietest autumn-time as ever I call to mind, neither rains nor fog. And often and often, as we was just droppin' up or down with the tide and a gentle draught, all sails set, I've stood at the tiller in the early mornin', and seen the sky and the water all turnin' white with the daylight, and maybe a bit of a mist just risin' off the river, and the *Warspite* and *Arethusa* trainin' ships lookin' big above it, and a gull or two flappin' around to see what they could get, and the sea-birds callin' and pipin' from the mud along the banks, and I've 'eard little sounds of movin' in the cabin under my feet, and I've knowed in myself as she was gettin' up, and washin' 'erself, and lightin' the fire for our breakfasts. And then I've seen the blue smoke comin' out of the little chimbley. And after that she'd slide back the 'atch, and put 'er 'ead out so smilin' and clean, for all the world to match the mornin'. But the rest o' the time when she wasn't workin', as she liked to call it, she was mostly layin' aft on the canvas, and at such times I always took the tiller myself, so as to be ready near 'er if wanted. And for the up journeys I mostly tried to get a cargo of 'ay, and put 'er on top of it for 'er to lay on, and then, if so be we fouled a buoy, or a lighter came into us, or we drew up 'ard agen the wharf, she'd never feel nothink but a soft kind o' jolt, as is the advantage of 'ay to lay on. And after a bit I sold up my little 'ouse at Maidstone, and brought a few bits o' things, more especial female clothing, aboard. And so I'd got no other 'ome but the barge, and with 'er there I 'adn't no need to think o' none else. And about Christmas-time she started cuttin' and sewin' all day long at little bits of things, as she stowed in the spare berth o' the cabin. But all the time she kep' 'erself uncommon quiet, barrin' sometimes of a frosty night I'd 'ear 'er come on deck, and lookin' out I'd see 'er walkin' up and down, up and down, with nothink but the stars and the river-lights to see, and praps a great furnace flarin' away in the dark with a mouth like 'ell-fire. But some'ow she always got kind of uneasy and unrestin' as soon as ever we put up to London Bridge, and as long as we lay along-side the wharf, she kep' 'erself in the cabin till the evenin'.

'Well, it might be about Easter-time or somethink earlier, she had a baby born on the barge—not a convenient kind o' place for such things to 'appen in, but I brought off a doctor from Rochester. And if it 'ad been a female, we'd 'ave called it Deborah Jane; but through its bein' a boy, there didn't seem nothink necessary to call it. So we called it all manner, and out of all its names one kind o' name some'ow seemed to stick best, and we mostly spoke of it as Lucky, "bloomin' little Lucky", and suchlike silliness, as pleases females. But the real wonder was to see the fuss as Erith made over it so soon as she was better, again, always dressin' and un-dressin', and washin' and 'uggin' at it, and takin' such care as if it was goin' to be the only one baby in the world, and people was to take a fresh start from it, same as from Adam.

'"Just look at 'is sweet little body", she'd say, and with that she'd undress it again, and spread it out naked on 'er lap, and kiss it all over by inches. And the mate said she made more to do with it nor the ordinary cos she'd paid 'igher for the gettin' it. But I some'ow think she'd got a kind o' notion as 'avin' 'ad the baby some'ow put 'er up on a level same as other women. After all them pains and the strangeness of 'avin' that bit o' live stuff to feed and fend for, all the rest, whatever it was as 'ad gone before, didn't seem much to matter, it bein' all kind o' sunk in the kid. And it was two things most as made me think so: fust cos when we put into London, she didn't never 'ide away in the cabin any more, but just fetched up the baby, and sat on deck, nursin' it and lookin' up at the bridge quite calm, as if nobody could say nothink at 'er now. And second, she came to look on me quite different. Before that, I might just as well 'ave been a saint or an angel or a parson from the way she treated me, makin' scarce no difference for me bein' there or not. But now she seemed to find out as I wasn't never any such-like person, but somethink quite different. And she grew kind o' shyer, and yet more sweeter, than before. It makes me squirm to think on it now; it do indeed.

'It took a long time comin' on between us—long on 'er side, is what I mean. Yer see, livin' on a barge ain't at all the same thing as livin' on shore and goin' out to work. Yer've mostly always got time on a barge, and there ain't no call to 'urry about sayin' anythink, more especial when the two of yer's livin' together on it, and tomorrer goes by much the same as today, only for the matter of the wind blowin' or not blowin'. So we went on without no change till the middle of the winter after the baby was born, and it was bitter cold with a frost as turned the river into great blocks of ice, joltin' up and down with the tide alongside of us as we sailed. One night we 'ad laid up for the evenin', and gone to bed with great fires blazin' in both cabins. But some'ow I couldn't get no sleep for thinkin' on 'er, she bein' so near and all. So I creeps out and along the deck, just to see if she and the kid was gettin' on all right. And I found 'er settin' in front of 'er fire as if waitin' for me. So I just puts these two arms round 'er, knowin' it wasn't no good for me speakin', and she ups and kind o' folds 'er 'ands round at the back of my 'ead—there's no other woman ever knew such a thing to do as that—and kissed me on my mouth.

'And all that night, till the flood began to run again, we 'eard the great blocks of ice scrapin' and strikin' with dull thuds agen the sides of our cabin close to where our 'eads was layin'. I've mostly been 'appy enough all my time, till this 'ere sickness took 'old on me, and at times I've been extraordinar' 'appy, as after winnin' the Doggett, and now and again with my mates or with females. But that night when I 'eard the flood comin' in, and went on deck, and 'auled up, and trimmed the gear, and felt the old barge startin' to move through the water, shovin' away the blocks of ice same as me shovin' through a crowd, and I knowed as she was just under my feet layin' still and thinkin' o' me, that time was worth all the rest o' my good times put together. And almost afore we'd made Woolwich, the fog came on that thick, we was tied up there two days and two nights, and nothink movin' on the water, barrin' praps a steamer feelin' 'er way from one light to another, and bellowin' all the time like the devil tryin' to catch us two under the dark, and 'e not able. And when at last the fog fell down on the water, same as soot round an unswep' chimbley, the days 'adn't seemed no more nor one night, for all me bein' so urgent, and losin' money beside.

'Well, mate, that's the one part o' what I got to say, and that's 'ow I came to be in love quite different to the ordinar'. And that's 'er as was the only female I ever came across to understand them things. I used to think it was praps only through 'er bein' a lady born, but I've set eyes on a deal o' ladies since that time, and 'ave quite give up that notion. I've sometimes seed one of our own females as I've thought might 'ave well risen to it, but what with workin' and cleanin', and not gettin' proper things to eat, and marryin' so soon, and 'avin' such a lot o' children, they mostly all on 'em don't some'ow do it, and it ain't no good pertendin', for all I've liked 'em well enough, and they me, same as all females. And I needn't be tellin' you, mate, as I meant quite honourable by Erith, and was just dyin' to marry 'er and make 'er an honest woman, same as other wives. But some'ow or another she wouldn't 'ear no word on it, I never knowed for why. Like enough she was stopt by somethink of 'er past times, she never tellin' of 'em, nor me never askin' out of a kind o' respeck. Married or not, I always thought on 'er as if we was makin' love, and that's ow' I thinks on 'er still. It wasn't only 'er keepin' the place so tight and clean, and doin' the cookin', and 'elpin' to swill down the deck after our teas to stop the planks from partin' in dry weather, and 'er likin' to see the dirty water runnin' out at the slits under the bulwarks. And it wasn't only 'er paintin' at the barge, for all she was a rare 'and at paintin', and covered over the 'atches and the tiller and rudder and the wooden casin' to the chimbley with red and white and green and all manner. Why, she even painted the sprete white at the ends and green in the middle. And she made me get the name of the barge changed from the *Deborah Jane* to the *St George*. And she painted a picture in white o' that there feller on the tops'l—a queer lookin' bloke 'e was, with scales of armour same as a crocodile, and a serpent's 'ead in one 'and and a long sword in the other, reachin' right out o' the tops'l altogether. Eh, and a rare lot o' chippin' I got over that picture, through folks not understandin' of it, and callin' it an eel-catcher, or Old Nick, or the Grand Old Man, or anythink else 'andy. But, as I was sayin', it wasn't all that, but the kind o' way she 'ad o' lovin' me as made the difference. So as if she'd took no care with the look o' the vessel at all, nor so much as boiled a kettle, I'd 'ave loved 'er just exackly the same by reason of the way she 'ad of lovin' me. Why, I've sometimes felt my blood workin' up and down same as the pistons on the *Jumnah*, when I've been after some job ashore, and was puttin' off to the barge again in my little dingey, me knowin' well what was waitin' for me in our bit of a cabin. And at times if things was runnin' slack up the river, we'd get sent out for another kind of cargo, and 'ud 'ave to make round to Ipswich or maybe as far as Dover, and then she'd start workin' the tiller accordin' as I kep' tellin' 'er, and me managin' the gear, as might be. And if so 'appen a bit o' wind got up, and we was beatin' up agen it, close-'auled with the lee-boards down, and the water lappin' all over the deck above yer ankles, she'd lay 'old on the tiller along of me, and laugh, and sing, and talk all manner o' things of what us two could do together. For, as I was sayin', she was a rare plucked un, she was, and it's my belief she just loved runnin' into danger almost as much as she loved me, and for the same kind o' reasons.

'But yer may be sure I got a rare chippin' from all my mates on the water at the first start off. In my own crew the man turned kind o' surly, and didn't do 'is work what yer'd call proper again. But the boy made up for it, 'e workin' just double, and bringin' 'er water to wash with and everthink she could dream o' wantin', and mindin' little Lucky for 'er whiles she was busy at the cookin' and that. And some'ow or other the story of us spread all down the river, and we sailin' past the other barges, my old mates 'ud 'oller out to me, wantin' to know 'ow Grace Darlin' was, or what price I'd take for the Piccadilly Belle. And if so 'appen she'd 'ung up bits of 'er underclothin' and little Lucky's to dry on a line after washin', they'd call out: "What, Timmo! Is them yer new Doggett coat and badge?" But they dursn't say much, by reason of their knowin' I could break their bloomin' bones as soon as look at 'em. And Erith she only laughed, and told 'em she was quite willin' for 'em to 'ave 'er, only they'd got to catch us fust, and then to settle it up with 'er man, meanin' me. And afore a year was out, the river was fair mad in love with 'er, and they'd used to watch for the white St George on the tops'l coming up be'ind 'em, and then stand all o' the one side, and say "Good-mornin'", and all manner o' things, mostly decent, as we went by.

'But with their females it wasn't the same thing, acourse not, and they soon enough found out as the way to 'urt 'er laid through the little lad. So they'd 'oller out, "'Ullo, Timmo! and 'ow's that little barstud of yourn gettin' along?" or, "Bought any more second-'and kids up the spank, Timmo?" or, "What price the little backstairs Dook?" And I couldn't do nothink agen them, barrin' by callin' of 'em undecent names, me never bein' any 'and at breakin' the jaws of females, nor yet carin' to give 'em what for, through fear of me doin' 'em some injury. And some'ow Erith she didn't show no pluck agen 'em either, but took the kid in 'er lap and said nothink, like as if she'd lost 'er spirit. Eh, but there was one thing she could always give 'em points over; for she grew to be a rarer beauty every day, turnin' a kind o' thin varnished brown on 'er face and arms with the sun and rain and wind, the rest of 'er remainin' as before.

'So we went on sailin' with the tides, up and down, for nigh on two year, and never a word between us, cos she didn't never make game of me, but only of them others, and she was always findin' out somethink new to say or do, each time sweeter nor before, as I've told. And she'd used to tell me we was so fond of each other through 'avin' been lovers a long time back, afore we was born, when everythink was different, and perhaps I'd been a king. That's as it may be, and I'm not sayin' nothink in regard to it either 'ere nor there. But I only know as I don't feel much like a king now.

'Yer see, it was all too nice to last, same as everythink else. Even trouble don't last, worse luck; for it's worst when it's kind of 'alf over. And since them days it's never been more nor 'alf over with me. And as for a kind o' joy as was in me them two year, it took and fair melted away into nothink, like the ice from a Norway ship when the wind's blowin'. And wind, mind you, is much worse for ice nor what the sun is, and many's the lighter-full of ice as I've took out o' Lime'ouse Basin in my time. So I ought to know.

'It came with little Lucky afore 'e was born, and it went with 'im when 'e went, and that was about the very 'eat of August, and ragin' 'ot it was. We'd just been unladin' a cargo of 'ay as usual at 'Onduras Wharf, and 'ad dropt down with the ebb, and fetched up alongside a lot o' lighters just below Southwark Bridge, so as to stand ready to take on our down-cargo next mornin'. And the tide was beginnin' to run almighty 'ard, and was 'issin' and bubblin' and foamin' agen the bows o' them lighters as they lay, with a swallerin' kind o' noise most terrible to 'ear ever since that day. And me and the crew was just settlin' the gear, and clearin' off the bits of 'ay, throwin' 'em into the water, so as to be straight agen supper-time comin'. But Erith 'ad gone below that very minute, and 'ad left the kid on deck for us to keep an eye on, 'e bein' able to waddle about pretty smart, and as artful as any young nipper in the streets. And by reason of the 'eat, she'd put 'im on nothink only a little shirt striped pink and white, and 'e kep' on pullin' of it up, and pattin' 'is little belly, and laughin' like mad, bein' pleased not to 'ave on nothink beside, and callin' 'imself 'is mother's only son and all manner o' silliness she kep' learnin' im.

'On a sudden I 'ears Erith callin' to me, and me goin' aft, she says: "I was only wonderin' if I'd go on lovin' you if you tied me to the burnin' stake." When we wasn't doin' nothink, she'd often go sayin' queer kind o' things like that, just to see what I'd say for answer. But afore I could think to say anythink, I looks up and see a great empty lighter driftin' down right on top on us, and the boy on it pullin' like 'ell at 'is long sweep, but makin' no way not enough to clear us. So I runs fore, and gets out the fender ready, and next second she comes full end on into us, and was away again, 'er stern swingin' round into mid stream, and me thinkin' no 'arm done, bein' well used to such. But just as the jolt passed off with a sort o' shiver, I see a kind o' pink flash fall into the water right under the bows of them lighters layin' at anchor on our port. Eh, yer may well suppose what is was. The little lad 'ad crep' for'ard, and was throwin' a bit of 'ay into the water, same as 'e 'd seen us doin', 'e bein' always that artful. And the whiles 'e was throwin', the jolt came, and it's my belief 'e went down with the bit of 'ay still stickin' in 'is little 'and. Afore you could speak I was down under them lighters, gropin' along over the mud at the bottom of the river where things looks white and green. And twice I swallered water so as to keep me down longer, a thing as a man mayn't do more nor once with any safety; and then I made a grab at somethink floatin' 'alf-way up, and racin' over the ground with me and the tide, same as if somethink was drivin' us all on from be'ind. But it wasn't nothink, only 'is little white cap as 'is mother 'ad made for 'im agen the sun. Then I forced myself to come to the top, for all me feelin' very sleepy and kind of satisfied to stop below. I was far away from the lighters and our barge by then, but I went on swimmin' and lookin' about, not darin' to go back without 'er little lad. I went under London Bridge and down through the Pool, the people all cheerin' at me, they not knowin' for why. But I knowed it wasn't no manner of good further. And at last a perlice boat with two black-beetles and a water-rat as we calls the Thames perlice and a sergeant, they pick me up, and take me back to the *St George* as now is. And I gets aboard, and goes straight up to Erith where she was standin', and I 'olds out the little white cap to 'er, all drippin' wet both me and it. And it was the same as she'd just done makin' to keep the sun off 'is little 'ead. But 'is little 'ead was now bein' rolled over and over with the tide along the bottom o' the river somewheres past the Tower, and cool enough, be sure —our little Lucky boy.

'And that evenin' and night we lay just driftin' up and down with the ebb and flood. And as soon as it was dark, she took all the lanterns and fixed 'em in the bows, and stood peerin' over into the water, never movin' nor sayin' nothink. And next mornin' we was late with the cargo, and that was the beginnin' of trouble twix' me and the firm. And so it went on for a fortnight or more. Instead of layin' up when we'd made our journey, we'd keep on movin' about with the tide, day and night the same, me and the boy just doin' whatsomever she told us to, and not sayin' much among ourselves nor to 'er, through bein' kind o' scared at the way she kep' seekin' and seekin'. Many a night when I've dropt straight asleep 'oldin' the tiller, me bein' so tired, and she still leanin' over the bows and never movin', I've woke up almost afore it was light, and found us laid up along shore at low water, and she wadin' about in the slimy black mud with 'er legs bare and 'er skirts pinned up round 'er waist, she goin' from one lump in the mud to another, and turnin' of it over ever so gentle with 'er 'ands, never usin' a 'ook or a pole to it, but just pullin' it out and rubbin' the mud off to see what it might be. And praps it 'ud be a keg, or a stone, or a bit of cargo, or an old iron pot, or a big drowned dog with the 'air rottin' off it; but it wasn't never the thing as she was lookin' for.

'But when a fortnight or three weeks was gone, she just gave up, and we went on sailin' same as usual, she doin' the cookin' and washin' and everythink as before, but keepin' one eye on the water through it all. And if anythink came floatin', she'd give it such a lookin' at as give us all a turn, she makin' as if she was thinkin' on some'ut else all the time. And now and again I'd 'ear 'er down in the cabin sayin' over to 'erself all the names as she'd called our Lucky boy, and all the bits of nonsenses she'd used to say to 'im. And it's my belief that no matter where she looked, wet or dry, she see 'is little body runnin' about or floatin' past.

'But the third time as we put up into London again, or maybe it was the fourth, through us losin' all count o' times, I some'ow woke up in the night, and felt as the pillow was wet. So I puts my 'and on 'er face, and feels the tears runnin' out at 'er eyes, but she never givin' a sound nor yet a sob. George, old man, you just be careful in yer dealin's with females as cry after that manner. They're the best to love yer, George: that's neither 'ere nor there, and there ain't no denyin' it. But there's always somethink terrible about 'em, same as with a wild beast, or maybe a more fearsomer kind o' spirit, for all I'm not denyin' as to love you there ain't none like 'em. And feelin' me awake, she puts 'er 'ands round my 'ead, as I told yer was one on 'er ways, and kisses me, and says:

'"I've given you some sort of 'appiness since I've been with you, 'aven't I, dear?"

'And I says:

'"All the 'appiness as ever I 'ad, the rest not countin' alongside of it."

'"And if I came again as at the first," she says, "you'd act the same, and stand by me the same as before?"

'"Yer know as that's a nonsensical kind o' question, darlin'," I says. "I wouldn't let nobody take yer away from me now, not if my life depended on it."

'Then she took and kissed my face all over, and me thinkin' she was 'appier and kind of sluein' round to 'er life again, I kissed 'er back, and then fell fast asleep, feelin' pleased and kind of easier.

'And in the mornin' she was gone, and I never set eyes on 'er again. She must 'ave climbed out over the other barges and up on to the wharf, she bein' always active as a cat. And she'd took nothink with 'er, only for little Lucky's cap and a few bits of things, tied up, as I s'pose, in a cotton 'an'kerchief. And ever since then, when I've not been thinkin' on other kinds o' things, I been mostly puzzlin' over why she went.

'Some 'ud say as what with 'er dwellin' so much on the boy and all, she got thinkin' about 'er own people again—'er father and that. But she wasn't never the kind o' woman to take much count o' blood, barrin' her own little lad. And some 'ud say as she was scared off through always seein' the ghost of 'im in the water or asleep in the cabin. And when she'd gone I found out for myself what ghosts are, and it was partly that as drove me from the barge. And some 'ud say as she couldn't abear to think of sailin' the barge alone of me till we got old, and never a child between us: for we didn't never get none of our own, worse luck. But it's my belief as there was a kind of a change in 'er nature, as came with the child and went with the child, same as the look o' the river changes with the tide rising or fallin'. And so long as that change kep' up, she thought 'erself all right. But as soon as the child went down with the ebb, it kind o' took the daylight off everythink, and she couldn't abide no more. That's my way o' lookin' at it, for all I can't bring myself to say as she thought the daylight took off me as well.

'I didn't stop long on the barge myself neither, me not carin' for it after that, and gettin' into trouble with the firm through 'angin' about so much, waitin' for 'er to come back. So I took to the lighters again, as is no more nor so many funeral 'earses alongside the old *St George*. But every Saturday afternoon I'd go up to the old wharf on chance of 'er comin' for want of my 'elp. And I've scarce missed a week ever since, for all me marryin' my second wife after a year or two, as was a good enough sort o' girl too till she went off, as I was sayin', with my old mate, as 'ad rose to be captain of the *St George* in my place. So me and 'im, we'd a bit of a row one night by reason o' that, and I broke 'im a rib or two; but, bless yer soul! it was more for the sake o' decency and what's called law-and-order nor for nothink else, me not much carin' what she did. And last I married my third, 'er as now is, and she's a good enough kind o' female too.

'And now, mate, as I was sayin', if so be I've got to go out this time, I wants to leave a kind o' message be'ind with yer. I wants yer to go every Saturday at the flood, s'posin' it should be as you can get off at the time, and to stand about by the old wharf I spoke on, just keepin' yer eye on the *St George*. Yer'll know 'er from a distance through a bit of my old tops'l bein' still left on 'er with two or three foot of St George's sword, as was painted by 'er I've been tellin' of. And if so 'appen you mark a woman keep lookin' at 'er too—tall and thin she'll be, and with a look to make you love 'er—you get up close alongside of 'er, and say "Erith", so as she can just 'ear it, but not as if you was meanin' to say nothink in purtikler. And if she looks round, just tell 'er about me, 'ow I kep' on waitin' for 'er till I'd got to go out, and when I'd got to go, I went bearin' 'er in mind. And, another thing, give 'er my Doggett badge, as she'd used to make shine in our cabin. It 'ud bring 'er in somethink, if needful, either melted down, or sold back again to the Fishmongers' Company, as gives such things. It's over thirty year since I won it, and praps they'd kind o' like to 'ear o' me again, seein' it was a grand race that year as I won it.'

With that my father promised, and we said good-bye and good luck, and came away. And 'is wife let us out at the door, and my father said as 'e 'oped her man 'ud soon be all right. And she started cryin' like anythink, and says:

'O, I only wish as the Lord 'ud take 'im to 'Isself, seein' as 'e ain't no further good to me, nor never will be, so the doctor says.'

And when my father 'ad told it over afterwards at 'ome, my mother says:

'Lord! what fools you men make of yerselves with thinkin' this and that! As if the woman wasn't mighty glad to get somewheres to 'ave 'er child in quiet, and a fine strong man workin' to feed 'em both. Lovin' of 'im, indeed! Ger along! Soon as she 'adn't got no more need on 'im, she's off, same as anybody else. And serve 'im right for bein' such a sorft-'ead. Now mind *you* don't get 'angin' about no wharves lookin' after artful females! Ladies, indeed! It ain't *that* word I calls 'em!'

'Well,' says my father, 'I'm a-goin' to do what my mate asks of me. And as to females, there ain't no danger o' that, cos why, she just be nigh on our age by now—not as we're to be called old, neither.'

Henry Nevinson

Sissero's Return

Just before that there Chris'mus time, when Mrs Simon was kind of gettin' used to 'avin' a baby same as other mothers, and the women was turnin' up chippin' 'er about it, and was lookin' round for somethink fresh, we 'ad a rare set-out in our street by reason of somebody else turnin' up unexpected. Leastways there wasn't only one as was expecting 'im, and she'd kep' on expectin' for three years gone, so as yer couldn't 'ardly reckon 'er as expectin' no more. She was a queer-lookin' woman with bright red 'air and a very white face, and a figure as neat and straight as Lina's own. Same as all red-'aired people, 'er name was Ginger. But after she got married 'er proper name was Mrs Sissero, but she wasn't never called that, only by the rent-collector and such as aimed at showin' an extry respeck. The rest on us used to call 'er Mrs Kentucky, or Tennessee, or Timbuctoo, or Old Folks at 'Ome, or anythink else 'andy as 'ad connection with niggers. For the thing as made 'er famous was she'd married a nigger and couldn't never get over it.

All on us knowed all about 'er well enough, seein' as she was Shadwell born and bred, through 'er father 'avin' been a stevedore i n London Dock. And more nor that, a woman as 'as got two nigger children, risin' three and four, with woolly black 'air and a skin the colour of an old boot afore it's cleaned of a Saturday, she can't 'ope to keep 'idden away same as ordinary people or rats. And all what the street didn't know for itself, my mother found out bit by bit. For she's got a rare knack of befriendin' people, 'as my mother. And there was points about Mrs Sissero as 'ud 'old all of 'em, men and women alike, argufyin' and wonderin' this and that, till their 'eads fair buzzed with tryin' to fix the rights of it.

Through 'er father bein' a stevedore, she'd got took on in the

Dock very young, so soon as ever she'd passed 'er Standards from the school. And she was mostly set to work as is good for females, more especial unpackin' mineral-water bottles, such as come over by the thousand in little steamers from Germany, where most things get made, and there's always plenty o' work through people livin' so poor. All day long them females as does the unpackin' stand down in the 'old on boards laid across row and rows of bottles. And they keep shiftin' row after row all round 'em one by one into great baskets as are 'auled up by a crane, and shifted again into railway trucks or carts. And they call it 'playin' the pianner', by reason of the rows bein' so reg'lar and their 'ands jumpin' about on 'em so quick, same as when a man's vampin' on the black and white notes, and the singer keeps on always changin' 'is pitch. And so soon as the females 'ave done talkin' about 'oo's makin' love—and that don't often last 'em till much past breakfast—there's nothink outside their work for 'em to do but fight over the number o' baskets they've sent up, and keep chippin' their boss, as is mostly an oldish kind of man, so as 'e may know 'ow to give back their sauce in the same way, and nothink come of it. And if they've got a feelin' for their boss, or if they can't abide 'im, their way of chippin' 'im is to stand and call 'im all manner of sweet and tantalizin' words, same as they call to babies and such, enough to drive any man wild, if 'e was to believe 'em. But if they've got no feelin' about their boss one way or other, they don't say nothink at 'im, and don't get 'alf as much work done. Only this 'appens as good as never.

What part o' the world Sissero fust come into, Gord only knows. 'E wasn't one o' them thin shiverin' niggers as crawl around in blue cotton and turbans with their knees bent, and look as if they was goin' to slip a knife into yer back, or else tell yer some almighty secret, and sometimes do a deal in raw walkin'-sticks. Nor yet he wasn't one o' them greasy niggers as mouch about, not feelin' nor sayin' nothink, bein' made suitable to the wild beasts of their native parts, as our teacher said don't so much as wink 'owever 'ard yer give 'em what for. But Sissero 'ad a mug almost as good as a white 'un to look at, only for its bein' black and shiny like a top 'at. And another thing as showed 'e wasn't white same as us, was 'is bein' always on the laugh. No matter for what 'e was doin' or sayin', nor what sort of day it was, you'd only got to look at Sissero and 'e'd start laughin'. 'E seemed to 'ave a kind of 'appiness always brewin' and workin' inside of 'im, as if 'e was just a-goin' to bust with it. And my mother said it came of 'is 'avin' been so near born a lower animal, same as a monkey. But all the monkeys as ever I see, on organs and such, didn't look purtikler 'appy, but mopy, same as other grown-ups.

Any'ow, no matter for where he sprung from, Sissero 'ad come to sail on one o' them there little steamers tradin' from 'Amburg. And like most niggers as takes to the sea, 'e was a stoker, cos bein' black they can stand the 'eat better, same as the devil. But for all 'is bein' nothink only a stoker, the contractors would at whiles put 'im on for boss, if there wasn't nobody else 'andy, seein' as 'e was always so obligin' to the women, and they kind o' liked to 'ave 'im laughin' around, and there was more sport to be 'ad chippin' 'im, cos of 'is bein' so black, and answerin' so funny. So bit by bit 'er as I'm tellin' on got to look for 'is ship comin' in, and to be always kind o' waitin' for it—a thing as she's 'ad plenty of practice in since that time, and no mistake.

There ain't no mortal sayin' 'ow it was she first came to take up with a nigger, she bein' very steady at the work, and not so bad to look at, and very respectable brought up, for all 'er red 'air. But in talkin' to my mother, she'd used sometimes to tell 'ow Sissero 'ud come up out o' the stoke-'ole, when the furnace was out, and put on a clean blue shirt open down the front, showing the great muscles on 'is chest all shiny and black as sin. And 'e was always most remarkable clean when 'e wasn't workin', either through a deal o' washin', or through the dirt not showin' on 'im same as on white flesh, and that's why it's good for slaves to be black. So when 'e'd smartened 'isself up, 'e'd come and stand be'ind 'er, and stroke 'er red 'air, and in place of callin' 'er Ginger same as the others, 'e called 'er Miss Sunshine, or Miss Guinea-Gold, or Miss Butterfly's Wing. And then he'd stand and laugh, till she and all the rest o' the women 'ad to start laughin' to keep 'im company, and all about nothink only through feelin' so 'appy. For 'e was always just about as 'appy as a man beginnin' to get, not exackly drunk, but what yer might call a bit round the corner, and the public is gettin' to 'ave a kind o' look of Buckin'am Palace about it. And for all that, Sissero didn't scarcely ever touch nothink, but kep' 'isself as sober as Aldgate pump, 'e livin' very reg'lar on board 'is ship, and not troublin' about girls to speak of neither, barrin' only if 'e caught sight on that red 'air, no matter for 'ow fer off, there wasn't no 'oldin' 'im but 'e must run and stroke it. And any time o' day as you passed 'is ship, you'd only got to sing out, 'What, Sambo!' or Jumbo, and any other enticin' word, and you'd see 'is black 'ead bob up, and 'ear 'im start laughin' as if 'e was worth five pound a week, and 'adn't never 'eard such a good joke in all 'is life. And maybe that's one o' the causes yer liked 'im so, cos 'is laughin' made yer think yer was so precious smart.

You may be sure there was a fine set-out when it got known as Sissero and Ginger 'ad started keepin' company. They was first seen together round by the fish-market after dock-hours, and then settin' of an evenin' on the pier-'ead of Shadwell basin. And next time as ever Sissero's ship put in, they went and took a walk arm-in-arm right down the 'Ighway of a Sunday afternoon, 'e in 'is dark coat and light-blue shirt and canvas trousers, and she all in white, and nothink on 'er 'ead but 'er orange 'air, so as, if seen from the top winders, the women said she looked like a poached egg. Yer couldn't ever guess which went most wild on 'earin' it, the men or the women. But my mother said it was the men, through none on 'em likin' a nigger to get the pull of 'em, not even with Ginger, she bein' a nice enough girl beside, always uncommon quiet and obligin', just goin' about 'er business and never meddlin' with nobody. I'll grant yer she wasn't purtikler smart by way of feathers and stuffs, through 'er 'aving never been thought nothink of, and called Ginger; but some'ow she turned 'erself out neater nor the ordinary, no matter for what she 'ad on. And for all its freckles, her skin looked some'ow as smooth and well-fittin' as a drum-'ead. So all the men was wild, for all they didn't exackly want 'er to their-selves. And all the women was wild, for all they didn't exactly want the nigger neither. But likin' to 'ave him about, they aimed at keepin' of him unmarried, same as old Spotter says all females aims, on a kind of off-chance of goodness knows what. So in the Dock and up and down the street they kep' worryin' and goin' on at Ginger, askin' what price a Darky, and if she curled 'is 'air for 'im, and 'ow about that banjo. And after a deal of goin' on, they 'it upon Mrs Simon as the proper person to carry a warnin', she bein' fond o' speakin' serious.

So Mrs Simon meets Ginger one afternoon on 'er way 'ome from work, walkin' alone, same as mostly. And she says:

'Look 'ere, Ginger, I'm come of my own good will to present yer with a solemn warnin'. And it's me as 'as a right to speak o' warnin's, through knowin' so many women un'appy, and my own man as good as a nigger as fer as the look on 'im goes.'

'Don't yer get sayin' nothink about niggers, Mrs Simon, or maybe yer'll wish yerself further,' says Ginger very quiet.

'I'm not a-goin' to say nothink of the sort you think for,' says Mrs Simon. 'But I'll just put one question fair and straight to yer; and you take it as my solemn warnin'. And it's this: Would yer like to see the Tower 'Amlets wake up one mornin' chock full o' little niggers? Cos, if so, yer'e goin' about the right way to do it.'

'Shut it!' says Ginger, gettin' a bit sharper. 'There ain't no talk o' nothink o' that 'appenin', I should 'ope.'

'Yus, yer'd hope; that's just it,' says Mrs Simon. 'Now, mine says as 'e's read somewheres in 'is book: "Do as yer'd be done by." And if we was all to start doin' same by you, as you aim at doin' by us, I tell yer all London 'ud be black afore you'd 'ad time to turn round and look. So that's my solemn warnin', and I leaves it *to* yer.'

'And I'm much obliged to yer for it,' says Ginger, and shouts after: 'And there's one thing certain, Mrs Simon, and I'll tell it yer to yer 'ead, and that's as, black or not, my man don't come off on my face when 'e kisses me, same as yers seems to on yer face from the look of it. Cos why, I've often tried, and many's the time I'll try again, please Gord.'

So, she 'avin' no mother, Ginger ran 'ome to get 'er father's tea ready afore 'e came up from 'is work. And after that the women gave it up as a bad job, and were only waitin' to see their warnin' come true. And one fine day Ginger and Sissero just went off, and set up 'ouse together. And from that moment till 'e died, 'er father never took no more notice on 'er nor if she'd been dead and buried before 'im.

They lived in a room in Middle Shadwell with some kind of a kitchin attached, did the Sisseros. It was top-back, and three-and-six, but Ginger chose it 'erself for its bein' 'alf-way down the bit of 'ill leadin' to the river. So she could set at the winder, and look over through a gap in the fish-market right away to the entrance of the Dock, and watch the ships and barges comin' up the river beside. And she knowin' about what time Sissero's boat was due to arrive, and makin' allowance for the set o' the tide, could mostly mark it on its way up from Lime'ouse, if so 'appen she wasn't at work in the Dock 'erself, and then run to the pier-'ead to get the fust sound of 'is laugh afore the draw-bridge swung round to let the steamer into the Dock. And then she'd off back 'ome again to get every-think ready agen 'is comin' in 'ungry and 'appy in the evenin'. And the other men, seein' 'er always look so decent and cheerful 'urryin' up and down, started thinkin' it wouldn't 'ave been so bad to 'ave a girl like that, for all 'er red 'air, and thought to theirselves what she wouldn't 'ave done for the likes o' them, considerin' what she did for a nigger. But some o' the women, by reason o' the vessel being mostly a fortnight out and no more nor a week at 'ome, kept' throwin' it up at Ginger as she was only one part married out o' three. And Mrs Simon told 'er she'd as leave 'ave been married to a commercial gent at Margate, as comes 'ome on Sunday evenin' and is off on Monday mornin' with 'ardly time to spit between. But Ginger only said there was two things as it's better to 'ave too little of nor too much—one was dirt and the other was a man. And not 'avin' nothink to say agen that, Mrs Simon only said she reckoned as Ginger 'ud soon 'ave less nor enough of one o' them things; but as to dirt, she didn't know nothink about that 'erself, through leavin' it to others to find out. And with that she cast 'er eye at my mother. But my mother took no manner o' notice, only for turnin' to talk to Ginger over the makin' o' babies' close, for all the world as if Mrs Simon didn't so much as count for a livin' woman, through never 'avin' 'ad cause to make any at that time.

At first, acourse, Ginger went on with 'er work in the Dock same as usual. But that was put a stop to by 'er first baby comin'. And it was most extraordinary 'ow people started makin' up to 'er, so as to get an early look at that baby. What with runnin' back-wards and forwards to inquire, and takin' round bits o' gruel and soup and packets o' sugar, so as to make sure of bein' let in, it 'ud 'ave come cheaper to 'ave gone to the Zoo straight off, and more to see for yer money. But as to talkin', a baby elingphant couldn't 'ave give 'em more to say, for all Mrs Simon 'eld out there wasn't nothink to be surprised at, nor nothink as she 'adn't expected, black wool on its 'ead and all, barrin' only it made 'er feel a kind o' sinkin' when she turned up the sheets from the bottom and caught a sight of the creature's feet, and they was all darky, same as its face. And if she'd 'ad 'er choice she'd sooner 'ave mothered the devil nor anythink else with black feet. But Ginger said nothink; only so soon as she was up, she went back to work, takin' the baby with 'er, and layin' it in a 'ole she cleared out among the bottles.

And so she went on a bit, till the second started comin'. And then Mrs Simon says to my mother:

'Speakin' for myself, Mrs Britton, I really shall 'ave to turn it up. The way these lower classes do go on is somethink too awful to think of.'

It was a girl, this second; darky, almost same as the other, but some'ow with a kind o' look o' Ginger on it. And by when it could just about move itself, there came a sort o' red shinin' all over its woolly 'air, if yer 'appened to catch it sideways agen the light. And old Spotter said the kid put 'im in mind of a mule canary. And 'e told Ginger 'e'd never seen no better cross in all 'is life. And she looked up so sweet at 'im from where she was settin', I almost thought she was goin' to kiss 'is weskit. And very likely 'e wouldn't 'ave said nothink agen it if she 'ad. O, but she was real proud o' that second baby, keepin' on askin' everybody if it wasn't almost as good as white, and whether she couldn't pass it off for an Italian, same as an organ-grinder. And whenever she see Mrs Simon comin' along that way, she'd stick out the baby's feet from under its close, all to show 'ow white they was, for all nobody, barrin' only 'erself, couldn't make out much difference in colour, not to speak on, 'twix' this new 'un and the fust.

When she got back to work again, through 'er not bein' able to take no more only the newborn with 'er, she left the boy in care of a neighbour, payin' 'er somethink by the day. But by the end of a week the neighbour said as she couldn't undertake 'im no longer, or else must charge the same as for three, seein' as 'e scared the other children away through bein' black, and them as wasn't frightened kep' on prickin' at 'im with pins to see whether 'e'd bleed red or what. So Ginger just turned up 'er work and stayed at 'ome with 'er children. And when Sissero put into Dock again, she says nothink about the boy bein' made game of through bein' black, but told 'im she wasn't strong enough to go on with the work no more, seein' as she 'ad to stand up all the time; but must find out some other ways o' makin' the money.

And 'e says:

'Now, don't yer be troublin' yer sunny 'ead about the money, darlin'. I'll make the double on it as easy as kiss yer, and then I'll love yer twice as much—cos why, yer'll be twice as expensive.'

And with that 'e laughed till the very babies on the bed started laughin' in company.

Anybody would 'ave thought as 'e only said it of a purpose to please 'er, cos it was 'is fust evenin' at 'ome after bein' away. But the queer thing was as 'e says the very same next mornin'. And not only says, but goes right off and changes into the British Injer, where 'e'd get twice the money, but be kep' at sea sometimes three months, sometimes six or more, without comin' 'ome at all. So 'e sailed away in a mighty big steamer, startin' from the Albert Dock this time, and Ginger she stopt at 'ome with what money 'e'd left, and what she could borrer in advance. And after the fust voyage 'e came back all right, and brought 'er a fine 'eap of earnin's. And she took and 'id some in the beddin' and some under a glass ornament on the chimbley-piece. So 'e went away agen to get more, and she didn't never cry to speak on, but just went about as if 'alf the life 'ad gone out of 'er body.

Now the queer part of it all came in cos that there street 'ad a Sheeny rent-collector. And 'e was like the rest o' Sheenies in aimin' to make money without doin' no work, and unlike the rest o' Sheenies in not keepin' 'isself *to* 'isself. 'E was a rare 'un to talk, more especial with women, and it's my belief 'e'd turned rent-collector, not so much for savin' 'isself doin' work, as to get carryin' on with the women on Monday mornin's, their men bein' gone out to think over startin' work again after the Sunday. 'E always wore a top-'at and a check coat with a glove on 'is left 'and and shiny boots runnin' up to a point, same as if 'e'd got no more nor one toe. And when 'e knocked at the door, and stood there takin' off 'is 'at and 'oldin' 'is silver pen in one 'and ready to dip in the little ink-bottle tied to 'is weskit-button, no wonder as females thought at fust 'e was somebody come for the votes, like a Member o' Parliament or somethink o' that. Any'ow 'e made 'isself uncommon pleasant to Mrs Sissero, and 'ud talk all manner to 'er darky kids, callin' 'em rosebuds and other silliness. And 'e bought a necktie as near as might be the colour o' Ginger's 'air, and 'e'd used to say 'e 'oped she admired it, cos it was 'is favourite colour, only 'e never couldn't get it bright enough. But at last, Sissero bein' then away on 'is fust long voyage, that Sheeny must 'ave tried on somethink as made Ginger fair wild, for she wasn't the sort to fly out about nothink, and this is what she did. She just waited till 'e'd got downstairs after collectin' 'er rent, and then she goes to the front winder in the passage, and whiles 'e was shuttin' the door and lookin' in 'is book to see what was 'is next call, she empties a bucket o' slops fair over 'is top-'at and check suit and all, she 'avin' just done scourin' out 'er rooms, and the water bein' still nicely warm and full as it could stick of soap and dirt.

Then she goes back and gives 'er children their dinners, and says not one word more about it to mortal soul. Only after that, whenever she 'ears the Sheeny comin' upstairs of a Monday mornin', she locks the door, and slips the three-and-six and 'er rent-book under it. And the Sheeny just signs the book, and dursn't do nothink else, through bein' frightened for 'is life of gettin' another duckin', and 'avin' to buy another second-'and top-'at up the Spank.

Now, any decent-minded man like my father or old Timmo would 'ave gone and broke the door in, and either got kicked out 'isself, or been asked to stop to tea, just accordin' to the state o' the woman's feelin's at the time. But that ain't the Sheeny way. There ain't no such man to wait as a Sheeny. That's likely the cause why, when they started out from Egyp' a long time back, it took 'em forty year to cover a bit o' ground as our teacher said any common crowd, to say nothink o' fightin' men, ought to 'ave covered in forty weeks, let alone forty days; and our teacher was a lance-corporal in the Fust Tower 'Amlets. But the truth is, as Sheenies, not reckonin' their bein' uncommon bad at walkin' and takin' exercise, fair love to keep on waitin' and waitin', till the thing as they're aimin' at just drops into their mouths.

So that Sheeny waited, pickin' up the rent reg'lar every week, and signin' the book. And so it went on till Sissero 'ad started out on 'is second voyage, and been away three months or more. And then one Monday mornin' 'e found no rent put out nor no book to sign. So 'e knocks, but nobody didn't answer. And next week it was same again; and the week after 'e slips a notice to quit under the door, and goes away and waits. And the next Sunday night, after it was dark, Mrs Sissero comes round to my mother, carryin' one nigger child and luggin' the other along. And she says to my mother:

'Mrs Britton, 'is ship's been in these three days, and 'im not in it, and me under notice.'

'And I'm sorry in my soul to 'ear it,' says my mother, 'for all not 'avin' no cause to be, seein' as yer can't say I didn't warn yer. It'll be somethink black 'e's after now. For black's in the blood, and it's blood as tells, as old Spotter says.'

'Mrs Britton,' she says, 'yer've no cause to speak like that, you not knowin' my man same as what I does. But tell us, what shall I do?'

'Well,' says my mother, tryin' to seem cheerful, 'yer might 'old out a week or two with puttin' yer things away, and by then praps 'e'll turn up.'

'Put 'em away already,' she says, 'only for what me and the children stand up in.'

And it's like enough my mother knowed that, seein' as Ginger 'ad got on a long coat down to 'er 'eels; and so soon as a woman takes to a long coat, it's sure there ain't never much left underneath.

'Couldn't yer go back to work?' says my mother; 'that's as good a way o' bringin' in money as any I knows.'

'Gone back already,' says she, 'and one-and-six a day's all I can make at it, through me bein' pulled down by reason of the baby, and never rightly gettin' over it. And what with three-and-six for rent, and 'aving to buy coal by the penn'orth, and payin' the caretaker extry to mind the boy, and gettin' soap and that to clean ourselves, it's no manner o' good to make out yer can live a life worth callin' on nothink but two bob a week for yerself and two children to eat, and the baby beginnin' to 'unger after solids.'

'Then yer must shift into a cheaper room,' says my mother. 'You'll likely get one 'ereabout or in Buildin's for eighteenpence. Then you'd 'ave somethink over sixpence to eat for every day in the week. And that's plenty for three mouths I should 'ope, two on 'em small.'

Then Ginger sat sayin' nothink for a long time, but kep' on strokin' at the baby's curly nut, and lookin' sideways to catch the kind o' red shinin' on it.

'Yus, Mrs Britton,' she says at last, 'it's only nature for yer to be sayin' that. But I can't bring myself to it. I tell yer, I'd sooner die nor do it. That's the room 'as 'e fust took me to, and that's where 'e always came back, knowin' I'd be standin' at the door and waitin' till 'e got to the top o' them stairs. And when 'e comes back again, and finds me gone, what's a man such as 'im to do? 'Ow's 'e goin' to set about findin' me, 'im as is so innercent, and all the people 'avin' a game with 'im, cos 'e ain't so white as some is, and tellin' 'im as there's plenty other red-'aired girls in the world. And that's true enough, and that's the worst on it, for all there's maybe none so red as me. But 'e'd easy enough get 'old on one o' them girls, for, yer see, when a girl's been nothink but laughed at all 'er life, she'll just fall down and wuship the fust man as beats 'er, and stamps on 'er chest, and pulls 'er in 'alves, and does everythink only don't laugh at 'er. Not as mine 'as ever laid a 'and on me, 'is manner o' makin' love bein' different. No, Mrs Britton; yer may say what yer like agen me, but I'll be burnt alive afore I leave my 'ome, and I wonder *at* yer for talkin' of it.'

'Then it ain't no good for me speakin' no more,' says my mother, standin' up. 'Only there's one thing I'd like to say, talkin' of red 'air. I've 'eard tell, for all nobody wouldn't believe it, as red 'air 'as a good sellin' price, by reason of so few of us 'avin' got it, thank the Lord. Now, I'll lay that 'air on yer 'ead reaches down to Gord knows where, and it's the one thing yer've got left as 'ud sell. Why, it 'ud pay yer rent for a month, and by that maybe 'e'll be ashore again.'

'Mrs Britton,' says Ginger, lookin' very white in the face, and takin' up the children to go away 'I dunno for why it was as yer 'usband fust liked *you*, but mine liked me all along o' that same red 'air o' mine. And, so 'elp me! I'd sooner sell my own soul and yers into the bargain nor part with one single inch of it for money. So it's no good for us talkin', thankin' yer all the same.'

So she goes back to 'er room to keep watchin' out for 'er 'usband, as never came. And next day bein' Monday, it seems as the Sheeny collector, comin' round to serve 'er with the second notice, found the door wide open, and walked in smilin', takin' off 'is new top-'at. And afore 'e come out again, 'e'd signed the book for three-and-six received that week and all the arrears as well. And so it went on, Monday after Monday, the book gettin' signed as reg'lar as if Ginger 'ad been an army-pensioner or a lady with money of 'er own. And the rest o' the week she went about 'er work same as usual, but never laughin' nor yet answerin' back when the other women chipped 'er. Only with 'er always keepin' one eye on the river, in 'opes 'er man might come back the old way, and turnin' round to stare at every steamer as put into dock, she some'ow got to 'ave the look of a curly Newfoundland bitch as I once see with stones and things tied to 'er, and they was just goin' to 'eave 'er over the dock-bridge, and she kep' lookin' round to see if 'er old master wasn't comin' along. So Ginger just dragged about from week to week, showin' no more spirit, only for once when Mrs Simon met 'er comin' back from work, and says:

'I do 'ear, my dear, as yer'e uncommon partial to furreigners still. And all I says is as yer'e quite right to make no manner o' difference between 'em all. A furreigner's a furreigner, no matter whether nigger or Sheeny, and there ain't no tellin' one from another, even by daytime, nor no need to.'

'You dare call my man a furreigner!' says Ginger, turnin' sharp on 'er as if to break 'er jaw.

''It me, my dear; 'it me, do 'e now,' says Mrs Simon, backin' out into the road pretty quick; 'there's many a worser thing as some women we know 'as to put up with nor bein' 'it.'

But at that, Ginger just dropt 'er arms down like a Volunteer standin' at ease, and goes up the bit of 'ill to 'er 'ome without a word, lookin' as limp as a bit o' cotton. And so it went on maybe for six or seven month. And the darky kids kep' growin' bigger, and swellin' over with fat, and their 'air curlin' like buffaloes. And to see 'er feedin' of 'em, and carryin' on, you'd 'ave thought she'd nothink else to do all day long, more especial with the youngest, the one she liked best, as I said, through thinkin' it almost as good as white.

So she 'ad 'er book signed reg'lar, and kep' 'er room nice, and started buyin' back 'er things bit by bit. And then all on a sudden the Sheeny left off comin', and for three weeks 'e never so much as brought the book. But on the fourth week 'e goes up again, and knocks at the door, for all it was standin' wide open to 'im, and when Ginger comes, 'e says:

'Very sorry, Mrs Sissero, but the landlord says 'e can't keep a tenant as doesn't pay rent no longer, and yer must either pay down for the month or go. So 'ere's yer notice, and I wish yer good-mornin'.'

With that 'e rammed the paper into 'er 'and, took off 'is top-'at, and went downstairs, and I can picture to myself the grin as 'e 'ad on 'is face as 'e looked away from 'er, where she stood leanin' agen the wall, too dazed to say one single word. Some women would 'ave flown out at 'im, and cursed all down the street, screamin' after 'im 'ow 'e 'ad treated 'er, for all the neighbours to 'ear. But some-'ow, I s'pose, Ginger felt too bad. She didn't even think of emptyin' slops over 'im same as before. There wasn't only but one thing for a woman like Ginger to do, and that was to slip a carvin'-

73

knife into 'is oily body. But she, 'avin' none in 'er 'and, did nothink at all; only stood and stared at 'im till 'e'd gone away, and then stood and stared at nothink. But the eldest darky kid runs out, and says:

'Ain't the nice gen'leman comin' in today to set with us a bit, and show me 'is tick-tick?'

And the next week neither no nice Sheeny didn't come, nor never again, but a stony old collector, as made no fuss, but served the notices, and put in the brokers, and sold all up, and turned Ginger and 'er babies out into the street without makin' no remark, 'e bein' 'ardened to the job, and taking it all in the day's work, same as yer sweep out fleas. So Ginger comes to my mother again, as is the way with most people when there ain't nothink else to do, and we puts up all three on 'em for that night in front of our kitchin fire. And next mornin', me comin' into the room early to get a bit o' breakfast on my way to work, I shan't never forget 'ow queer they looked. Ginger 'ad set a darky on each side of 'er, one wrapt in 'er skirt and the other in 'er coat. And she was layin' on the 'earth-rug in the middle, covered 'alf-way up with our table-cloth. And all 'er red 'air was loose and 'eaped about over the boards, and the darkies' 'eads was mixed up in it. And the sun comin' through 'oles in the winder-blind made it shine like something worth the 'avin'. But in the middle of it all 'er face was as pale as a dead woman's at a wake. And then was a kind o' peaceful look on it, same as on Florrie Branton where we went to see 'er in the 'orspital, and 'er leg 'ad been took off, and it was all over and done with.

Next day my mother went bail with our landlord, and got 'er one o' the top rooms in the same 'ouse with us at eighteenpence, for all the natural rent bein' one-and-nine. So there she lived with 'er two kids, keepin' 'erself very quiet, and never stoppin' to talk beyond just answerin' with a civil word and a bit of a smile, if anybody spoke 'er kind, as wasn't often. For the women leastways used to make out as they felt the Sheeny stickin' in their throats, and stoppin' 'em from sayin' anythink when they went to speak to 'er. And mostly all day long she was at 'er work, and often 'er own father 'ud pass 'er in the Dock, and 'e not so much as look at 'er. But in the evenin', as reg'lar as the clock, the minute she'd 'ad her tea, away back she went to 'er old 'ouse, and set down on the door-step, the very same place where she'd swilled the Sheeny, and just

waited hour after hour till everybody 'ad gone to bed, and the lights
in the winders 'ad been put out one by one. And nobody never
raised no objection to 'er settin' there, cos they knowed she was
waitin' for 'er man comin' 'ome. In summer time she used to take
the two kids with 'er, and they'd play in the dust or go to sleep, as
convenient to theirselves. But in winter she put 'em to bed, leavin'
the door open so as my mother could listen for 'em yellin', and
'erself always went and set on that doorstep, for all the cold bein'
sometimes enough to freeze 'er tight to it, like a lighter stuck up in
the ice.

When she'd gone on like that for some time, acourse nobody said
nothink more about it, beyond sayin' as she was goin' a bit queer.
But what made us know she was real dotty was a notion she took
to pay off all 'er arrears to the landlord of 'er old 'ome from the very
time when the Sheeny started signin' for nothink in purtikler.
And this is 'ow she set about. There was a friend of 'ers as worked
at piecin' flags together for a big firm in the City, and they paid 'er
fivepence for doin' each large flag, same as a Jack or a ship's pennon,
as reached across 'er room many times over. And about that time,
seein' as somebody of the Royal Family was goin' to 'ave 'is dinner
in the City, or somethink o' that, this friend 'ad got more work nor
she could get through with. So she sublets to Ginger at thruppence
a flag, stickin' to the spare twopence for the goodwill. And on fine
nights Ginger worked at the flags on that doorstep, usin' the street
lamps when the evenin's closed in too dark to see by. And she got
so artful at it that the work stuck to 'er, and one way and another
she put by a shillin' a week to pay off 'er arrears. So she took and
left the money at the landlord's in a bit of newspaper once a
month, never tellin' 'er name nor nothink beyond sayin' it was 'er
arrears. And what I'd like to know is 'ow that landlord contrived
to live through 'is surprise when 'e got 'em.

'Er bein' so dotty about those same arrears acourse kep' 'er
room very bare. There wasn't nothink in it to speak on, bar only a
picture of a mountain bustin' itself out with fire over the sea, as 'ad
been a special fancy with Sissero, cos there was somethink almighty
about it. But outside that, she 'adn't got only a chair and a table.
She'd so much as sold the bed, and the mattress was 'eaped in one
corner on the floor, and for beddin' she mostly used them flags she
was workin' at, coverin' 'em over in newspapers to keep 'em clean.
And many's the time, me goin' up with 'er late to give 'er a light

when she'd come in from waitin' for 'er man, I've seen the two little darkies curled up together under a Union Jack or the flag with lions and iron railin'-tops on it, and I've thought on what our teacher 'ad used to tell us about the flag o' the Empire standin' for a sign o' purtection to all the different kinds o' people round the world; for all that a good blanket would no doubt 'ave been warmer, but not so cheap at the price. But there was always one thing as Ginger didn't never stint 'erself in, and that was food.

'It's all very well, Mrs Britton,' she'd say to my mother; 'but where's the good of all as I've done, if 'e only comes 'ome and finds me turned as lean and ugly as Mrs Simon, and 'e never one o' them as 'as a fancy for dry bones?'

So there wasn't no change to speak on for nigh on two year, barrin' only the little darkies kep' growin' bigger, and Ginger more 'appy-lookin', cos she said the longer 'er waitin' lasted, the nearer she must be to the end on it. And whether with this or somethink else, there came a look on 'er as made 'er seem kind o' different. And I've 'eard the women say as she was gettin' almost as decent-lookin' as any of 'em. And as for the men, there was plenty willin' to take 'er now, babies and all, through 'avin' a kind of an interest in the way she'd been goin' on. And one on 'em 'avin' lost 'is wife some weeks earlier, makes bold to go up to 'er and offer to take 'er on till Sissero came 'ome, and then give her up again; or to keep 'er, for good and all, if 'e didn't never come 'ome. But she just laughed, and told 'im it wasn't 'ardly worth while makin' no change for the little bit of 'er waitin' time as was left, but thankin' 'im for 'is kindness, as she was willin' to be grateful for.

And so at the last, one Saturday night, just afore that Chrismus time I was tellin' on, my father was comin' 'ome from 'is Trade Union Lodge, and I'd met with 'im after watchin' the gamblin' at the end of the Stag and Bull stairs leading down to the river, and on a sudden we 'ear a noise comin' along our street more like the neighin' of a 'orse nor nothink else, and my father cops me by the arm, and says:

'Gord love us! I ain't never 'eard no man but one as could make a noise same as that!'

And sure enough, there comin' down the middle o' the street was Sissero, kind o' walkin' sideways, 'avin' one arm round Ginger's neck and the other round 'er waist in front, and all the time kissin' at 'er most shameful, as if 'e couldn't never get enough

of 'er, and not lookin' where 'e was walkin' to, but lookin' only in
'er face, and now and then burstin' out laughin', as I said. But
Ginger she didn't laugh, nor say nothink; only walked straight on,
lookin' in front of 'er almost the same as if she'd been asleep, bar
sometimes she kissed 'im back so 'ard on the mouth 'e 'ad to stop
'is laughin'. And some'ow 'e 'd loosened 'er red 'air, and it 'ad all
fell down so as pretty nigh to cover 'em both over.

So my father stood back to let 'em pass up through our doorway, and 'e fetches the nigger one on the shoulder, and says:

'What, Sissero! 'Ere's luck!'

But Sissero took no manner o' notice, no more nor a fly, 'e only
keepin' on kissin' the woman. And she just put out one 'and, and
kind o' touched my father's. And I never see 'im turn red afore nor
since. So them two went to the bottom o' the stairs, and then
Sissero just tightened 'is arms round 'er, and carried 'er right up
to the top o' the 'ouse, same as yer'd carry a little baby.

And when we went in, and told my mother, she was near on
cryin', and she says:

'Lord love 'er! if I'd been 'er, I'd 'ave been willin' to wait
twenty year for such a night, bar only for 'is bein' black—or even
black and all.'

You lay there was a rare turn-up in our front room next day,
bein' Sunday, so soon as the word went round as Sissero 'ad come
'ome. And for once most people seemed to be kind of agreed to be
pleased about it. Only the queer part was as for nigh on eighteen
month nobody 'adn't said never a word regardin' that there
Sheeny man, but now all the women started talkin' about 'im
straight off, the men standin' at the door, and shakin' their 'eads,
and spittin'. And some says one thing, and some another, but
mostly they 'ad turned agen Ginger now as she was 'appy again,
only for Mrs Sullivan and one or two others stickin' out there
wasn't no 'arm done, she bein' druv to it from necessity and not
from 'er choice. And soon they was in a fair way to tear each other
in pieces, let alone Ginger. But on a sudden Mrs Simon ups and
says:

'All I've got to say is as she's a disgrace to our sex, and it's
nothink but right as 'er lawful 'usband should know it. So it's me as
is goin' to tell 'im, and this blessed day as ever is.'

'And if yer do, my dear,' says Mrs Sullivan, 'I'll just break yer
jaw for yer this blessed night.'

'Yes,' says Lina, 'and I'll just take that bloomin' little baby o' yern, and ram it in a sack along of all yer cats, and drownd the bloomin' lot.'

'Go it, Lina! Good old Lina!' said the men, all laughin' and lookin' at each other. And it was likely there'd be fair bloodshed, when my mother starts sayin':

'Mrs Simon might very well be right enough in what she says, if we was dealin' with an ordinary man same as other people. I'm not sayin' nothink about that. But the thing we've got to deal with is a nigger, and 'e bein' black makes a difference. Cos, as fer as I make out, them as is black ain't by no means purtikler. And that's cause why gentlefolks sends 'em missions and such for the purpose o' makin' 'em more purtikler—same as they sends 'em at us, through thinkin' we ain't purtikler enough neither. But that ain't the truth, as Mrs Simon knows very well.'

So that kind o' settled it, and it was agreed as nobody shouldn't let out nothink about the Sheeny, but leave it to Ginger to speak if she wanted.

'And 'er not one to talk uncalled for, no more nor me,' said Mrs Crips.

'Well,' said old Spotter, 'all I can learn from this 'ere talk of Sheenies and niggers is what I've said all along, as it's blood as tells. The nigger's a nigger, and the Sheeny's a son o' Jacob, 'im as I was learned about in my school-days down in Devon. Eh, I can 'ear old Jacob sayin' to that Sheeny: "Well done, my son! Yer'e a true child o' mine, *you* are!" And mind you, as fer as I know, Jacob was the very fust as understood the meanin' o' blood and breedin'.'

With that old Simon moved to go, lookin' as fierce as was in 'im to look, and that was about the same as a sheep lookin' at a dorg. And 'e says:

'It's the Chosen People as ye're speakin' on, you just bear that in mind. And it's written they shall possess the earth, so it ain't no good for you talkin'.'

'Yus,' says old Spotter, 'and it seems like enough they will possess the earth, anyways the Tower 'Amlets. But as for bein' chosen, there ain't many 'ud choose 'em again in these days any'ow.'

So when Sissero comes down the stairs in the afternoon, just about as the lamps was bein' lighted, we all stood there ready to wish 'im luck, and shake 'ands with 'im, and give over disputin'. And 'e seemed to be runnin' over with 'appiness at every inch of 'is body, and I couldn't for the life of me tell which was whiter, 'is teeth or 'is eyes. So 'e stood there laughin' and talkin', tellin' us 'ow 'e'd got stuck up in China nigh on two year through missin' 'is ship, and then couldn't get no ship to take 'im off, but 'ad been forced to work on a rice plantation, and 'ad lived all the time with a Chinee girl, till at last 'e'd managed to slip off in a British Injer ship again, and so 'ad worked his passage 'ome in course o' time.

'And now there ain't nothink only one bad thing in it all,' 'e says, 'and that's as them two child'en of ours upstairs they start 'owlin' and yellin' so soon as they set eyes on me, cos of me bein' so black. And them my very own child'en, as any bloke can see for 'isself by only lookin' at 'em,—as whose else should they be, I'd like to know?'

And with that 'e starts off laughin' again, enough to bring the 'ouse down.

George Gissing

Lou and Liz

The great bell at Westminster was striking nine. Sunlight streamed into the garret window, bathing a robust, comely girl, who stood half-dressed before a looking-glass and combed out her tawny hair. In bed lay another girl, seemingly asleep, and on the pillow beside her perched a baby boy of eighteen months, munching at a biscuit.

'Now then, Liz!' cried the girl who was dressing, as she took a hairpin from between her lips. 'Goin' to loy there all d'y? Wike up, do!' She began to sing in a strident voice, '"J'yful, j'yful will that meetin' be,—when from sin our 'arts are pure and free." Jacky, give mummy one on the 'ead. Liz, git up! 'Ow d'yer suppose we're goin' to git to London Bridge by eleven?' Again she sang: '"You can 'ear 'em soigh, an' wish to doy, an' see them wink the other eye,—at the man that browk the benk at Monty Car—lo!" Say, Liz, did you 'ear Mr Tunks come 'ome last night? Same old capers; fallin' down all the time he was goin' up—Wike up, I tell yer!'

Liz raised her head with a drowsy laugh.

'Stop yer jaw, Lou! What a chatter-mag you are!'

A rejoinder came in the shape of a pincushion, aimed sharply at the remonstrant. It missed Liz, and hit her child full in the face. The room rang with an infantile shriek of alarm and pain. In a moment Liz had jumped out of bed, had hurled back the missile with all her force at Lou, and in the same breath was trying to soothe the baby and to revile her friend. This time the pincushion knocked over the small looking-glass, which shattered upon the floor. For five minutes there was tumult—screaming, railing, scuffling; the storm of recrimination only ended when Lou discovered in her pocket—amid keys and coppers and dirt—a broken stick of chocolate, which she presented as peace-offering to Jacky.

''Ow'm oi to do my 'air?' asked Liz, as she stood in her night-gown and ruefully regarded the broken glass.

'Oi'll do it for you,' Lou replied, giving her own locks a final slap.

'An' now we've got to buy Mrs 'Uggins another glawss!'

'Don't fret yer gizzard about that. I can get a measly little thing like this for sixpence. What's the odds s'long as y're 'eppy!—"The man that browk the benk at Monty Car—lo!"'

'I dreamt it was rinin',' said Liz, as she drew the blind aside, and looked with satisfaction at the cloudless sky. 'Somethin' loike weather, this, for a benk 'oliday. Say, Lou, you might give Jacky's face a wipe whilst I'm dressin'.'

Discord between the two (it happened about once every half-hour when they were long together) always ended in a request for some favour, urged by the younger girl and cheerfully granted by her companion.

They were nothing akin to each other, but had shared this garret for about a year. Liz worked at home, making quill toothpicks, and earning perhaps a shilling a day; Lou was a book folder, and her wages averaged eleven shillings a week; their money, on a system of pure communism, went to discharge their joint expenses. Alone, Liz could barely have supported herself and her child; as it was, they made ends meet, and somehow managed to save a few shillings against a bank holiday.

Lou wore a gold wedding ring, and round her neck, hidden by her dress, hung a little wash-leather bag which contained a marriage certificate. It was her firm belief that on the preservation of these 'lines' depended the validity of her marriage. Three years had elapsed since, at the birth of a child, her husband saw fit to disappear; the baby died, and Lou went back to her old calling.

Liz wore a brass wedding ring, and had no marriage certificate to show. She was known as 'Mrs Purkiss', but was entitled only to 'Miss'. As to Jacky's father, his disappearance was as complete as that of Lou's husband.

In their way they had suffered not a little, these two girls. But the worse seemed to be over. With admirable philosophy they lived for the day, for the hour. Liz was never burdened by a sense of gratitude to her friend; to Lou it never occurred that she herself was practising a singular generosity. They laughed and sang, squabbled and abused each other, drank beer when they could afford it, tea when they couldn't, starved themselves occasionally to have an evening at the Canterbury or at the Surrey (the baby, drugged if he were troublesome, sleeping now on his mother's lap, now on Lou's), and on a bank holiday mingled with the noisiest crowd they could discover.

Today they were going to Rosherville.

Jacky wasn't very firm on his feet; considering the child's diet and his bringing up in general the wonder was that he trod this earth at all. He weighed very little, and the girls were so much in the habit of carrying him about wherever they went, that they rarely grumbled at the burden.

It would have pleased them best to go down to Rosherville by steamer, but that cost a little more than the journey by train and every penny had to be considered. Their tickets, both together, came to three-and-sixpence; eighteenpence apiece remained for refreshment at the Gardens. Dinner they took with them—bread and slices of tinned beef; for tea, of course, there would be 'srimps and creases'. Before and after, those great mugs of ale which add so to the romance of Rosherville.

What an Easter! Day after day, scarce a shadow across the sun. And so deliciously warm that one had been able to save no end of money from firing. On Good Friday they had lain in bed until dinner-time—'doin' a good sleep', as Lou said; the rest of the day they spent in patching up their hats and jackets. On Saturday, it was work again. Sunday, another good sleep, and an afternoon ramble just to show that they had some Easter finery, like other people. And now had come the real holiday. They were in wild spirits. On setting out, they ran, and leapt, and shouted. Lou, as the elder and stronger, took Jacky upon her shoulder, and rushed off with him, singing the great song of the day, about the man who, etc.;—the man's feat, by the by, signifying to Lou nothing more nor less than a successful burglary, perpetrated at some bank in a remote country where the police were probably deficient.

It rejoiced them to get far away from the familiar region, and to indulge their gaiety amid a revelling throng. They had few acquaintances they cared about. With the people who knew her story Liz could not be altogether at ease; the morality of her world pressed anything but heavily upon her, yet she was occasionally aware of slights and covert judgments. Lou, again, though strong in the possession of her amulet, was too proud to invite people's pity in the character of a deserted wife, and her sharp temper had before now subjected her to insults. 'No wonder y'r 'usband run aw'y an' left yer', was a natural retort from any girl whom Lou's tongue had wounded. Except, of course, from Liz; who, however angry, could not permit herself that kind of weapon. This necessity of mutual forbearance made a strong link in their friendship. And the fact that Lou considered herself her friend's superior, morally and even socially, doubtless helped to keep them satisfied with each other.

Everything was fresh to them; even familiar posters acquired a new interest seen in the light of holiday. A wrestling lion and a boxing kangaroo, large and vivid on hoardings by the railway, excited them to enthusiasm. 'Look at it landin' 'im one in the jawr!' cried Liz, pointing out the kangaroo to Jacky, with educational fervour. And the monkey-faced little fellow seemed to understand, for he leapt on his mother's knee, and smote his sticky little hands together.

The grounds at Rosherville were a pretty show in this warm spring weather. Fresh verdure had begun to clothe the deciduous trees, and the thick-clustered evergreens made semblance of summer against a bright blue sky. From the cliffs of quarried chalk hung thick ivy; up and down and all about wound the maze of pathways, here through a wooded dell, there opening upon a lawn of smooth turf, or a terrace set with garden shrubs and flowers. Liz had never been here before; Lou not for several years. First of all they must needs scamper from place to place, uttering many an 'Ow!' of rapture. The bear-pit entertained them for long; so did the aviaries. But at length the sight of many people thronging about a liquor bar reminded them that it was nigh dinner-time. They found a spot within the area of beery odour, and sat down to eat and drink.

Jacky was encouraged to sip from the ale-mug; his wry face moved the girls to shrieks of laughter, interspersed with 'Pore dear! What a shime!' and the like exclamations. In her bag Liz had brought a bottle of milk; it was churned into acidity, but the infant, after his alcoholic thwartings, imbibed it eagerly. Bits of meat, too, he consumed, and lumps of heavy cake; and, by way of dessert, coloured sweets in considerable mass. The girls would have deemed it downright cruelty to refuse him any eatable thing that he appeared to relish.

Two or three hours went by. The pair encountered no acquaintance and gave only brief encouragement to exhilarated
youths who sought to make themselves agreeable. Rough banter,
even a dance, they were quite ready for, but Lou's amulet and Liz's
child forbade them to pursue flirtation beyond a certain discreet
limit. When Jacky began to wail from weariness, indigestion and
need of sleep, they came to a rest within sight of the dancing platform, where a band made merry challenge to crowding couples;
Liz, very red and perspiring, sat down with the baby on her lap,
and tried to hush him into slumber.

A sudden exclamation from her companion caused her to look
up. Lou was standing with eyes eagerly fixed on the round platform, her lips open, her face and attitude expressing some intense
excitement.

'Liz!' she ejaculated. 'If there ain't *my 'usband!*'

In an instant the other girl was on her feet. The child, left to
roll upon the grass, made an unregarded outcry.

'Where is 'e? Which is 'im, Lou?'

'That fellow in the brown pot 'at dauncin' with the girl in a blue
dress. Down't yer see?'

'I see!'—Liz quivered with sympathetic agitation, and balanced
forward on her toes. 'What are you goin' to do?' she added, in
quick undertones.

The other made no reply. She took a step forward, looking like
some animal about to spring. Her fists were clenched at her sides.

'Are you quite sure?' asked Liz, following her.

'Sure? D'you think I'm a bloomin' fool?' was the fierce answer.

'Down't make a row, Lou!' Liz entreated, looking anxiously at
the people around them. 'You always said you didn't care nothin'
about 'im.'

'I ain't goin' to mike no row. Shut up, and go an' look after the
child.'

She approached the dancers. It was several minutes before the
man on whom her eye was fixed came out from amid the stamping,
whirling and shrieking throng; his companion in the blue dress
followed him. Lou went steadily up to him, met his look, and stood
expectant, without a word.

He wore the holiday attire of a rowdy mechanic; had a draggled
flower in his coat, and in his mouth the extinct stump of a cigar.
He was slim, and vulgarly good-looking; his age appeared to be not

more than thirty. The flush on his cheeks told of much refreshment, but as yet he had not exceeded a fair bank holiday allowance. Only for a moment did the sight of Lou disconcert him; then he gave a broad grin, and spoke as if no encounter could have pleased him more.

'Thet *you*? Why, you've growed out of knowledge.' He turned to the blue dress, and said, 'Old friend o' mine, Sal. See y' again before long.' Then, going close up to Lou, 'You've growed that 'endsome, I shouldn't 'ardly 'ave known you. Let's heve a bit of a stroll.'

He caught her by the arm, and drew her towards a part where there were fewer people.

'That's 'ow you tike it, is it?' said the girl in a thick voice, her eyes still fixed upon him.

'I always said you was good-looking, Lou, but to see you now fair tikes my breath away, s'elp me gawd! What 'a' you been doin' with yourself all this time?'

'What 'a' *you* been doin', that's what *oi* want to know?'

The delinquent affected compunction. He lowered his voice.

'I couldn't 'elp myself, Lou. Times was 'ard. I went off after a job an' I meant to send you somethin' to go on with, s'elp me I did. But it was all I could do to get grub for myself an' a fourpenny lodgin'. I've thought about yer d'y and night, an' 'oped as you wouldn't come to no 'arm. I knew your uncle 'ud look after you—'

Lou at length found her tongue, and for several minutes used it vigorously, but without creating a public disturbance. The man— she knew him by the name of Bishop—cast uneasy glances round about; he saw that his late partner remained at a distance, but that a girl with a child in her arms was following them.

'Who's that?' he asked at length, indicating Liz.

'It's a friend as I live with,' Lou answered, sharply. 'She knows all about *you*—no fear.'

'An' d' you mean to say as you 'aven't found another 'usband all this time?'

The reply was a fresh outburst of wrath. When it had spent itself, Bishop said in a wheedling voice:

'I behaved bad to you, Lou; there's no two ways about that. But I didn't mean it, an' I've always wanted to make things right again between us. 'Ev a drink, old girl. I've got something to say to you— but 'ev a drink first, and your pal, too. Let's be friendly together.

There ain't no use in making a bother. I cawn't 'elp lookin' at yer, Lou. You're that 'endsome, I wouldn't 'a' believed it.'

In spite of everything, this flattery was so pleasant to Lou's ear that she had much ado not to smile. Old feelings began to revive as she regarded the man's features, and his insinuating talk tempted her to forget and forgive. Such an event as this was in harmony with the joyous nature of the day. Abruptly she turned round and beckoned Liz to approach.

'Moy oye, what a bebby!' exclaimed Bishop, as if in admiration. 'You don't mean to say as that's yours, Lou?'

'If you want to know,' Lou answered, sullenly, 'mine didn't live only three weeks.'

'Pore little thing! I'm sorry for that. But it's all for the best, I dessay. Come an' let's 'ev a drink. Let's be friendly. What's the odds, s'long as it all comes right in the finish.'

Liz, meanwhile, was suffering much mental disturbance. From the first moment, she had dreaded lest Lou and her husband should be reconciled: that would mean a parting with her friend, and how was she to get on alone? Obliged to disguise her uneasiness, she kept in the rear of Bishop, and glanced now at him, now at Lou. It became more obvious that the deserted wife was exulting in what had happened; her eyes had a strange gleam; she tossed her head, and walked with much swinging of the arms.

Bishop persuaded them to sit down on the grass whilst he fetched liquor from the neighbouring bar.

'Are you goin' back to him?' Liz asked of her friend in a hurried whisper.

'Me?' was the scornful reply. 'What d'you tike me for?'

'But you're goin' on as if you meant to.'

'He's my 'usband, I s'powse, ain't he?' Lou rejoined with a fierce glare.

'I wouldn't drink with a 'usband as had served me like 'e has.'

'Shut up!'

'Shut up yerself!'

The quarrel was interrupted by Bishop's return with two foaming pint mugs. They were speedily emptied and replenished. Liz quaffed the beverage without delight, for she saw that her objection only had the effect of making Lou stubborn in disregard of wrongs. One of many concertina players who rambled about from group to group suddenly shrilled out a summons to dancing.

''Ev a turn, old girl?' said Bishop, who, as he sat, had already stolen an arm about Lou's waist.

After due show of snappy reluctance, the girl consented, and with dismay in her heart Liz saw the pair twirl away. This was Bishop's opportunity for private speech. After again assuring Lou of his penitence for past injury, he told her that in a day or two he was to begin work on a job at Woolwich, a job likely to last for some months, with good wages; he had lodgings out there already. His proposal was that Lou should return with him this evening. They would go together, at once, to her home, carry off her belongings, and tomorrow find themselves comfortably established as man and wife once more. The fiery colour in Lou's cheeks betrayed her mood of eager excitement, the disposition to forget everything but this unhoped-for chance of resuming her dignity of wifehood. Yet she could not, in fact, lose sight either of the risk she ran (for Bishop would as likely as not forsake her again when he grew tired of her), or of the distress she would inflict upon poor Liz. The dance, the seductive murmurs of her partner, told strongly in one direction; but every time she cast her eyes on Liz and Jacky, fears and compunctions renewed their grasp upon her.

Just as breathlessness was compelling her to pause, she became aware that her friend and the child had disappeared. She stopped on the instant and looked in every direction; nowhere amid the moving clusters was Liz discoverable. She must have gone off in a sulk. Lou resented this behaviour. It diminished her anxiety on the girl's behalf, and when Bishop continued to urge an instant departure she sauntered slowly away with him.

But Liz had not purposely withdrawn. Sitting disconsolate on the grass, she happened to catch sight, at a distance, of that young woman in blue, with whom Bishop had first of all been seen. A thought flashed through her mind; she caught up Jacky and darted in pursuit of the conspicuous person.

Not, however, to overtake her readily, for in front of them was the Baronial Hall (name redolent of the Old Vic and of the Surrey Theatre), and the blue-clad girl vanished through its portals before Liz could come up to her. Within was the high scene of Rosherville riot. A crowd filled the long room from end to end, a crowd that sang and bellowed, that swayed violently backwards and forwards, that stamped on the wooden flooring in wild fandangoes, and raised such an atmosphere of dust, that on her attempt to enter, Liz began to cough and felt her eyes smart. Jacky, terrified by the din, burst into a howl, here inaudible. But the blue dress was once more in sight, and Liz would not relinquish her purpose; she crushed onward, until an opportunity came of touching and addressing the object of her pursuit.

'Miss,' she said, speaking close to the young woman's ear, 'would you mind tellin' me somethin'?'

She of the blue robe seemed to be alone, but was stamping, like those around her, to the nearest concertina, and had a look of supreme good humour on her blowsy countenance.

'What d'you want to know?' she shouted back.

'That gentleman as you was dancin' with out there on the platform—'

'What of 'im?'

'Is he a friend of yourn?'

''Course he is. Known him since't I was a choild.'

'But you don't know 'is wife, do you?'

''Course I do.'

'What—my friend Lou?'

The reply was a stare of astonishment.

'His wife ain't no Lou!' exclaimed the young woman. 'Her name's Marier. What d'you mean?'

Liz uttered a shriek of delight. She had hoped to discover something to Bishop's discredit, but nothing as good as this had struck her imagination.

'If you'll come along o' me,' she said, 'I'll tell you somethin' as you'd ought to know.'

Readily enough the stranger followed, and with a struggle they got into the open air. In the conversation that ensued, Liz learnt that the man of whom they spoke was not in reality named Bishop, and that he could not be legally Lou's husband. Some ten years ago he had married in his true name of Wilcox, and his wife, with four children, lived at Enfield. More than once he had left Mrs Wilcox to her own resources; but she, having a little shop, did not suffer much from her spouse's neglect.

Liz had now to rush in pursuit of her friend; the stranger, much interested by what she had heard, accompanied her. But Lou was by this time far from the spot where she had danced with her nominal husband.

'She'll have gone off with 'im!' cried Liz, in despair which was not wholly selfish. 'Where's the w'y out? If I 'edn't this baby to carry! I cawn't go no faster!'

Tears began to trickle down her cheeks, where dust had mingled muddily with perspiration. She saw before her a life of loneliness and want. The homely garret would have to be forsaken; she must shelter herself and Jacky in some miserable hole—well if it didn't end in their going to the workhouse. Oh, why had she been so snappy with Lou! Perhaps that very last bit of quarrel had decided her friend to go off without remorse. Yet, even amid the distress, Liz experienced a brief, intermittent comfort in the reflection that, after all, Lou was not really a married woman, that the 'lines' of which she so often boasted were worthless, and her gold ring no better than one of brass.

Her companion offered to take a turn at carrying the child whilst they hurried on in search. They made for the exit, and asked if such a couple as Lou and the brown-hatted man had been seen to depart in the last few minutes; answers were vaguely negative. Back again into the gardens; hither and thither amid the folk who were enjoying themselves—drinking, dancing, love-making, shooting in the rifle gallery, watching acrobats and niggers on the lawn, and a performance in the open-air theatre. Liz seemed to herself the only unhappy creature in this assembly of thousands. Presently it occurred to the pair that one or other of them ought to have remained at the exit; they had forgotten this. Liz, utterly wearied and woe-begone, stood still and let her tears have their way.

High up on the tops of the tall elms, nesting rooks uttered their 'Caw, caw' undisturbed by the uproar of humanity in lower regions. Grave, domestic rooks, models of reason and virtue in comparison with the rampant throng they wisely ignored.

Ultimately, half an hour after the beginning of their search, Liz and the blue girl found themselves near the spot whence they had started; and there—there in the very place where they had danced to the concertina—stood Lou and Wilcox-Bishop. Liz, now again with Jacky in her arms, bounded forward.

'Lou! Dear old Lou! Thenk Gawd! Come 'ere and let me tell you somethin'.'

'Where have you been?' cried the other impatiently.

'Lookin' for *you*, everywheres. Ow, Lou! Don't 'ave nothin' to do with 'im.' She spoke in a subdued voice, not to be heard by passing strangers. 'He ain't what he calls himself! He ain't *your* 'usband!'

The man had drawn near, not without a look of misgiving, for he saw the young woman in blue regarding him ominously, and observed Liz's agitation. There followed a lively scene, brief, dramatic. Wilcox, made heedless by long impunity, and overcome by amorous temptation, had loitered about with Lou merely because she was unwilling to go away without seeing Liz; he had met no one except the blue girl who could imperil his project, and it seemed to him most unlikely that she would have an opportunity of learning what he was about before he got safely off. It was true that he had work at Woolwich, and he saw no risk in living there with Lou, whilst he kept up communication with his legitimate wife at Enfield, whose little shop was too valuable to be definitely forsaken. But the unexpected had befallen. Face to face with him were three accusing women, one of them furious, the second exultant, the third scandalized. Useless to attempt denial; evidence could now be obtained against him at any moment. He stood at bay for two minutes, then, with a burst of foul language, turned tail and fled.

Lou would have pursued him. She was beside herself with rage, jealousy, humiliation. But already a little crowd of amused observers was gathering, and followed her with whoops as she started after the escaping man. Upon these people Liz suddenly turned in wrath, asked them what business it was of theirs and so brought them to a standstill. Her voice had a restraining effect on Lou; she also stopped, turned, and glared savagely at the spectators, who fell back.

'See 'ere, Liz,' she said, 'you can do as you like; oi'm goin' 'ome.'

'So'm oi,' was the answer.

Jacky had been roaring incessantly for the last quarter of an hour, and would continue until he fell asleep. The day was hopelessly spoilt. Wherever they went in the Gardens they would feel that people were pointing at them and talking about them; the blue girl would of course make known their story. So they moved dolefully towards the exit, exchanging not a word.

When they were out in the high road Lou paused.

'You don't think I meant to go with him, do you?' she asked

fiercely. "'Cause if you do, you're bloomin' well wrong. Think I'd a' gone back to a feller like that?'

There followed a string of violent epithets. Liz, though convinced that only an accident had saved her friend (and herself), was politic enough to protest that of course she had never feared anything so foolish; and when this assurance had been repeated some fifty times, the injured girl began to take comfort from it. Her wrath turned against the man once more. She would be revenged upon him; she would go to the police station, and have him 'took up'; he should be sent to prison like the bigamist they had read about in *Lloyd's* only a week or two since.

'Where's a p'liceman?' she exclaimed, looking about her. 'He ain't far off yet, an' I'd like to see him copped, and took off with 'andcuffs.'

The policeman was not difficult to discover, but for all that Lou did not carry out her menace. She railed copiously but decided that it would be better to go to the 'station' when they got home, and make her charge with all formalities. Meanwhile Jacky kicked, struggled, and roared in his mother's arms.

"'Ere, give 'im to me,' said Lou at length, when her companion was but dropping in exhaustion. "'Ow can y' expect to enjoy yerself when you 'ave to tike babbies out! We 'aven't had no tea, nor nothin'. Come on, an' let's git 'ome.'

They missed a train at Rosherville Station, and had to walk to Gravesend. The return journey was miserable, for very few people were going back at this early hour, and none of the accustomed singing in the carriage helped to restore their spirits. Relieved from personal anxieties, Liz could now sympathize with her friend's distress. They squabbled as a matter of course, and the necessity of postponing talk about what had happened until they were alone again exasperated the tempers of both.

By eight o'clock Jacky lay fast asleep in bed, and Liz was preparing tea. Lou had not entered; she went off somewhere by herself, promising to be back before very long. Within the house was perfect quietness; down in the street an intoxicated youth roared out a song which contested popularity with that concerning the bank-breaker of Monte Carlo—an invitation to a bride to take her marriage trip 'on a boycyle mide for two'.

Three hours later Lou was still absent. Liz grew fearful once more. But perhaps her friend had really visited the police station, and was detained there all this time by the gravity of her business. At half-past eleven there was an unfamiliar step on the stairs, ascending noisily. Liz threw open the door, called out, and was answered with a laugh which she recognized, though it had a strange note. Lou had not spent her evening with the police.

In the light of early morning Jacky's clamour for breakfast awakened the two girls. Having given the child some cold tea (left in the pot all night), and a hunch of bread, Liz spoke to her companion. For a while there was no answer, but presently came muffled words.

'Say, Liz, you won't let on to nobody about it?'

'Not oi! I tike my *hoath* I won't, Lou.'

A pause, then Lou's voice was again heard.

'I woke up in the night, an' thought I'd burn them marriage-lines. But I won't neither. I'll keep somethin' to show.'

'Oi should, if oi was you. You was married, all the sime.'

'But I can git married again now, if I want.'

'Course you can,' Liz replied, half-heartedly.

'All right. Let's do another sleep. What's the odds s'long 's y're 'eppy?'

And they dozed till it was time to get up and begin the week's labour.

Edwin Pugh

The First and Last Meeting of the M.S.H.D.S.

One evening Phil Evers, Jack Cotter and Watty Staight called on me. They filed into my room with solemn faces, and sat down in a row on my sofa. Usually they distributed themselves. Their demeanour impressed me.

'What's the matter?' I asked.

'Oh, it ain't nothin' serious, y' know,' said Watty. 'Jack'll tell yer what it is.'

Jack gave Watty a reproachful glance which Watty carefully avoided.

'If I must I must, I s'pose,' said Jack Cotter heavily. 'But seein' as 'ow Watty's the one as mentioned yer nyme—'

''Old on,' said Watty. 'Don't go ashiftin' it all on ter me. We're all as bad as one another. The fac' is,' he added, turning to me, 'we've took a liberty, an' you're the pusson as we've took the liberty with.'

''Tain't sech a orful lib'ty, y' understand,' said Jack Cotter. 'It jest amarnts ter this: Mister Bannin, the noo minister at the 'All, y' know—is agittin' up a Debatin' Serciety for young men. 'E 'appened ter mention ter me that 'e was 'ard up fer a speaker ter open the fust debate. Watty an' young Evers was wi' me. An' we all plumps art, simultaneous, wi' your nyme. "D' yer think 'e will?" Mister Bannin sez. "I'm sure 'e will", sez Watty. An' there we left it. We can on'y 'ope you won't give us away.'

'Though we're aweer o' the lib'ty we're atakin',' supplemented Watty.

'What have you three got to do with this Debating Society?' I asked.

'Oh, we're stooards,' said Watty. 'We keep order—'

'And hold the coats,' added Phil Evers.

'You're ter choose yer own subjec', an' treat it 'ow yer like,' said Jack Cotter. 'Mister Bannin 'opes it'll be a subjec' as we're all interested in, thet's all. Some'ink perlitical, fer ch'ice.'

I promised to do my best, and they departed.

The day fixed for the first meeting of the Marsh Street Hall Debating Society arrived. I went early to the Hall to avoid the crush. I was there first. A woman had just lighted the fire, and clouds of smoke filled the room. Only one small gas-jet was lighted. I had come hot from my own fireside, and the chill gloominess of the place oppressed me. I sat down and read my notes. The woman who had lighted the fire pretended to have forgotten me. She took up a broom and began to sweep the floor. I sneezed in weak protest, and she desisted. She gathered up her brooms and pails and brushes, and went out, slamming the door behind her.

I did what every human man does when he is left alone in a strange place with a fire and a scuttle of somebody else's coals. I kicked the fire into a blaze and piled on fresh fuel. I was doing this when the door opened suddenly and Mr Bannin entered. He came up to me and shook hands. He was a little, round-faced man, with thin lank hair, and a short neck. He wore semi-clerical garb and spectacles.

A minute later Watty Staight, Sheckles, Jack Cotter, Hiram Slike and Phil Evers came in together.

They crowded round me and shook my hand as if they were sorry for me.

'Feel fit?' asked Watty.

'If yer break darn, tip me the wink, an' I'll say "'Ear, 'ear!" lard,' said Slike. 'That'll paws it off.'

'Wotever else yer do,' said Jack Cotter, 'don't say "er—er" when yer 'ard up fer a word.'

'No; to "er" is inhuman,' said Phil Evers.

'Do you think I might let them in now?' said Mr Bannin, coming up to me. 'They seem to be getting a little obstreperous.'

He referred to my audience, which was indulging in horse-play just outside the door.

'Certainly,' I said; and he crossed over to admit them.

They came trooping in with stretched mouths and loose

shoulders, and sat down in a body as near to the door as they could get.

Their ages ranged from sixteen to twenty-five. They were undersized, ill-looking fellows, for the most part. There was an air of shabby smartness about them. They all had their hair brushed down in an oily fringe over their pimply foreheads: they all wore cheap watch-chains and soiled dickies: those dickies that are collar and dickey in one, and cost sixpence halfpenny.

As each man sat down, he spread out his great red hands on his thighs, and twirled his hard felt hat between his knees.

'I think,' said Mr Bannin, rising, 'we may now open the proceedings.'

As he spoke, a fresh instalment of audience entered. It was heavily booted. The noise that it made whilst seating itself drowned every other sound. At last there was comparative silence, and Mr Bannin rose again.

'You all know,' he said, 'why we have met here this evening.'

'No, we don't,' cried someone in the back row.

'We have met here,' said Mr Bannin, disregarding the dissentient voice, 'to debate whether the House of Lords should or should not be abolished. A gentleman has very kindly consented to come and open the debate for us. He is not connected with the Hall in any way, so I hope you will give him your best attention until he has finished. Then, if any of you have anything to say, you will be at perfect liberty to say it. These gentlemen,' indicating Watty Staight, Jack Cotter and Phil Evers, 'are stewards, who will decide all points of order outside my jurisdiction as Chairman. Now, sir,' to me, 'if you are ready—'

I stepped forward, and made my speech, the audience listening quietly. When I had done, Mr Bannin rose again and said—

'Now, who will oppose the opener?'

There was much nudging of ribs and shaking of shoulders at this.

'Go on, Bill,' one fellow's mates would say. 'Wipe 'im up.'

'Go on yerself,' Bill would probably reply. 'Yer bloomin' slippy a-tellin' other pipple ter git up, but I don't notice as yer so enxious ter git up yerself.'

Finally Phil Evers rose.

'Mr Chairman and Gentlemen,' he said. 'I am afraid I know little or nothing of the matter in hand. But as a similar lack of knowledge has not deterred my friend from opening the debate, I don't see why I should hesitate to reply to him.'

''Ear! 'ear!' from Watty Staight.

Phil adjusted his pince-nez.

'First as to what my friend, the opener, said about—about various things,' he continued, smiling blandly on his auditors. 'He said, if I remember rightly, something about the House of Lords. He said that the House of Lords should or should not be abolished: I have forgotten which; but it is immaterial. Now, do you know, I agreed entirely with what he said. I felt, as he said it, that he was expressing my views exactly. That is why I rise to oppose him. For I know that anything that I agree with or that agrees with me must be bad for humanity generally. Now I, as a child, liked soap; applied internally, of course. I used to eat soap as easily as you drink beer. It agreed with me. If my parents had not fostered artificial tastes in me, I believe I could return today to my old diet of brown Windsor, and thrive on it as well as I could thrive if the House of Lords was—was disposed of in accordance with my friend's suggestions. Ergo: I am an irrefutable argument against any cause I espouse.'

Mr Bannin coughed uneasily. Somebody in the audience asked Phil to leave off talking and say something.

'But,' Phil said, oblivious alike to signs and portents, 'there were parts of the opener's speech with which I certainly did not agree. I did not hear those parts; I am naturally inattentive. But I have no doubt those of you who did hear them disagree with him as heartily as I do.' He paused, and the audience showed a disposition to cheer. 'I must confess,' he said, 'to feeling a little ashamed of myself. You all know well what that feeling is. . . . I beg your pardon.' He laughed. 'I say that I feel ashamed of myself merely to please my friends,' he continued presently. 'If I told the truth I should say: I think I have been more amusing tonight than they will ever—intentionally—be. But I have no reverence for truth. Its strictest adherents always seem to me to be lacking in brain development. It is so fatally easy for a truthful person to be truthful always; it is so hard for an untruthful person to be truthful occasionally. Then, too, Truth, as typified in an indelicate lady— Truth is nothing if not indelicate—Truth, I say, lives in such an unhealthy atmosphere—at the bottom of a well, you know. She is so eminently foolish, too, for she is always looking into a hand-mirror that noxious vapours must have irremediably obscured ages ago, and that, too, in a place where no natural light ever penetrates, and the air is too heavily charged with carbon dioxide to admit of artificial illumination.'

'Time, Mr Evers, if you please,' said the Chairman. And Phil sat down.

There was no applause.

Mr Bannin rose with a weak smile. 'Now, if there is any *serious* opposition,' he said.

At first there was not. Then a red-headed man rose with the air of an iconoclast and addressed the chair.

'Concernin' wot the lawst speaker said,' he began. 'Ez fur ez I could mike art 'e wuz on'y atryin' it on. Nar, I arst yer, mates all, is thet fair pl'y? We come 'ere ter be elevated, an' a bloke gits up an' talks a lot o' bloomin' rot.'

'Order! order!' cried a little man at the end of the front row.

The Iconoclast turned on him and regarded him fiercely. Then he addressed the Chairman again.

'I never knoo,' he said, 'ez 'ow the little bandy-legged man on the roight wuz a stooard before.'

'W'y don't yer set darn, Ginger, an' give someb'dy else a chawnce?' cried a lean man in a plaid choker.

The lip of the Iconoclast curled.

''Ullo! 'ere's another bloomin' stooard!' he exclaimed.

'Wot d' *you* know abart the 'Ouse o' Lords?' the lean man demanded. 'A-chuckin' yer fat abart ez if you wuz the G. O. M.'

'Gentlemen, please,' cried Mr Bannin. 'This will never do!'

'You really ought to know better, you know,' said Phil Evers mildly.

'You be blowed!' said the Iconoclast. 'Who're you? 'Think I don't know yer? Garn! I'd clip yer one under the lug fer 'alf a pin.'

'It's not a deal,' said Phil feebly, and subsided.

'Mister Chairman,' said a very strong voice from the rear of the Hall. 'Mister Chairman and Gentlemen, I wish ter make a few remarks.'

Everybody turned to look at this new speaker. He was a short man with small black eyes and wing-like ears.

'Excuse me, guv'nor,' said a pale-faced boy in a light-blue suit, who had been furtively making cigarettes ever since the proceedings opened. 'But are you the Prince o' Wales? No? Then thet's all roight, an' I don't mind. You kin go on. But if the Prince o' Wales is 'ere, I give 'im fair warnin', once for all, as I won't 'ave none of 'is sauce. If 'e sez anythink I object to, I shell go an' tell 'is mother. . . . It's all roight, Chairman, 'e ain't the Prince o' Wales. . . . Go on, guv'nor.'

The man with the ears stared in the daze at the boy in the blue suit.

'It's no use: thet's done me,' he said. And he sat down and pondered.

There was a lull. At last a young man in a fur waistcoat rose.

'Mister Chairman, lyedies and gen'l'men,' he began. 'Leastways there ain't no lyedies, but you know wot I mean. I got up ter s'y— I got up ter s'y. . . . I s'y, Bill, wot did I git up ter s'y?' Bill whispers in his ear. 'Ho, yuss. Er. The 'Ouse o' Lords is a' institootion as I ain't partial to meself I—I——'

'Sussussussussussus?' whispered Bill.

'I didn't ketch it, ole man,' said the fur waistcoat. 'Tell yer wot, mates, as my pel knows s' much abart it, I'll give in, an' let 'im 'ave a go. 'E's all roight, you take my tip.'

Mr Bannin rose wearily. 'I really must insist,' he said, 'on some little order being maintained. It is not usual for speakers at debates to speak twice in one evening. And they do not, as a rule, rise when they have nothing to say. I throw out these suggestions merely for your guidance, as I know that most of you are enjoying a new experience tonight.'

'Brayvo!' yelled the audience.

He sat down. There was a tense silence. For five minutes we sat looking at one another, and nobody spoke above a whisper. At last Mr Bannin said, 'What! is there no one?'

Another five minutes passed. Then a queer, misshapen youth, with a satchel slung across his shoulders, rose.

'Chairman and Gentlemen,' he said breathlessly. 'I feel that in addressing you I am taking a great liberty; but nevertheless I hope you will pardon me. I am a stranger in these parts. I happened, an hour ago, to be passing this door, and seeing a crowd of people squeezing in here, I squeezed in too. That's my way. I have listened with great interest to the discussion, and I think it has been most ably carried on. But, after all, gentlemen, why should we trouble ourselves with abstract questions? Is it that we may learn the way to be happy?'

He paused for breath. Everybody stared at him in silent wonderment. His fluency was so remarkable, and he had such a queer, high-toned voice.

'Yes; I suppose we trouble ourselves with these and kindred abstract questions for just that reason,' he continued. 'We see the end, and take a semi-circular course towards it, instead of following the broad highway. And that broad highway? Is it named Political Place? or Ambition Alley? or Work Road? or Money Crescent? No. It is the Highway of Health. The only thoroughly happy man is the thoroughly healthy man. Gentlemen, I have in this little satchel a preparation—'

But we rose in a body and howled him down. To think that we should have listened thus eagerly to an itinerant quack-doctor!

Mr Bannin rose with white lips. 'I think we had better disperse,' he said.

We dispersed.

As Phil Evers and I descended the steps in the wake of the crowd, we saw that the quack had gathered round him half our late audience. He seemed to be doing good business.

Edwin Pugh

A Small Talk Exchange

The Marsh Street Provision Stores is owned by one Mrs Luzzell. It is a very little shop, and stands at the corner where Marsh Street and Marsh Place join. It is called a Provision Stores because there are no 'shops' in our neighbourhood, and Mrs Luzzell is tender of popular prejudice. At the opposite corner is a 'Coal and Potato Emporium'. Three doors to the right is a 'Farm Dairy'. I lodge over a 'Shaving Saloon', and by cricking my neck can see a 'Fish Supper Bar'. But we have no shops. And I tremble for the Vandal who tries to plant one among us.

A man did this once. His name was Brown, and his ruin was speedy. He occupied the 'Fish Supper Bar' before its present owner took it over, and sold newspapers and stationery. The trade in newspapers and stationery is one that lends itself gracefully to euphemistic description, but this Brown man called his shop a 'news-shop', which was a flight in the face of Providence too culpable for condonation.

Brown was a little red-faced man, with a husky voice and a showy wife. He took everything easily—except money. His stock in trade was large, and grew steadily larger. His 'front' was arranged in a way that shocked Mrs Luzzell's commercial instincts by reason of its prodigality. He had a trick of hanging comic weeklies on a string, so that half the pictures in them and not a little of the reading matter could be enjoyed for nothing. He also pasted penny recitations to the windows where they could be read free of charge at all times, save at night. At night the gas behind them made the print invisible.

I think we were rather sorry when Mr Brown left us, because his wife had helped to eke out our conversation. Topics of general interest are not too common in Marsh Street; and Mrs Brown, by reason of her showiness, was an inexhaustible subject of comment to the gossips in Mrs Luzzell's shop. Mrs Luzzell's shop is to the ladies of Marsh Street what my landlord's shop is to the gentlemen: A Small Talk Exchange.

It is easier to define things than to describe them sometimes. If this were not so I could not make one definition do duty for such unlike concerns as 'The Marsh Street Provision Stores' and Mr Tully's 'Shaving Saloon'. Mr Tully's 'Shaving Saloon' appalled one by its appearance of emptiness. Three chairs and a long bench for waiting customers were all the furniture it contained. There were numerous sporting prints and play-bills and mirrors on the walls, of course; but such things, though they discount the appearance of emptiness in a room, do not fill it. Whereas 'The Provision Stores' was stuffed to repletion with every conceivable article of commerce that blows or grows or is produced by art or nature. If you were short of cash, Mrs Luzzell could supply you with seven pounds of coal or a peck of coke for a penny. If your collar-stud broke unexpectedly you could buy three bone ones on a card for a halfpenny, or a metal one for a farthing. She sold patent medicines of the cheaper sort, too: ointments, boxes of pills, corn-plasters, menthols in wooden cones, camphor, alum and gold-beaters' skin. Flanking the door were two large boxes. One contained Spanish onions at three a penny; the other, broken biscuits at twopence halfpenny per pound. Half of one of the windows was sacred to sweetstuff: the other half, to toys: all at a penny each. Mrs Luzzell rarely sold more than a pennyworth of anything.

Yet she thrived: though she had a large family and a lazy husband. She was a little woman, with dimples in her chin and cheeks and wrists and elbows. A merry little woman despite her manifold cares, and comely withal. Her face was round and plump, and her complexion still retained much of its pristine redness and whiteness. She was short in the neck. Her hair matched her eyes, which were black, and she wore it smoothed down tightly over her scalp. Her bust was ample, and she had no waist worth mentioning: nevertheless she moved with grace and lightness. At times, when her babies fell sick or her husband threw boots at her, she was a trifle short in her speech; but ordinarily she exuded good humour just as easily as she exuded perspiration in the summer-time. She was the mother of twelve children, and had room in her heart for twelve more.

She always claimed to have invented 'farthing dips'. 'Farthing dips' are not candles, as you may perhaps suppose; they are a species of lottery. They first boomed in 1885; but long before then Mrs Luzzell had made them a speciality. This is how the thing is worked.

A number of envelopes, each containing a piece of coloured paper, are placed in a long box. You pay your farthing and make your selection. You can take any one envelope from the box. If your envelope contains

A piece of blue paper you are entitled to $\frac{1}{2}$ oz. of sweets.

	green	„	1	„
	yellow	„	2	„
	white	„	3	„
	brown	„	4	„
	red	„	8	„

All the sweets in Mrs Luzzell's shop are sold at the rate of four-pence per pound. There are no blanks, so the most you can lose is half an ounce.

I remember being in 'The Provision Stores' one morning when a little girl, attended by three other little girls, came in for a farthing dip. There was a stiffness in the neck of the little girl with the money, and an unwonted elasticity in her gait. She came forward, followed closely by her three very friendly little friends, and laid a halfpenny on the counter.

'Farthin' dip 'n' a farthin' out, please, mem,' she said shrilly.

Mrs Luzzell took the fateful box from its shelf and extended it towards the child. The other three children pressed forward eagerly.

'S'posin' yer git de 'alf-ounce, Liz,' one said.

Liz drew back her hand.

'Come, my dear,' said Mrs Luzzell; 'I can't hold the box out all day, yer know. Pipple are awaitin' ter be served.'

Liz faltered, and put forth her hand again very unsteadily.

'Take de end one, Liz,' one of her companions said. 'Min got a four ounce in de end one once, didn' yer, Min?'

Min, a tiny child, with her long white hair combed down into her eyes, nodded. The tenseness of the situation had almost overcome her. She was very pale.

Liz took the end envelope and opened it with trembling fingers. It contained a piece of blue paper.

'On'y 'alf-ounce,' she whimpered.

'You can't alwis git 'alf a pound, y' know,' said Mrs Luzzell consolingly. 'What'll you 'ave?'

''Ave eggs an' bacon, Liz.'

'No; 'ave fishes.'

'Don't you 'ave fishes. There ain't no taste to 'em. 'Ave stick-jaw. It lasts so.'

Liz chose musk drops. As the sweets were handed to her she burst into tears.

'There, there, my dear,' said Mrs Luzzell, greatly distressed; 'gimme 'em back. You shell 'ave yer ounce. But mindjer, all on yer, I don't do it agin.'

So Liz got the worth of her farthing. As she went out we heard her say to her companions—

'I believe they're all 'alf-ounces, don't you?'

Which was distinctly ungrateful in Liz.

Mrs Luzzell smiled pathetically and turned to attend to the other customers crowding her shop.

It was a cold raw morning. Snow had fallen during the night, and Marsh Street was clogged with it. It lay, all scored with black lines, in the road, and trampled down and sullied on the pavement. The sky above was grey, and the smoke from the chimneys rose in straight black columns towards it. There was no sound of traffic audible out of doors, and even such sounds as were audible—the rasping of shovels on the stone flags; the shrill calls of the milk-boys mingling with the pessimistic cries of the sweeps and the rat-tat of the mercurial postman—rose muffled and thick in the heavy damp air.

Mrs Luzzell's customers were inclined to be exacting. Their noses and their tempers were alike inflamed by the inclemency of the weather. They were all women, and their ages ranged from six years to sixty. The little women were the most exacting.

'Not too much fat wi' them rashers, please, mem,' said one, aged ten. 'The lawst wuz nea'ly all fat. It blazed up in the pan an' caught the chimley afire almost. An' it ain't good fer the childring either.'

'In my opinion,' quoth another little woman, who had much

ado to keep her eyes on a level with the counter, 'bacon shouldn't never be give ter childring at all. It spiles 'em. Give 'em a good hunk o' bread an' drippin', wi' plenty o' weak tea or milk an' water, if yer want 'em ter grow up straight an' tall an' proper, I say. Look at me on bacon. Thet comes o' bein' father's fav'rit. 'E would gimme it, though mother wuz agin it all along. On the sly too. An' I enkirridged 'im. But there! men's all alike—enkirridgement or not.'

This moral reflection terminated in a muscular sniff.

'"Ere y' are, my dears,' said Mrs Luzzell, handing them their purchases. She seemed oppressed by their grotesque aping of adult speech and manners.

'"Ow much?' they asked in a breath, with much acrid sharpness of tone.

'Fourpence 'a'p'ny you, an' thrippence three farthin's you,' said Mrs Luzzell. 'Thank yer.'

'Good-mornin', mem,' said the two little women, and walked out together.

I watched them through the glass panels of the door as they crossed the road. Their frocks were old and thin, and their boots had gaping wounds in them, through which their dirty stockings bulged. One of them wore a woman's bodice that hung slack over her warped chest and bellied out behind her. The sleeves of the other one's dress were too short, and the arms they did not protect were raw and bleeding. Their lank hair, falling in unkempt elfin locks about their ears, fluttered in the wind, and their tiny ill-fed bodies seemed to wither and wilt in the rough cold morning air.

'A nice time them two pore little things 'as!' said a big, hollow-cheeked woman, with a black eye and a cloven lip. 'The way they're set upon, too! It's disgraceful! . . . There they go,' turning round and looking after them. 'Look at 'em. Ain't it orful! . . . An' never a noo rag ter their backs from year's end ter year's end.'

'Pore little things!' said the other women.

They watched the two little women till they were out of sight, and then turned and gave their orders.

Most of them were women who should have been in the prime of life. But bad food, hard work, and the over-hasty production of large families had hastened their physical decay. They were all haggard and thin, or florid and blowsy. Not one of them was even warmly dressed. A few were tidy, but the majority looked dirty and unwholesome. Their faces were sallow, their eyes dull, their hair rusty. Yet they did not seem unhappy. They talked and laughed as if life still mattered to them, and death were not their only chance of rest and peace.

They talked. How they talked! In what a ceaseless flow of slip-shod syllables the words poured forth. And not one single gleam of wit or appreciation of humour, not one spark of wisdom or even an original phrase, relieved the dreariness of the whole output. Nobody listened. Each was eager to hear only herself. When breath failed or an untimely 'What for you, please?' from Mrs Luzzell disturbed the colourless current of their thoughts, they would pause irresolute—grudging the semblance of attention of another's discourse that their silence implied; and when for ten consecutive seconds they could think of absolutely nothing to say, it seemed to me once or twice that they were on the verge of weeping.

They talked of the weather; of the price of coals; of their husbands; their children; their sicknesses; their quarrels with con-tumacious neighbours and relations; of School Boards; of marriages and births and deaths that had lately happened or were on the *tapis*; of funerals; of clothes and boots; of the dearness of pro-visions; of Mrs Nemo's new bonnet; of Mr Nemo's profligacy; of the decadence of filial love and duty; of Heaven and Hell; of the fine dinners they had eaten; of murders, suicides, fires, divorces, breaches of promise, wife-beating and husband-beating; the stupidity of country folk—a favourite theme; and their own sharpness and intelligence. It was interesting to hear them speak, too, of a class they designated 'low people'. Heaven guard their offspring from intermarrying with 'low people', they said. And when the woman with the black eye and the cloven lip heard that another woman's son showed a tendency to contract 'low habits', she entreated the mother to 'keep 'im right'.

'Once let 'im git really low, an' there's no higherin' of 'im agin,' she said.

She was saying this as I left the shop.

Edwin Pugh

The Inevitable Thing

(i)

Moll lay sleeping in the sun, with her crumpled bonnet under her head, and her dishevelled hair trembling in the wind. Her face was red and swollen and dirty; her dress was torn and bespattered with mud. In the grime on her cheeks were furrows that tears had made; and on her forehead lay clots of black blood that had oozed from a broken bruise above her temple. One of her gloved hands clutched a shabby little reticule; the other was thrust into her bosom.

She lay on a clayey slope, with her feet jammed hard against some tarred palings. Behind her stretched a tract of waste land abutting on a railway. This was called 'The Tips'. 'The Tips' was part of that ever-widening belt of neutral ground which engirdles all great cities, and is the line of demarcation between town and country. Hoops of iron, the staves of barrels, rusty pots and pails and kettles, broken crockery, fragmentary boots and hats, old clothes sodden and stained with mire, infected bedding, putrescent carcases of dogs and cats, bricks, worm-eaten beams of timber, nettles, a scanty crop of thin reedy grass and here and there a bloated dandelion, were the products of this strange territory. Years ago a row of houses had been projected there, and symmetrical holes cut in the ground. But nothing further had been done. The holes had lost their rigid angles and degenerated into mere puddles of stagnant rain-water, in which imaginative urchins floated untrustworthy rafts, and mimetic little girls washed their dolls' clothes.

On the other side of the tarred palings, and separated from them by a narrow strip of roadway, was a row of houses called colloquially 'Tips' Tenements'. These houses had once been villas and rejoiced in distinctive names, as a close inspection of the miniature pediments over their porches proved. But latterly they had fallen on evil days, and were now let out in flats to whomsoever could afford a rental of five shillings a week. Unmentionable things happened in these houses, and untranslatable language was sometimes used. Fights were of frequent occurrence, the average allowance of black eyes being usually one and a fraction to each adult tenant.

On the morning when Moll lay sleeping in the sun, there emerged from the door of the last house in Tips' Tenements a tiny yellow-haired girl. She was bareheaded, and she wore a frock that was too small even for her small body, so that her dirty little knees and a few inches of her mottled thighs were plainly visible. The Tips' tenants had not yet risen from their beds, and the street was consequently silent and deserted. The hour was six o'clock. All the sky behind 'The Tips' was radiant with the glory of the morning, and something of that glory was reflected in the child's face.

For some seconds she stood hesitating on the kerb, with her wide eyes roving over the cheerless expanse of 'The Tips'; then, as she caught sight of a fluttering something behind the tarred palings, she crossed the dusty road, and, clutching a rail in each of her chubby hands, thrust her yellow head through a gap in the fence and looked down into Moll's sleeping face.

Moll stirred uneasily under the scrutiny and opened her eyes. The child clapped her hands, and her lips parted in a smile. Moll stared at her with an expression of drowsy half-inquiry on her face. Presently, she sat up and began to arrange her tumbled hair.

'Come 'ere,' she said.

The child still smiled at her, but made no attempt to approach, though the gap in the fence was amply wide enough to admit her.

Moll laughed with noisy vehemence.

'You can't hear what I say to you, can you, Bet?' she said, shaking her head at the child. The child nodded. Moll laughed again. 'An' you couldn't answer me if you did 'ear, could you?' she continued, 'because yer quite deaf an' dumb, ain't yer, Bet?'

The child uttered a harsh, crooning murmur, and squeezed through the gap. She sat down beside Moll and drew from her pocket a very dirty, sticky piece of pink sweetstuff. This she offered to Moll with an air of charming invitation. Moll put it aside.

'Sweet little dear!' she said, and stooped forward and kissed the child. 'Though I ain't no right to kiss 'er,' she murmured. 'Me so 'orrible an' vile, an' 'er such a little angel.'

She sighed, and began to brush the mud from her dress with her gloved hands.

'Lawd!' she exclaimed, as a sudden spasm of nausea overcame her. ''Ow bad I do feel, to be sure! 'Ere, Bet!' The child sidled up closer to her. 'You ain't afraid o' me, are you, Bet? You don't throw things at me when I'm drunk, or pull my dress, do you? You're a little angel, Bet, that's what you are, though you can't never 'ear me say so. . . . I wish you belonged to me, Bet. I think there'd be a better chance fer me to git religion an' keep straight then.' She blinked her swollen eye-lids and began to snuffle. 'I did git religion once,' she said, 'but it wasn't no good to me. I broke out again. An' every time I break out I break out wuss'n ever I did before.'

She began to sob and dab at her eyes with a ragged handkerchief.

The child, seeing her distress, again offered the piece of pink sweetstuff to Moll. Moll pretended to nibble it.

'There, my dear!' she said. 'I won't cry any more.'

She wiped her eyes with an air of finality, and rose.

'Run back to yer mar, now, Bet,' she said. The child looked into her face. 'Yer mar wouldn't like you to come wi' me, you know,' Moll added. But Bet, divining the purport of her words, shook her shoulders petulantly, and nestled closer to her strange friend. She put her short arms about the woman's neck and kissed her. Moll reciprocated passionately, then sank down once more on the ground and began to rock herself to and fro in a paroxysm of weeping.

(ii)

For some minutes Moll continued to weep. At last Bet touched her on the shoulder, and when Moll looked up, pointed with a dingy digit over the tarred palings. Advancing toward them was a red-faced, slatternly woman. Her aspect was threatening. She wore a coarse brown apron, and her sleeves were rolled up above her skin-less elbows. At sight of her, Bet trembled visibly.

''Ere's yer mar come to look for you,' said Moll.

Bet began to cry. Her mother crossed the road and reached the palings.

'What are you doin' wi' my child, Moll Matters?' she bawled. 'Ain't you got enough sins o' yer own to answer for without con-taminatin' other people's children?'

'Who's contaminatin' anybody?' demanded Moll fiercely. 'I don't want yer brat.'

'Then don't inkerridge 'er to go wi' you. This ain't the fust time, you know. I s'pose you want to make 'er like yerself?'

'Gawd forbid!' said Moll.

'So I should think. 'Ere, Bet.'

The child, in obedience to her mother's gesture, left and ad-vanced towards the palings. Her mother seized her by the arm and dragged her through the fence.

'What're you doin' out at this time o' the mornin'?' she cried, angrily shaking the child. 'Can't you stop in bed till yer told to git up? 'Ere's me bin a-lookin' for you all over the place. Git along wi' you,' and she pushed her towards the opposite side of the road-way. Bet gave one forlorn backward glance, and trotted towards her home. On the doorstep she was seized by her elder sister, a lank girl of fourteen, and bundled out of sight.

'Well, Moll Matters, so you've bin up to yer games again, 'ave you?' said Bet's mother with fine scorn.

Moll made no reply.

'Missis Marting's swore she won't 'ave you for 'er lodger any more. She's chucked all yer furniture out, and says she'll do as much for you if you try to go back. An' quite right, too, I say. Yer a disgrace to the street, that's what y'are.'

'Chucked my furniture out?' cried Moll, aghast.

'Yus. It's in the road now—what's left of it, that is. Some o' the things got broke an' some's bin stole. But you'll find a few odds an' ends that'll prove I ain't tellin' you no lies.'

Moll rose with a lame attempt at dignity.

'I don't want to 'ave nothin' to say to you, Missis Grewles,' she said. 'An' I don't believe a word you've uttered.'

'Go an' see for yourself, then.'

'I will,' said Moll.

She turned away and began to climb the slope. Mrs Grewles laughed and yelled after her a torrent of abuse, of which Moll took no heed. She stumbled over the uneven ground until she came to a spot where the fence had broken down, and stepped over the débris into the street. One agonized glance down the deserted roadway was sufficient to assure her that Mrs Grewles had spoken truly. Piled up in the gutter and scattered over the pavement were the sorry remnants of her household goods. The tables and chairs and bedding—all that was worth keeping—had been purloined. Some rusty broken saucepans, a legless stool, and other useless trifles, were all that remained. She stood contemplating the desolation of her home with a twitching face, then becoming conscious of the fact that every window in the street was opaque with eager, interested faces, she lifted her chin disdainfully and walked away.

She did not return until late in the evening, and during her absence the female half of the Tips' tenants discussed her at some length on the doorstep of the house in which she had lodged.

'Mrs Marting,' Moll's ex-landlady, a heavy-bodied, light-headed young matron, was overwhelmed with shrill sympathy.

'It's not a bit more'n she deserved!' said Bet's mother.

'I'd ha' done it long ago,' declared another lady with hair that could hardly be termed false, because it was such a palpable wig.

'It do seem a bit 'ard, though, don't you think so?' ventured a stout old woman, who had only lately become a Tips' tenant.

'Ah, my dear! you don't know 'er!' Bet's mother said.

'Is she so orful bad, then?'

'Bad? Bad ain't the word. She's wuss'n bad. An' the good 'usband she 'ad, too! 'E left 'er so much a year when 'e died—eighty poun's, wasn't it, Mrs Kwitt?'

'Mor'n that, I believe.'

'Yuss; more'n eighty poun's a year. Jest think of it. Enough to live comfor'ble on in a 'ouse o' yer own. I on'y wish some one'd leave me eighty poun's—'

'More'n eighty poun's.'

'Well, we'll say eighty poun's a year. I'd show you all 'ow to 'old yer 'eads up. But what does Moll do? Spend it all, or nearly all, on rum. Rum, too. Gin I could understand, or beer with a good body in it. But rum—ugh!'

'An' she don't eat 'ardly anythink,' interpolated Moll's ex-landlady; 'or ever buy 'erself a noo dress, even.'

''Orrid!'

'We've all tried to git 'er to turn over a noo leaf. But it ain't no manner of good—not a bit. I'm sure dear Mister 'Oward—round at the Mishing 'All—'as talked to 'er that feelin' you wouldn't believe. On'y a day or two ago 'e was on at 'er to sign the pledge, and give 'er 'eart to Gawd. She said she would try, an' she did sign the pledge. But las' night she broke out again. I 'appened to be on the doorstep about seving, an' I see 'er a-coming round the corner between two o' the men from Mead's factory. She was 'alf bosky then, an' kep' singin' an' laughin' like a mad thing. She went into the Lion wi' the two men, an' there she stuck till chuckin'-out time. When I went acrost to git my supper-beer she was sittin' in one of the men's laps with 'er arm round the other man's neck, an' 'er dress all open an' 'er 'air all down.'

'The beast!'

'I didn't see what become of 'er. But it seems she climbed onter the Tips and slep' there all night. She was there this mornin', anyway.'

'Pore thing!' murmured the new Tips' tenant.

'Pore thing!' cried the other women in chorus. 'I like that. Pore thing, indeed!'

'I was on'y thinkin', p'r'aps, if 'er 'usban' 'adn't died she mightn't 'a' gorn wrong.'

'I don't see that's any excuse. I'm a widder myself, but I don't go boozin' with a parcel o' men,' said the lady with the wig.

'Some people takes things different, o' course,' said Moll's champion apologetically. 'But I must be goin' in, or I shall be 'avin' my man comin' out arter me.'

'So must I,' said two other ladies simultaneously, and half an hour later the meeting broke up.

(iii)

Late that night Moll knocked at Bet's mother's door. Bet's father came in answer to her summons. He was a shock-headed, good-natured man, with a sleepy face and watery blue eyes.

'Well?' he said.

'I've come about Bet,' said Moll breathlessly.

'What about her?'

'I want 'er.'

Bet's father stared at her in mute perplexity.

'You ain't bin gittin' drunk again, 'ave you, Moll?' he said.

'O' course not,' Moll replied indignantly.

'I ain't a-castin' out no insinuations, you know,' Bet's father hastened to say. 'I jest inquired . . . Well?'

'I want Bet.'

'You want Bet? 'Ow do you mean—want her?'

'I want her to keep—to 'ave all to myself. To take away an' provide for.'

'You do?' Bet's father scratched his thick head. 'Seems to me this is a case for the missus, ain't it?' he said.

'You're the 'ead o' the family, you know,' Moll reminded him.

'Well, if I'm the 'ead, she's the neck, an' the 'ead can't move without the neck, can it?'

'Bosh!'

'Oh! it's easy to say "Bosh!" '

'As easy as it is for the 'ead of a family to move without the neck.'

Bet's father bit his ragged moustache doubtfully. 'I don't know so much about that,' he said. Then he turned round and yelled up the passage, 'Annie!'

'She'd a-bin takin' a 'and in this conversation 'erself,' he said to Moll, 'if she wasn't a-bathin' the kids.' He chuckled. 'If there is one thing that riles the old dutch more 'n another, it is to 'ear people a-talkin' an' not to be able to chip in 'erself. . . . An-nee-ee!'

A door at the farther end of the passage opened outward with a bang, and the voice of Bet's mother rose shrilly to the rafters.

'What on earth's the matter?' she exclaimed. 'An' why don't you shut that door? A-letting in a draught on the children while I'm a-bathin' 'em. How'd you like to set naked with yer feet in 'alf-bilin' water, and a north wind a-blowin' on yer back?'

She came forward and stared at Moll contemptuously.

'So yer back again, are you?' she said. 'I wonder you dare show yer face arter the way you was carryin' on yes'day. What d'yer want?'

'I want Bet,' said Moll.

Bet's mother laughed in high derision.

'Oh, you want Bet, do you?' she cried. 'An' d'you think yer likely to get 'er?'

'I don't know,' said Moll.

'Well, I do. So you can sling yer tross.'

'Wait a bit. 'Ear me out.'

'I don't want to 'ave nothin' to do with you.'

'But look 'ere.'

She thrust her hand into the pocket of her skirt, and drew it out filled with gold.

'There's a matter o' twenty-two pound there,' she said.

Mr and Mrs Grewles stared at the glittering heap with gaping mouths and lifted eyebrows.

'My!' said Mr Grewles.

'Where'd you get it?' his wife asked suspiciously.

'I've jest draw'd it out o' the bank, o' course,' said Moll. 'It's my quarter's allowance.'

Mr Grewles drew a long breath.

'I wish it was mine,' he said.

'Some of it shall be yours,' said Moll, 'if you'll let me 'ave Bet.'

''Ow much of it?' asked Mrs Grewles.

'Five poun's of it.'

'Five poun's?'

'Well, say six.'

'It's a sight o' money,' said Mr Grewles, whose face was haggard with longing.

Mrs Grewles stood looking alternately at her husband's face and the gold. The temptation was as great as her needs.

'What d' you think, Sam?' she asked her husband.

'It's a sight o' money,' Sam said again.

Mrs Grewles clutched her chin, and regarded the floor with a vacant stare.

'Would you be takin' Bet away altogether?' she inquired at last.

'Yuss,' said Moll. 'I should want 'er all to myself. Oh, Mrs Grewles, do let me 'ave 'er. I'd be that loving to 'er, I would. An' you've got such a many.'

'Such a many!' echoed Sam.

'But what d'yer want 'er for?' Mrs Grewles asked, temporizing. 'She wouldn't be no comp'ny for you.'

'Yuss, she would. I'd rather 'ave 'er then any o' the others. She's so sweet!'

'She *is* a sweet little bit,' murmured Sam.

'You will let me 'ave 'er? Jest think, you with eight of 'em an' me without one. Me that's naturally so full o' love, too, I can't 'old myself. Me that's pray'd to Gawd on my bended knees night arter night for years an' years to send me a little baby. It's on'y 'cos I ain't got nothin' to love that I go on the booze. Gimme little Bet an' I'd be as good as anybody.'

Mrs Grewles drew a long breath and her lips tightened in a thin red line.

'No!' she said. 'You ain't no right to ask it.' Then the tears overflowed her eyes, and her face was suffused with a flush of passion. 'Oh, you wicked creature!' she cried, 'to come 'ere temptin' me to sell my own children as if they was 'eathen slaves. An' you, too,' turning on her unfortunate husband. 'Ow dare you stand by and not say a word the 'ole time? You that calls yerself a man an' a father! Oh, I ain't got no patience with either of you, that I ain't.'

She stamped her foot and menaced Moll with her hands.

'D'y'ear?' she screamed. 'Get away!'

'You'd better go away,' said Mr Grewles.

And Moll went.

(iv)

'I almost wish we 'ad took that Moll's money, arter all,' Mrs Grewles said to her husband two or three days later. 'There's Bobbie wantin' boots again an' Alice without a rag to 'er back, to say nothin' o' myself.'

'Ah!' said her husband.

'An' where the rent's to come from I don't know.'

'Nor me.'

'I wish you wouldn't sit there blowin' smoke all over the place, for all the world like a stuck pig that ain't got no gumption, instead o' usin' yer brains,' Mrs Grewles exclaimed irritably.

'I ain't never seen a pig smokin',' said Sam; 'but that don't matter, o' course. The subject is, Moll, an' 'er money.'

'An Bet.'

'An' Bet—yuss. Well, it ain't too late, is it?'

'I expect it is. She ain't bin 'ere since, an' nobody ain't seen 'er.'

'Well, if nobody ain't seen 'er, I've seen 'er.'

'Then nobody 'as seen 'er.'

'If you like to call me nobody—yuss.'

'Where did you see 'er?'

'She's waited on me outside the workshop every night.'

'Oh, she 'as, 'as she? So that's wot's made you late a-comin' 'ome! 'An why ain't you told me nothink about it?'

'I didn't see as there was any call to tell you,' Sam stammered.

Mrs Grewles put her arms akimbo and nodded her head with ferocious emphasis.

'So that's it, is it?' she cried. 'As she can't get my children, she thinks she'll 'ave my 'usban' instead, eh? We'll see about it, though. Let me lay 'ands on the beauty, that's all!'

'Now don't you go a-losin' yer temper all at once, 'cos you might find it 'andy some day, an' not 'ave it about you,' Sam said pacifically. 'There ain't likely to be nothink between me an' 'er, an' you ought to know it.'

'What did she want with you, then?'

'She wanted Bet, o' course. "Can't you spare 'er?" she says. "I'll give you ten poun's if you'll let me 'ave 'er."'

'Ten poun's?'

'Yuss.'

'What else did she say?'

'What else?'

'Yuss, looney! what else?'

'Well, there was a lot more, o' course, but it jest amounted to that. She wants Bet, an' she'll give us ten poun's for 'er.'

'Why didn't you tell me?'

'What was the good? I didn't want to upset you. An' I thort you was dead set against it.'

'So I am; but still—'

'It's a sight o' money. That's jest 'ow I feel. But it's no good. We didn't ought to do it, an' if we did do it we'd be sorry for it arterwards—when all the money was spent.'

'I don't know,' said Mrs Grewles dejectedly. 'I can't 'elp thinkin' about Bobbie's boots an' Alice's clo'es.'

'You mustn't think about 'em.'

'I won't.'

'That's right.' Mr Grewles rose and kissed the back of his wife's neck as she was stooping over the kitchen grate.

'Oh, get away!' she exclaimed, making a dab at him with a great metal spoon. 'It gives me the 'orrors to be touched there.'

Nevertheless, it was evident that she had enjoyed the caress.

'Ain't it about time them kids was in?' Sam asked presently.

'Yuss, it is,' said Mrs Grewles. 'Go an' call 'em—dear.'

'I will—dear,' said Sam. He hovered round his wife with a grinning face, intending to kiss her again, but she ran away into the washhouse and left him disconsolate.

He went to the gate and beckoned to his children, who were playing on 'The Tips'.

'Where's Bet?' he cried as they came running towards him.

'Bet?' they exclaimed with one voice.

'Yuss, Bet. Don't yell out as though you ain't never 'eard o' Bet before. Where is she? Bob, where is she?'

''Ow should I know, father? It ain't my place to look arter 'er. I'm a boy.'

'Alice, where is she?'

'I don't know. She was playin' hopscotch with Lil Smith las' time I see 'er.'

'Don't any of you know where she is?'

There was an uneasy silence.

'You'd better go an' find her, if you want any supper,' Mr Grewles said. 'Go an' see if she's in Missis Smith's.'

The children ran off. Sam stood at the gate with a rueful countenance, looking after them. Presently they returned.

'She ain't in Missis Smith's,' they announced. 'An' Missis Smith says she ain't set eyes on 'er since six o'clock.'

'Where was she at six o'clock?'

Again there was an uneasy silence.

'Where was she? Answer me.'

'She was roun' the corner wi' Moll.'

'With who?'

'Moll.'

Mr Grewles' face turned pale. 'Good Gawd!' he exclaimed. 'What'll the missis say?'

He stood with puckered brows munching his pipe and breathing heavily.

'You'd better all git indoors,' he said to the children.

They trooped past him into the house. He heard their shrill voices, mingled with the shriller voice of his wife. Presently Mrs Grewles came out. Her face, too, was pale, and her hands trembled.

'What's all this about Bet?' she asked.

Her husband shuffled his feet.

'I'm afraid,' he began, and then paused.

'What 're yer afraid of?'

'I'm afraid—'

'Out with it, for Gawd's sake!'

'I'm afraid Moll's took Bet.'

'What?'

'I'm afraid she 'as.'

Mrs Grewles began to cry. 'It's a judgment on me!' she sobbed. 'I never ought to 've thort o' partin' with 'er.'

'O' course I may be mistook,' said Sam, 'an' I 'ope I am. Still, I'll tell you what I'll do. I'll go round to the police station an' make inquiries.'

''Ow much will it cost?'

'It won't cost nothink. It's the best thing I can do. An' look 'ere, Annie, don't you go upsettin' of yerself. It'll be all right. They'll put the 'tecs on 'er track, if so be as she 'as took Bet. Stealin' kids is arson, you know. I was readin' a case in the paper on'y las' Sunday. She's liable to git five year.'

'She deserves ten—or more!'

Sam went indoors and donned his hat and coat. Mrs Grewles sat down in the kitchen and yielded herself unreservedly to tears.

'Oh, Sam!' she cried. 'If we don't never git 'er back any more!'

'Oh, that's all right. Don't you fret. The tecs'll find 'er.'

'I 'ope so,' said Mrs Grewles. 'But I feel a presentiment that we've lost 'er now for good an' all.'

Sam, in great distress, left the house. Half-an-hour later he returned.

'It's all right,' he said, 'I've seen the inspector, an' 'e tells me the 'tecs is bound to find 'er. You see, Bet bein' deaf an' dumb makes it so much easier for 'em to trace 'er.'

'It's all very well for you to talk,' said Mrs Grewles. 'You're on'y a man, an' ain't got no presentiments like I 'ave.'

(v)

While Mrs. Grewles was lamenting the loss of Bet, Bet herself was eating fried fish in a little shop near Tottenham Court Road. Moll sat opposite her with her eyes fixed on the child's face and her fingers drumming nervously on the greasy table. The air was heavy with the heat from the fire over which the fish was cooking, and thick with oily odours. Moll's plate of fish was untouched. She rarely ate anything even when she was in a normal state of mind; now that she was oppressed with a heavy sense of guilt, the mere idea of food was eminently distasteful to her. She was racked with fears, too, for she thought she had committed an irredeemable crime in kidnapping Bet. Nevertheless she was resolved that nothing save the strong, long arm of the law should deprive her of her delicious booty. Every toil-worn face in the shop seemed to her to express suspicion. 'How quiet the little thing is!' a woman who was sitting at the same table with them had said to Moll. Moll had given the woman one quick, frightened glance and shrunk away from her in mortal dread. She wished she had not gone into the shop, and longed to quit it.

At last Bet finished her meal, and they rose and went out into the streets. They turned into Tottenham Court Road. It was a clear, cold night, and in the white light of the electric lamps every face showed distinctly. When anyone looked at Bet, Moll drew the child closer to her, and hurried along faster than before. She had made definite plans for the future. And so, when they came to the Euston Road she stood hesitating on the kerb, torn with indecision.

She gazed around at the pinchbeck splendour of the great shops and warehouses, and her troubled eyes, rising above them, looked into the depths of the dark, starlit sky. Its grand remoteness thrilled her with a sense of awe, and filled her heart with indefinable long-ing. She wanted to be away from the squalor of this mighty city, to sit under those stars with the night wind playing on her. . . .

Her mind was made up. She would go to one of those great railway stations in the Euston Road and ride away from London in a devil-driven train. Before another day had dawned she would be in the midst of wide, tree-dotted fields—far beyond the reach of malignant pursuit and capture. She would find a little cottage with roses blowing in its garden—it was October, but she was a cockney —and ivy trailing over its walls; and there she would live with the child Bet for ever and ever.

Suddenly there sounded behind her the heavy tramp of many feet, and a great crowd surged past. She turned and saw that in the midst of the crowd, between two policemen, was a kicking, biting, shrieking woman. The sight fascinated her.

'What's the poor thing done?' she asked a man.

'Poor thing!' cried the man. 'I like that! She's the drunkenest woman in London, she is! But they ain't lockin' 'er up becos' she's drunk.'

'What then?'

'She's bin stealin'.'

'Stealin'?'

'Ah! drink leads to more things than drunkenness, you know.'

'What's she stole?'

'I dunno. Some money, I expect, to buy booze with.'

'P'r'aps she's stole a baby?'

'Not much fear o' that, missis. Babies is too plentiful for people to steal 'em.'

'You don't know—you don't know,' Moll said earnestly.

The man edged away from her under the impression she was mad.

Moll turned to take Bet's hand and lead her away. To her horror she discovered that Bet had disappeared. She ran along the Tottenham Court Road after the crowd, thinking that perhaps the press of people had carried Bet along with it. She caught the crowd, passed it, and struggled back through it, but she could not find Bet. As she hurriedly retraced her steps, looking distractedly to the right and left, she again saw the man who had said that people don't steal babies. He was pointing her out to a mate. What if he suspected her of stealing a baby? She faltered and clutched at a post for support. The man and his mate moved toward her. Then her strength returned to her, and she ran, panting, from them.

She ran for more than 100 yards before she dared to pause, though she knew that by so doing she was attracting much attention. When at last she looked back the awful man was nowhere to be seen, and she slackened her pace.

But Bet! Where was Bet? The splendid shops and warehouses still remained in all their aggravating impressiveness, the struggling crowd of wayfarers still passed and repassed under the white light, and above, the stars still shone in the deep sky. But Bet was gone! Bet was utterly, irrevocably lost to her for ever!

'Oh, what shall I do? what shall I do?' she moaned.

Her lips became salt with tears, and she wrung her hands.

'What's up, missis?' a policeman asked her.

She gave him one startled glance, and then, as her eyes swept the long vista of road, she cried out, 'There she is! There she is!

Oh, Bet, Bet!' and started to run away. The policeman ran after her.

'Come, what is it?' he demanded, laying a heavy hand on her shoulder.

'You leave me alone. I ain't done nothink,' she said, struggling frantically under his grasp, for she had seen Bet standing in the road not fifty yards away, and was eager to reach the child before she again became lost in the crowd.

'Wait a bit! What 're you runnin' away for if you ain't done nothink?' the policeman asked her.

'I ain't runnin' away,' Moll said. 'I—'

But the policeman had suddenly released her. His face wore an expression of horror.

'Oh, my Gawd!' she heard him exclaim, and then he pushed her aside and dashed past her. She turned then, and saw that a huge crowd had gathered round the spot where lately she had seen Bet standing. Everyone was rushing to swell the crowd, and on every face was reflected that expression of horror which she had seen on the face of the policeman. With a cold heart and quaking limbs, she too ran towards the crowd.

It was fifty humans deep, and she could not reach its centre, though she fought and struggled towards it with the strength of madness. For ten horrible minutes she stood with her arms pressed hard to her sides and her face flattened against a bricklayer's fustian coat, unable to do aught but moan despairingly. At last there was a convulsion in the heart of the crowd and she was lifted forward. ... Some policemen, and one painted woman, were bending over a tiny heap in the roadway. She caught a glimpse of a shabby red frock, and knew that the tiny heap was Bet.

'Is she dead?' she gasped.

'Dead!' exclaimed a lank artisan, laughing—he was not heartless, but felt a little sick and hysterical. 'I should think she was dead. The 'bus went right over 'er 'ead. I see it myself.'

'Now then, stand back, some of you!' cried one of the policemen, and Moll was engulfed in the crowd. She struggled desperately to gain another glimpse of the dead child. She wanted to claim it, to hug its crushed face to her heart, to kiss it, and weep over it. She could not believe that Bet was really dead. She felt—nay, she knew—that the child could yet be kissed back into life.

'Let me go to 'er,' she moaned.

Someone in the crowd asked her: 'Does the poor little thing belong to you ?'

Moll looked at her interlocutor with frightened eyes, and hung her head. 'No,' she said.

'P'r'aps you know 'er ?'

But a terrible consciousness of her real position had overcome Moll, and she could not answer. She tried to escape from the crowd, but it was as hard to retreat as to go forward. She wondered whether she were legally responsible for Bet's death—she did not doubt that she was morally responsible for it—and soon persuaded herself that she was. For Moll was a woman with a strong, untrained imagination. Even as she stood panting in that writhing phalanx, she could see herself, as in a vision, arraigned behind the spikes of a prisoners' dock before a buzzing court, and heard the voice of Bet's mother rising in shrill denunciation of her. She was more afraid of Bet's mother than of any higher tribunal.

So, when the ambulance came and the crowd broke, she fled guiltily away.

(vi)

Moll was the unhappiest woman in London that night. And unhappy women are not scarce in the gay metropolis. As she walked through the streets she whimpered like a child.

'If I could on'y cry,' she told herself, 'I should feel better. But there don't seem to be a tear in me.'

She crossed Oxford Street and struck southward through a labyrinth of shabby byways till she reached Charing Cross. Here the hurrying throng and the ceaseless tumult forcibly reminded her of that other busy thoroughfare she had lately quitted. She started at the recollection, and, quite involuntarily, crossed over to the kerb, and looked to the right and left along the vista of glazed asphalte for the figure of poor dead Bet.

''Ere y' are, mem,' cried a grinning newsboy as he thrust a paper under her nose. 'All the winners an' all the murders, mem. *Noos, Ekker,* er *Star !*'

A drunken roysterer stumbled against her, and the wheels of a passing hansom brushed her dress.

'Come, move on,' said the omnipresent policeman. 'This side o' the Strand belongs to the parsons; yours is the other side.'

A laugh followed this sally, and Moll slunk away.

Where should she go? What should she do?

She felt miserably weak and foolishly peevish. Her head ached and she was cold. She did the inevitable thing.

The barmaid who took her order was a big, tawdry woman with dropsical yellow earrings and brassy hair. She surveyed Moll with huge contempt, and served her leisurely. There were a good many people in the bar: barbers' assistants, clerks, and birds of prey in gaudy plumage. She could see that some of them were being funny at her expense, and withdrew into a corner. She disposed herself on a plush-covered seat and began to sip her rum. It was hot and strong, and imparted to her chilled body a comfortable warmth.

For more than an hour she sat there, going to the bar whenever her glass was empty to get it replenished, and emptying it again with automatic regularity. At last the potman yelled: 'Time, please,' and she was hustled out.

A light rain was falling. The quivering pavements were shiny with wet; impalpable horses slipped and stumbled on the nebulous roadway; the tall houses nodded fantastically. Somebody with a strident voice was trying to sing. Moll wondered who the some-body could be until she discovered it was herself. She stopped then, and the silence was more oppressive than the singing.

She staggered across the widest road in the world and wandered on through a maze of kerbs till she found herself under dripping trees on the Embankment. Shivering, she sat down on a seat and watched the dancing lights on the river till her eyes closed and she fell asleep. A bull's-eye flashed in her face and awoke her.

'Come,' said a voice from the blackness behind the bull's-eye; 'you can't sleep 'ere, you know.'

She knew it and rose wearily. She toiled up an interminable staircase and found herself on a bridge spanning the river, with the rain beating in her face and fluttering her skirts. She rested her arms on the slimy parapet and looked down into the dark water. A shudder convulsed her. Ugh! How cold and uninviting it looked—down there! There were great black masses—barges, probably—floating on the stream; and puffing, grunting monsters with fiery eyes that belched forth smoke and flame. The lights on the Embankment threw paths of molten gold across the river, and it seemed to Moll that she could see myriads of dead faces gleaming up at her through the yellow brightness of its rugged surface.

Someone touched her on the shoulder. She turned with a start and a little scream.

'What d'you want?' she gasped.

It was a woman who had touched her: a woman with ghastly white hair and a weary, withered face. Her head was bare. She wore a shiny black bodice, trimmed with mangy fur, and a light summer skirt, sodden with rain.

'Are you cold?' she asked Moll.

Moll stared at her and nodded.

'So am I,' the woman said. 'I am as cold as charity—charity which is love—love which is a burning, blasting passion.' She laughed. 'Why do you think I touched you just now?' she said.

'I dunno,' Moll muttered, half attracted, half repelled by the woman's personality.

'I wanted you to come and sleep with me. My bed is under the bridge. It's a stone bed, but it's dry, and I have slept in it every night all through the summer. But, unfortunately, my clothes are wet, and I cannot sleep tonight, because I am so cold. I thought that perhaps if I could find someone to share my bed, we might huddle up together, and so warm one another. Will you come?'

Moll took the hand the woman extended towards her, and together they sought the shelter of the bridge.

'Here is my bed,' said the woman.

She pointed to a dark flight of steps leading down to the river. Moll shrunk back.

'Don't be afraid,' the woman said, with a wan smile. 'The water never reaches my bed, though sometimes, on a rough night, it just splashes it. And no policeman's bull's-eye ever shines down here. . . . I often wonder,' she said, 'why the laws of England have ordained that no one shall sleep in the streets by night, whilst everyone is at liberty to sleep in the streets by day. . . . Let me go first. That's right.'

''Ow orful the river sounds!' said Moll.

'It's a very harmless old river, and it sings better lullabies than any mother. Are you very wet? Never mind. Keep close to me and we shall soon be warm. . . . May I put my arms round you? Put your arms round me. . . . Good-night, my dear.'

'Goo'-ni'.'

'Good-night.'

At the Dock Gate

There was a big crowd waiting for the dock gate to open that morning, a gaunt, hungry-looking crowd that for the most part smoked sullenly in the dismal drizzle of rain, with coats buttoned tightly and collars turned up, against the nipping air.

Hunger is no aid to cheerfulness, and work had been terribly scarce among the dockers for some months past. Two men in the crowd, however, after standing moodily side by side for the better part of an hour, seemed to find the silence more unbearable than speech.

They were brawny, well-set fellows, with the same pinched look on their features as characterized most of the rugged, apathetic faces in that forlorn company; young men still, bronzed and bearded, and by no means ill-favoured, either of them, though the elder of the two was not without lingering traces of dissipation in his dulled eyes, and in the unnatural warmth of his complexion.

He was the first to speak.

'Well, Harvey,' he began abruptly, as if he had only just noticed who was his neighbour, 'bin havin' a spell o' bad luck lately, ain't yer?'

'Like the rest of 'em,' returned the other. ''Ow ha' you bin doin' yerself, Bonce?'

Bonce vouchsafed no other reply than an indefinite combination of oaths, which, nevertheless, had a sufficiently definite meaning, and added gruffly, after a further interval of stagnation:

''Ow's Meg? 'Ow's the missus?'

'Bad.'

'An' the kid? Bin quisby, ain't 'e?'

'Him?'

There was a sudden huskiness in Harvey's voice; he looked away, and spat deliberately, and made an effort to clear his throat.

'You can't expect a kid to live long on nothin', eh?—an' when 'is mother don't get food enough for herself,' he said, with a rapid and disjointed utterance. 'He's got *his* ticket,' he concluded, forcing a laugh, 'an' he ain't had long to wait for it. Jolly little chap, though, he was. Grin at us 'e used to, 'fore he got so bad—he—Blarst the rain! Got a match?'

'Poor little beggar!' growled Bonce, indifferently. ''Ow's *she* take it?'

'She? Oh, she's worryin' her 'art out about it.' Harvey laughed again with an affectation of carelessness. 'Women always do, y'know.'

They relapsed into grim silence, and smoked stolidly, each occupied with his own thoughts.

Bonce wasn't a bad-hearted man, but there was a subtle sense of vague gratification rising sluggishly through his reflections. He had been in love with Meg himself at one time; he had loved her with a pure intensity he was half ashamed now to remember; but she had preferred Harvey, and it somehow soothed a certain sense of injury within him to think that perhaps now she would regret her choice. He wasn't good enough for her, but—had she got anything better?

He and Harvey had quarrelled savagely about her at first; they had been open enemies for months; then they tacitly abandoned active animosity, and were contented to contemptuously ignore each other, and now, at last, they had spoken; time had toned their old feelings down to quite a neutral tint.

Bonce was not a bad-hearted man, and when that devilish glow of momentary satisfaction passed, a relenting afterthought touched him, a sense of dim pity even, that exasperated him and brought a strange tingling sensation into his eyes, so that he was doubly relieved when the loud clang of a falling bolt sent a thrill through the crowd, and they closed up quickly as the door in the great gate swung open.

'Steady, there, steady!' called the two policemen from inside. 'No shoving!'

But the anxious, hungry throng surged forward, elbowing and struggling in dumb, desperate eagerness towards that narrow entry, as if it had been the very gate of heaven.

One after the other the fortunate front ranks passed in, received their tickets at the little window of the wooden office inside, and hurried on in a straggling line towards the vessel that was waiting to be unloaded.

The two men who had been talking together arrived at the gate abreast; there was a hasty, dogged shove for precedence. Bonce passed in first, and Harvey was following him, when the little window of the office slammed down, and a voice ejaculated:

'Last ticket!'

'Last ticket!' echoed the policeman. 'No more wanted. Stand back there! Outside!'

Bonce turned with the ticket in his fingers. He had a brief glimpse of the man he knew backing out before the two policemen —his wan, haggard face, the gleam of wretchedness in his eyes.

'It's nothin' to do with me,' he muttered between his teeth, but even as he said it that dim afterthought of pity touched him again— not pity for the man before him, though he ran back as if a sudden frenzy had seized him, and shouted:

'Harvey! Harvey!'

The policeman paused and glanced round. Bonce wrenched the door wide again, grasped the man's arm, and dragging him through into the yard, thrust something roughly into his hand, his lip quivering, and inexplicable fury in his looks and manner.

'Damn you, take hold of it!' he cried hoarsely.

The disappointed crowd outside made way for Bonce as he shouldered his way out, cursing them for blocking up the entry, and the door shut heavily behind him.

Clarence Rook

Young Alf

On this particular occasion we met by appointment at the Elephant and Castle. He had a kip in the vicinity; that is, there was a bed, which was little better than a board, in one of those places where your welcome extends from sunset to sunrise; and to this he had recurred for some five nights in succession. For some reason or other he was unwilling to conduct me to his precise address for the current week. So we met, by appointment, where the omnibuses converge and separate to their destinations in all parts of South London, on the kerbstone at the Elephant.

I was in a sense a pilgrim. Good Americans, when they come to London, may be seen peering about in Bolt Court and eating their dinner at the Cheshire Cheese. I was bound on an expedition to the haunts of a more recent celebrity than Dr Johnson. My destination was Irish Court and the Lamb and Flag. For in the former Patrick Hooligan lived a portion of his ill-spent life, and gave laws and a name to his followers; in the latter, the same Patrick was to be met night by night, until a higher law than his own put a period to his rule.

Moreover, my companion was one on whom a portion at least of Patrick Hooligan's mantle had fallen; a young man—he was scarcely more than seventeen—who held by the Hooligan tradition, and controlled a gang of boys who made their living by their wits, and were ready for any devilry if you assured them of even an inadequate reward.

Young Alf—this is not the name by which the constable on point duty at the Elephant mentions him to his colleague who comes along from St George's Road—young Alf was first at the meeting-place. He had, he explained, an evening to spare, and there were lots of worse places than the Elephant.

Young Alf beckoned; and while I hovered on the kerb, watching the charging 'buses, the gliding trams, and the cabs that twinkled their danger signals, he had plunged into the traffic and slithered through, dodging 'buses and skirting cabs without a turn of the head. He went through the traffic with a quiet, confident twist of the body, as a fish whisks its way through scattered rocks, touching nothing, but always within a hair's-breadth of collision. On the other side he awaited me, careless, and indeed a little contemptuous; and together we made our way towards Bethlehem Hospital, and thence in the direction of Lambeth Walk.

As we swung round a corner I noticed a man in the doorway of a shop—a bald-headed man with spectacles, and in his shirt-sleeves, though the night was chilly.

'Ain't caught yer yet?' was the remark that young Alf flung at him, without turning his head half a point.

'You take a lot o' catchin', you do,' retorted the man.

Young Alf looked round at me. I expected to hear him laugh, or chuckle, or at the least seem amused. And it came upon me with something of a shock that I had never, so far as I could remember, seen him laugh. His face was grave, tense, eager, as always.

'That's a fence,' he said. 'I lived there when I was a nipper, wiv my muvver—and a accerabat.'

'Was that when—' I began.

'Don't talk,' he muttered, for we had emerged upon Lambeth Walk. The Walk, as they term it to whom Lambeth Walk is Bond Street, the promenade, the place to shop, to lounge, to listen to music and singing, to steal, if opportunity occur, to make love, and not infrequently to fight.

The moon was up, and struggling intermittently through clouds; this was probably one of the reasons why young Alf allowed himself an evening of leisure. But Lambeth Walk had no need of a moon: it was Saturday night, and the Walk was aflare with gas and naphtha, which lighted up the street from end to end, and emphasized the gloom of the narrow openings which gave entrance to the network of courts between the Walk and the railway arches behind it.

The whole social life of a district was concentrated in the two hundred yards of roadway, which was made even narrower by the double lines of barrows which flanked it. There was not a well-dressed person to be seen, scarcely a passably clean one. But there was none of the hopeless poverty one might have seen at the same hour in Piccadilly; and no one looked in the least bored. Business and pleasure jostled one another. Every corner had its side-show to which you must turn your attention for a moment in the intervals of haggling over your Sunday's dinner. Here at this corner is a piano-organ, with small children dancing wildly for the mere fun of the thing. There is no dancing for coppers in the Walk. At the next corner is a miniature shooting-gallery; the leather-lunged proprietor shouts with well-assumed joy when a crack shot makes the bell ring for the third time, and bears off the coco-nut.

'Got 'im again!' he bawls delightedly, as though he lived only to give coco-nuts away to deserving people.

Hard by the bland owner of a hand-cart is recommending an 'unfallible cure for toothache' to a perverse and unbelieving audience. As we pass we hear him saying,

'I've travelled 'undreds of miles in my time, ladies and gentle-men—all the world over; but this I will say—and let him deny it that can, and I maintain he can't—and that is this, that never in the 'ole course of my experience have I met so sceptical a lot of people as you Londoners. You ain't to be took in. You know—'

But young Alf was making his way through the crowd, and I hurried after him.

Literature, too, by the barrowful; paper covers with pictures that hit you between the eyes and made you blink. And music! 'Words and music. Four a penny, and all different.'

You may buy anything and everything in the Walk—caps, canaries, centre-bits, oranges, toffee, saucepans, to say nothing of fried fish, butchers' meat, and green stuff; everything, in fact, that you could require to make you happy. And a pervading cheerful-ness is the note of the Walk.

On that Saturday evening there were probably more people in Lambeth Walk who made their living on the crooked than in any other street of the same length in London. Yet the way of trans-gressors seemed a cheerful one. Everybody was good-humoured, and nobody was more than reasonably drunk.

Lower down we came to the meat stalls, over which the butchers were shouting the praises of prime joints. As we passed, a red-faced man with sandy whiskers suddenly dropped his voice to the level of ordinary conversation.

'You ain't selling no meat tonight, ain't you?' he said, cocking a knowing eye at my companion.

Young Alf glanced quickly at the butcher, and then round at me.

'I'll tell you about that presently,' he said, in answer to my look of inquiry.

''Ere we are,' said young Alf, a few moments later, as we turned suddenly fron the glaring, shouting, seething Walk, redolent of gas, naphtha, second-hand shoe-leather, and fried fish, into a dark entrance. Dimly I could see that the entrance broadened a few yards down into a court of about a dozen feet in width. No light shone from any of the windows, no gas-lamp relieved the gloom. The court ran from the glare of the street into darkness and mystery.

Young Alf hesitated a moment or two in the shadow. Then he said:

'Look 'ere, you walk froo'—straight on; it ain't far, and I'll be at the uvver end to meet you.'

'Why don't you come with me?' I asked. I could see that he was looking me up and down critically.

'Not down there,' he said; 'they'd think I was narkin'. You look a dam sight too much like a split tonight.' Then I remembered that he had been keeping a little ahead of me ever since we had met at the Elephant and Castle. I had unthinkingly neglected to adapt my dress in any way to the occasion, and in consequence was subjecting my friend to uneasiness and possible annoyance.

I expressed my regret, and, buttoning my coat, started down the court as young Alf melted into the crowd in Lambeth Walk. It was not a pretty court. The houses were low, with narrow doorways and windows that showed no glimmer of light. Heaps of garbage assailed the feet and the nose. Not a living soul was to be seen until I had nearly reached the other end, and could just discern the form of young Alf leaning against one of the posts at the exit of the court. Then suddenly two women in white aprons sprang into view from nowhere, gave a cry, and stood watching me from a doorway.

'They took you for a split,' said young Alf, as we met at the end of the court. 'I know'd they would. 'Ello, Alice!'

A girl stood in the deep shadow of the corner house. Her head was covered by a shawl, and I could not see her face, but her figure showed youth and a certain grace.

''Ello!' she said, without moving.

'When you goin' to get married?' asked young Alf.

'When it comes,' replied the girl softly.

The voice that falls like velvet on your ear and lingers in your memory is rare. Wendell Holmes says somewhere that he had heard but two perfect speaking voices, and one of them belonged to a German chambermaid. The softest and most thrilling voice I ever heard I encountered at the corner of one of the lowest slums in London.

Young Alf was apparently unaffected by it, for, having thus accorded the courtesy due to an acquaintance, he whipped round swiftly to me and said:

'Where them women's standing is where Pat Hooligan lived, 'fore he was pinched.'

It stood no higher than the houses that elbowed it, and had nothing to distinguish it from its less notable neighbours. But if a Hooligan boy prayed at all, he would pray with his face towards that house half-way down Irish Court.

'And next door—this side,' continued young Alf, 'that's where me and my muvver kipped when I was a nipper.'

The tone of pride was unmistakable, for the dwelling-place of Patrick Hooligan enshrines the ideal towards which the Ishmaelites of Lambeth are working; and, as I afterwards learned, young Alf's supremacy over his comrades was sealed by his association with the memory of the Prophet.

'This way,' said young Alf.

The girl stood, still motionless, in the shadow, with one hand clasping the shawl that enveloped her head. Here was stark solitude and dead silence, with a background of shouting, laughter, rifle-shots, and the tramp of myriad feet from the Walk thirty yards away. I hesitated, in the hope of hearing her voice again. But I was not to hear it a second time for many days; and she remained silent and motionless as we plunged again into obscurity.

Under the railway arches it was as black as pitch.

''Sh!' said young Alf warningly, as I stumbled. It was too dark to see the lithe, sinewy hand that he placed on my own for my guidance.

In a few seconds we had turned—as my nose gave evidence—

into a stable-yard. Upon one corner the moon shone, bringing a decrepit van into absurd prominence.

''Ere's where me and my pal was—up to last week,' said young Alf in a whisper.

He slipped across to a dark corner, and I followed. A stable dog barked, and then, as we stood still, lapsed into silence.

'Got a match?' said young Alf.

I handed him a box of matches, and he struck one, shading it with his hands so skilfully that no glimmer fell anywhere but on the latch of a door.

'Awright,' he muttered, as the door swung back noiselessly. Then he turned and put his face close to mine. 'If anybody wants to know anyfink, you swank as you want to take the room. See?'

The stairs were steep and in bad repair, for they creaked horribly under my feet. But young Alf as he ascended in front of me was inaudible, and I thought I had lost him and myself, until I ran into him at the top.

From utter blackness we turned into a room flooded by moonlight, a room in no way remarkable to the sight, but such a room as you may see when you are house-hunting in the suburbs, ascend to the top floor of a desirable residence, and are told that this is a servant's bedroom. The walls were papered; it had a single window through which the moonlight was streaming, and it was quite empty, save for something lying in the corner of the window —apparently a horse-cloth.

'This is where we was, me and 'im,' said young Alf. 'There's anuvver room across the landing.'

'Who was him?' I asked.

Young Alf walked over to the window, looked down into the yard below, and made no reply. There were things here and there that he would not tell me.

'Why did you leave?' I resumed. 'It seems a convenient sort of place to live in. Quiet enough, wasn't it?'

'Well, it was like this,' he said. 'Me and 'im was making snide coin; least 'e was making it, and I was planting it—'ere, there, and everywhere. See?'

'Made it in this room? How did he make it?'

''E'd never show me the way. But it didn't take him long. Well, we got planting it a bit too thick, 'cos there was more'n one on the same fake, and the cops come smellin' about. So we did a scoot. Time enough it was.'

'Smelling,' I said; 'I should think they did. It's enough to knock you down.'

'I fought I noticed somefink,' he said sharply, and in an instant he had pounced upon the object in the corner, and from underneath the horse-cloth drew a joint of meat, which at once proclaimed itself as the origin of the awful stench.

'Wonder how that got left 'ere?' said young Alf, as he opened the window gently and heaved the joint into the yard below.

'Better leave the window open,' I said as he was about to close it.

'Didn't I never tell you,' he said, 'how we waxed things up for that butcher as come down to the Walk? Battersea he come from.'

I had not heard the story, and said so.

'It was that what give the show away,' he said. 'You 'eard what that butcher said jest now?'

I nodded.

He leaned against the window sill, and, with one eye on the stable-yard, told me the story.

'It was Friday night last week,' he began, 'and me and two uvvers was coming along the Walk, down where the butchers are. There was one butcher there that I tumbled was a stranger soon as I ketch sight of 'is dial. He wasn't selling 'is meat over-quick, 'cos 'alf the time he was necking four-ale in the pub 'cross the way. He'd got 'is joints laid out beautiful on a sort of barrer. Well, we 'ung about, watchin' 'im go 'cross the road and come back again, and presently I says to the uvvers, "That bloke don't seem to be doin' no trade worf mentionin'. Let's 'elp 'im." Well, the uvver boys didn't want asking more'n once to do a pore bloke a good turn, so we just scatters and waits a bit till the butcher went 'cross the way again for 'is wet; nor we didn't 'ave to wait long neither. Soon as he goes into the pub we nips round and shifts his old barrer, and 'fore you could say knife we had it froo the arches and in the stable-yard here. We got the meat upstairs, and then we run the empty barrer outside, and left it standin' in Paradise Street, where it couldn't do no one any 'arm.'

'But didn't anyone see you shift the barrow?' I asked.

''Ow was they to know we wasn't in the employment of the butcher?' he retorted. 'Besides, the uvver butchers wasn't likely to make a fuss. They didn't want no strangers comin' and inter-ferin' wiv their pitch.'

'And did you see any more of the butcher?' I inquired.

'What do you fink?' he said. 'Presently we went back again to the Walk, and it wasn't 'alf a minute before we saw the butcher tearin' up and down lookin' for his barrer. Of course nobody 'adn't seen anyfink of it. Then he started on the pubs, and went into every pub in the Walk askin' after his barrer. He had a lot of wet, but he didn't find no barrer, nor no meat neither. We went into one or two of the pubs after 'im, and gave 'im a lot of symperfy, jest abart as much as he could do wiv. One of the boys says: "Sims to me your legs 'ave taken to walkin' again, guv'nor." And the butcher couldn't 'ardly keep 'is 'air on. Then anuvver of the boys says he never was so sorry for anyfink in all his life. Come all the way from the Angel up at Islington, 'e 'ad, purpose to get a prime joint at the new butcher's in the Walk. That butcher's joints was the fair talk round Upper Street way, he says. What 'e'd say to the missus when 'e come home empty-'anded he didn't know, he says.

'Then I chipped in.

'"Well, guv'nor," I says, "they tell me you've beat all them uvver butchers tonight. You've cleared out all your stock 'fore anyone else, 'aven't you? And you ain't given none of it away, neither."

'Wiv that he fair got 'is monkey up, and he went off down the Walk ragin' and roarin'; and me and the uvver boys went back to where we'd planted the meat. There was meat goin' cheap that night down our way—less than cawst-price, wiv no error. And some of them butchers wasn't quite so pleased as they fort they was, when they found legs of mutton sellin' at frippence a pound.'

'And what became of the unfortunate butcher?' I asked.

'Last thing I see of him he'd had more'n enough already. And then he got into a 'ouse—not what you might call a resky 'ome—and there they put him to sleep, and went froo his pockets, and pitched him out in the mornin', skinned—feer skinned 'e was. The cops found 'is barrer next mornin', and wheeled it off. But the butcher never showed 'is dial again in the Walk. Bit too 'ot.'

'Rather rough on the butcher, wasn't it?' I suggested. 'But you probably didn't think of that.'

His eyes glanced quickly from mine to the yard below, and back to mine again, and for a moment—perhaps it was the moonlight that caught his face and gave it a weird twist—but for the moment he looked like a rat.

'I got meself to fink abart,' he said; 'and if I went finkin' abart uvver people I shouldn't be no good at this game. I wonder which of them silly young blokes it was that forgot that leg of mutton I chucked outer winder.'

He peered over the sill, and the dog began barking again. But the step in the lane outside passed on. And young Alf turned again to me and expounded his philosophy of life.

'Look 'ere,' he said, 'if you see a fing you want, you just go and take it wivout any 'anging abart. If you 'ang abart you draw suspicion, and you get lagged for loiterin' wiv intent to commit a felony or some dam nonsense like that. Go for it, strite. P'r'aps it's a 'awse and cart you see as'll do you fine. Jump up and drive away as 'ard as you can, and ten to one nobody'll say anyfink. They'll think it's your own prop'ty. But 'ang around, and you mit jest as well walk into the next cop you see, and arst 'im to 'and you your stretch. See? You got to look after yourself; and it ain't your graft to look after anyone else, nor it ain't likely that any body else'd look arter you—only the cops. See?'

A cloud came over the moon, and threw the room and the yard outside into darkness. Young Alf became a dim shadow against the window.

'Time we was off,' he said.

He shut down the window softly, and, by the shaded light of a match with which I supplied him, led me to the door and down the stairs. The dog was awake and alert, and barked noisily, though young Alf's step would not have broken an egg or caused a hare to turn in its sleep. He protested in a whisper against my inability to tread a stair without bringing the house about my ears. But the yard outside was empty, and no one but the dog seemed aware of our presence. Young Alf was bound, he said, for the neighbourhood of Westminster Bridge, but he walked with me down to Vauxhall Station through a network of dim and silent streets.

I inquired of his plans for the night, and he explained that there was a bit of a street-fight in prospect. The Drury Lane boys were coming across the bridge, and had engaged to meet the boys from Lambeth Walk at a coffee stall on the other side. Then one of the Lambeth boys would make to one of the Drury Lane boys a remark which cannot be printed, but never fails to send the monkey of a Drury Lane boy a considerable way up the pole. Whereafter the Drury Lane boys would fall upon the Lambeth boys, and the Lambeth boys would give them what for.

As we came under the gas-lamps of Upper Kennington Lane, young Alf opened his coat. He was prepared for conflict. Round his throat he wore the blue neckerchief, spotted with white, with which my memory will always associate him; beneath that a light jersey. His trousers were supported by a strong leathern belt with a savage-looking buckle.

Diving into his breast pocket, and glancing cautiously round, he drew out a handy-looking chopper which he poised for a moment, as though assuring himself of its balance.

'That's awright, eh?' he said, putting the chopper in my hand.

'Are you going to fight with that?' I asked, handing it back to him.

He passed his hand carefully across the blade.

'That oughter mean forty winks for one or two of 'em. Don't you fink so?' he said.

His eyes glittered in the light of the gas-lamp as he thrust the chopper back into his pocket and buttoned up his coat, having first carefully smoothed down the ends of his spotted neckerchief.

'Then you'll have a late night, I suppose?' I said as we passed along up the lane.

''Bout two o'clock I shall be back at my kip,' he replied.

We parted for the night at Vauxhall Cross, where a small crowd of people waited for their trams. We did not shake hands. The ceremony always seems unfamiliar and embarrassing to him. With a curt nod he turned and slid through the crowd, a lithe, well-knit figure, shoulders slightly hunched, turning his head neither to this side nor to that, hands close to his trouser pockets, sneaking his way like a fish through the scattered peril of rocks.

Clarence Rook

Concerning Hooligans

There was, but a few years ago, a man called Patrick Hooligan, who walked to and fro among his fellow-men, robbing them and occasionally bashing them. This much is certain. His existence in the flesh is a fact as well established as the existence of Buddha or of Mahomet. But with the life of Patrick Hooligan, as with the lives of Buddha and of Mahomet, legend has been at work, and probably many of the exploits associated with his name spring from the imagination of disciples. It is at least certain that he was born, that he lived in Irish Court, that he was employed as a chucker-out at various resorts in the neighbourhood. His regular business, as young Alf puts it, was 'giving mugs and other barmy sots the push out of pubs when their old swank got a bit too thick'. Moreover, he could do more than his share of tea-leafing, which denotes the picking up of unconsidered trifles, being handy with his fingers, and a good man all round. Finally, one day he had a difference with a constable, put his light out, and threw the body into a dust-cart. He was lagged, and given a lifer. But he had not been in gaol long before he had to go into hospital, where he died.

There is little that is remarkable in this career. But the man must have had a forceful personality, a picturesqueness, a fascination, which elevated him into a type. It was doubtless the combination of skill and strength, a certain exuberance of lawlessness, an utter absence of scruple in his dealings, which marked him out as a leader among men. Anyhow, though his individuality may be obscured by legend, he lived, and died, and left a great tradition behind him. He established a cult.

The value of a cult is best estimated by its effect upon its adherents, and as Patrick Hooligan is beyond the reach of cross-examination, I propose to devote a few words to showing what manner of men his followers are, the men who call themselves by his name, and do their best to pass the torch of his tradition undimmed to the nippers who are coming on.

I should perhaps not speak of them as men, for the typical Hooligan is a boy who, growing up in the area bounded by the Albert Embankment, the Lambeth Road, the Kennington Road, and the streets about the Oval, takes to tea-leafing as a Grimsby lad takes to the sea. If his taste runs to street-fighting there is hope for him, and for the community. He will probably enlist, and, having helped to push the merits of gin and Christianity in the dark places of the earth, die in the skin of a hero. You may see in Lambeth Walk a good many soldiers who have come back from looking over the edge of the world to see the place they were born in, to smell the fried fish and the second-hand shoe-leather, and to pulsate once more to the throb of a piano-organ. On the other hand, if his fingers be lithe and sensitive, if he have a turn for mechanics, he will slip naturally into the picking of pockets and the rifling of other people's houses.

The home of the Hooligan is, as I have implied, within a stone's-throw of Lambeth Walk. Law breakers exist in other quarters of London: Drury Lane will furnish forth a small army of pickpockets, Soho breeds parasites, and the basher of toffs flourishes in the Kingsland Road. But in and about Lambeth Walk we have a colony, compact and easily handled, of sturdy young villains, who start with a grievance against society, and are determined to get their own back. That is their own phrase, their own view. Life has little to give them but what they take. Honest work, if it can be obtained, will bring in but a few shillings a week; and what is that compared to the glorious possibility of nicking a red 'un?

Small and compact, the colony is easily organized; and here, as in all turbulent communities, such as an English public school, the leader gains his place by sheer force of personality. The boy who has kicked in a door can crow over the boy who has merely smashed a window. If you have knocked out your adversary at the little boxing place off the Walk, you will have proved that your friendship is desirable. If it becomes known—and it speedily becomes known to all but the police—that you have drugged a toff and run through his pockets, or, better still, have cracked a crib on your own and planted the stuff, then you are at once surrounded by sycophants. Your position is assured, and you have but to pick and choose those that shall work with you. Your leadership will be recognized, and every morning boys, with both eyes skinned for strolling splits, will seek you out and ask for orders for the day. In time, if you stick to work and escape the cops, you may become possessed of a coffee-house or a sweetstuff shop, and run a profitable business as a fence. Moreover, your juniors, knowing your past experience, will purchase your advice—paying for counsel's opinion—when they seek an entrance to a desirable house in the suburbs, and cannot decide between the fan-light and the kitchen window. So you shall live and die respected by all men in Lambeth Walk.

The average Hooligan is not an ignorant, hulking ruffian, beetle-browed and bullet-headed. He is a product of the Board School, writes a fair hand, and is quick at arithmetic. His type of face approaches nearer the rat than the bull-dog; he is nervous, highly strung, almost neurotic. He is by no means a drunkard; but a very small quantity of liquor causes him to run amuck, when he is not pleasant to meet. Undersized as a rule, he is sinewy, swift and untiring. For pocket-picking and burglary the featherweight is at an advantage. He has usually done a bit of fighting with the gloves, for in Lambeth boxing is one of the most popular forms of sport. But he is better with the raws, and is very bad to tackle in a street row, where there are no rules to observe. Then he will show you some tricks that will astonish you. No scruples of conscience will make him hesitate to butt you in the stomach with his head, and pitch you backwards by catching you round the calves with his arm. His skill, born of constant practice, in scrapping and hurricane fighting, brings him an occasional job in the bashing line. You have an enemy, we will say, whom you wish to mark, but, for one reason and another, you do not wish to appear in the matter. Young Alf will take on the job. Indicate to him your enemy; hand him five shillings (he will ask a sovereign, but will take five shillings), and he will make all the necessary arrangements. One night your enemy will find himself lying dazed on the pavement in a quiet corner, with a confused remembrance of a trip and a crash, and a mad whirl of fists and boots. You need have small fear that the job will be bungled. But it is a matter of complaint among the boys of the Walk, that if they do a bit of bashing for a toff and get caught, the toff seldom has the magnanimity to give them a lift when they come out of gaol.

The Hooligan is by no means deficient in courage. He is always ready to fight, though he does not fight fair. It must, indeed, require a certain amount of courage to earn your living by taking things that do not belong to you, with the whole of society, backed by the police force, against you. The burglar who breaks into your house and steals your goods is a reprehensible person; but he undoubtedly possesses that two-o'clock-in-the-morning courage which is the rarest variety. To get into a stranger's house in the dead of night, listening every instant for the least sound that denotes detection, knowing all the time that you are risking your liberty for the next five years or so—this, I am sure, requires more nerve than most men can boast of. Young Alf has nearly all the vices; but he has plenty of pluck. And as I shall have very little to disclose that is to his credit, I must tell of one instance in which his conduct was admirable. One afternoon we were at the Elephant and Castle, when suddenly a pair of runaway horses, with a Pickford van behind them, came pounding into the traffic at the crossing. There was shouting, screaming and a scurrying to clear the way, and then I saw young Alf standing alone, tense and waiting, in the middle of the road. It was a perilous thing to do, but he did it. He was used to horses, and though they dragged him for twenty yards and more, he hung on, and brought them up. A sympathetic and admiring crowd gathered, and young Alf was not a little embarrassed at the attention he commanded.

'The firm oughter reckernize it,' said a man in an apron, looking round for approval. 'There's a matter of two 'underd pound's worth of prop'ty that boy's reskid.'

We murmured assent.

'I don't want no fuss,' said Young Alf, glancing quickly around him.

Just then a man ran up, panting, and put his hand over the harness. Then he picked up the reins, and, hoisting himself by the step, peered into his van.

'You're in luck today, mister,' said a boy.

The man passed the back of his hand across a damp forehead, and sent a dazed look through the crowd.

'One of them blarsted whistles started 'em,' he said.

'That's the boy what stopped 'em,' said a woman with a basket pointing a finger at young Alf.

'That's awright,' muttered young Alf. 'You shut yer face.'

'Give the gentleman your name,' persisted the woman with the basket, 'and if everybody 'ad their rights—'

'Now then,' said a friendly policeman, with a hand on young Alf's shoulder, 'you give him your name and address. You want a job, you know. You bin out of work too long.'

Young Alf's brain must have worked very quickly for the next three seconds, and he took the right course. He told the truth. It required an effort. But, as the policeman seemed to know the truth, it would have been silly to tell a lie.

The next day young Alf had the offer of employment, if he would call at headquarters. For a day or two he hesitated. Then he decided that it was not good enough. And that night he went to another kip. By this time he might have been driving a Pickford van. But he never applied for the job.

Regular employment, at a fixed wage, does not attract the boy who is bred within sound of the hawkers in the Walk. It does not give him the necessary margin of leisure, and the necessary margin of chance gains. Many of them hang on to the edge of legitimate commerce as you may see them adhering to the tail-boards of vans; and a van-boy has many opportunities of seeing the world. The selling of newspapers is a favourite occupation. Every Lambeth boy can produce a profession in answer to magisterial interrogation. If you ask young Alf—very suddenly—what his business is, he will reply that he is a horse-plaiter. With time for reflection he may give quite a different answer, according to the circumstances of the case, for he has done many things; watch-making, domestic service, and the care of horses in a travelling circus, have stored his mind with experience and given his fingers deftness.

Young Alf is now eighteen years of age, and stands 5 feet 7 inches. He is light, active and muscular. Stripped for fighting he is a picture. His ordinary attire consists of a dark-brown suit, mellowed by wear, and a cloth cap. Around his neck is a neatly-knotted neckerchief, dark blue, with white spots, which does duty for collar as well as tie. His face is by no means brutal; it is intelligent, and gives evidence of a highly-strung nature. The eyes are his most remarkable feature. They seem to look all round his head, like the eyes of a bird; when he is angry they gleam with a fury that is almost demoniacal. He is not prone to smiles or laughter, but he is in no sense melancholic. The solemnity of his face is due rather, as I should conclude, to the concentration of his intellect on the practical problems that continually present themselves for solution. Under the influence of any strong emotion, he puffs out the lower part of his cheeks. This expresses even amusement, if he is very much amused. In his manner of speech he exhibits curious variations. Sometimes he will talk for ten minutes together, with no more trace of accent or slang than disfigure the speech of the ordinary Londoner of the wage-earning class. Then, on a sudden, he will become almost unintelligible to one unfamiliar with the Walk and its ways. He swears infrequently, and drinks scarcely at all. When he does, he lights a fire in the middle of the floor and tries to burn the house down. His health is perfect, and he has never had a day's illness since he had the measles. He has perfect confidence in his own ability to look after himself, and take what he wants, so long as he has elbow-room and ten seconds' start of the cop. His fleetness of foot has earned him the nickname of 'The Deer' in the Walk. On the whole, few boys are better equipped by nature for a life on the crooked, and Young Alf has sedulously cultivated his natural gifts.

Clarence Rook

Billy the Snide

So young Alf took service with Billy the Snide, and felt that he had his foot well on the first rung of the ladder whereby a boy may mount to an honoured old age as a publican or a fence.

On the evening after the conversation recounted in the previous chapter I pushed open the swing-door of the public house off the Walk, and found young Alf engaged in conversation with the can. He nodded to me, and led the way through the door at the far end of the bar. As I reached the door, I caught the eye of the can.

'Same line?' he said, jerking his head towards the door through which young Alf has disappeared.

'Just at present,' I replied.

I was not quite certain for the moment as to his meaning, but I think I told the truth. For the present young Alf and I were a pair of literary men.

We had the pleasant room to ourselves, for we were rather early, and there was a race-meeting somewhere in the neighbourhood of London, and the boys had not yet returned to town.

'I been finkin'!' said young Alf, rubbing his close-cropped head with a grimy hand. 'I said I'd tell you 'ow we worked the biz, me an' Billy, an' I fink I can remember most about it.'

'What was his real name?' I asked.

He hesitated for a few moments.

'Bill Day was 'is name,' he said presently. 'But we never called 'im nuffink but Billy, or Billy the Snide. Everybody'd know who you meant. If you'd sent a tallygram to 'im by that name, 'e'd a' got it. But you couldn't tallygraft to Billy no more. His number's up awright, wiv no error.'

Bill, as I have implied, has pegged out, a victim to sundry

disorders, mostly of his own creating. I inquired of his appearance in the flesh, but young Alf, though frequently graphic in the delineation of events, is not an adept at describing personalities. It was only by careful cross-examination that I gained any idea of Billy the Snide's outward aspect, and my idea may differ entirely from the photograph which has been buried somewhere in Scotland Yard. I have the impression of a man above the middle height, clean shaven, of stern and perhaps forbidding exterior; a man who limped slightly in one foot, owing to a sudden leap from a first-floor window on to the area railings; a man observant, but reticent; a man who said nothing but what he meant to be believed; a man who always wore a bowler hat. Such is the impression of Billy the Snide that I have brought away. It is too meagre. I regret exceedingly that I never saw him before he snuffed out, for he was a leader of men, and his memory is still green in the Walk, where there is nothing green but is plucked.

Billy the Snide was in a pretty big way of business; he did not, you will understand, depend on his day's takings for the price of his kip. He was the owner of a pony and a barrow, as well as of a missus. He managed to feed and clothe himself, as well as certain people who had a more or less illegal claim upon him on the margin of profit left by counterfeit half-crowns, enjoying, too, ample intervals of leisure. Karl Alley was his address. Karl Alley lies cheek-by-jowl with Irish Court, runs off China Walk, and is a nasty corner for a green hand to find himself in after dark. Here Billy the Snide had a room; and by means of a few simple appliances he imitated the products of the Mint. But snide coin takes a bit of passing, and Billy was glad of the help of a smart youngster, who had done something class in the way of nicking to show he was up to the work; a youngster, too, whose appearance disarmed suspicion, for young Alf tells me that, in those days his face was almost saintly in its purity more especially when he was permitted to wear an Eton suit. We may suspect that a touch of worldliness was added to his aspect when he wore his new overcoat and his new cap, and was smoking a cigar.

Henceforth, for a few days of crowded life, it was the office of young Alf to throw bad money after good. He still lived with his mother and the acrobat, but every morning he went round to Karl Alley to arrange the work for the day; and there was a lot of jealousy among the boys who had never got beyond tea-leafing, which is creditable, but not class. He looks back upon this period of his life with considerable pride, for promotion went by merit alone in the circle of which Billy the Snide was the centre, and no boy would have been taken on to work with him unless he had given evidence of capacity. Young Alf was not yet thirteen, and very young to occupy so responsible a position of trust.

So young Alf was a proud boy when he turned into Karl Alley on the first morning of his engagement, and sought out the dwelling of his chief.

In order to try his hand and acquire confidence, young Alf was sent out on a small job alone. Billy the Snide produced a wrong 'un, and bade young Alf plant it at a big house near the Walk—the house to which you take mugs who have been marked for skinning.

Young Alf set forth, while Billy the Snide awaited the result in Karl Alley. It was nervous work, for young Alf was aware that they knew a bit at that house; moreover, he felt that his future depended on his present success. He waited a bit outside until he saw through the swing-doors that the can was busy. Then he entered, gave his order, planked his bull's-eye on the counter, and came out with four and elevenpence change.

Billy the Snide expressed approval, gave young Alf a shilling for himself, and for the next day proposed an expedition on a far more sumptuous scale.

The next morning they started, a pleasant family party, from the Walk, in Billy the Snide's pony-barrow; Billy and the missus in front, and young Alf sitting on the empty baskets at the tail-board. You would have said, had you met them trotting along the Brixton Road, that they were going to market. Indeed, Billy the Snide was wont to describe himself, when publicly invited to declare his occupation, as a general dealer.

Round Brixton, Stockwell and Clapham they drove on a career of uninterrupted prosperity, pulling up at public houses, and now and then at a likely-looking small shop. The best kind of small shop is one which is looked after by a woman whose husband is working elsewhere. Meanwhile Billy's right-side trouser pocket was growing rapidly lighter, and the left one, containing honest metal, was pleasantly heavy. Young Alf, too, had half-a-sovereign as his own share in his waistcoat pocket.

It was past noon when they reached Wandsworth Common, and Billy the Snide pulled up the pony at a house he had decided to

THE POLYTECHNIC OF WALES
LIBRARY
TREFOREST

work. Young Alf and the missus entered together, while Billy the Snide remained without by the pony-barrow so as to be ready in case of a scoot.

'What are you takin', missus?' asked young Alf.

The missus said that her call was for the usual—half-a-quartern of gin and two out. Young Alf slashed down a bull's-eye for the drink and the can, being suspicious, picked it up and put his lamps over it. Young Alf, being about to gargle, set down his glass.

'Missus, we're rumbled,' he said.

For the can had walked up to the bung with the coin, and the bung was walking with the coin to the tester. The tester was consulted, and for answer split the bull's-eye into halves.

The bung slid up to young Alf and the missus.

'That's a bad 'un,' said the bung, holding out the two halves of the detected coin. 'D'you know that?'

'Bad!' exclaimed young Alf.

'Good Gawd! To think of that!' said the missus, looking struck all of a heap.

'Well, guv'nor,' said young Alf, 'I'm in for a bit of a loss out of my 'ard week's graft froo that coin gettin' in wiv the uvvers; an' if I've got any more I shall look what ho!'

Young Alf pulled from his waistcoat pocket the half thick 'un which was his share of the profits.

'D'you mind puttin' one of these in the fake?' said young Alf.

The coin was put through the tester and came out intact Whereupon the bung reckoned it was a shame that young Alf should have been taken in with the five-shilling piece.

'It's very kind of you to symperfize wiv us, boss,' said Young Alf, finishing his ginger-beer.

'Now you 'ave one with me,' said the bung, looking at the empty glasses.

The missus said she would have another of the same. But young Alf, noting the sudden absence of the can, concluded that he had gone for a cop. It was clear that the bung was having some of his old swank.

'Step short, missus,' said young Alf. And wishing the bung 'good-afternoon', they scooted.

'It didn't take us 'arf a mo to shift soon as joinin' Billy,' said young Alf in concluding his narrative of the day's adventures. 'An' sharper'n any cop ever put down 'is daisy roots, we was round the corner an' out of sight.'

Altogether it was a day of pleasure and of profit.

To this succeeded three days of joy and gain; days on which young Alf viewed the world as it stretched southward to Denmark Hill, and eastward to the 'Bricklayer's Arms', sitting proudly upon the empty baskets at the tail of Billy the Snide's pony barrow. Impartially and conscientiously they worked South London; and young Alf's share of the swag ran into something like fifteen shillings a day, on the average. Young Alf confesses that these were among the happiest days of his life, for fresh air is good, and driving is good, and fifteen shillings a day is very good indeed, so long as it lasts; much better than three-and-six a week as an honest errand-boy.

'I don't ever fink I made more'n that since, not day in, day out,' said young Alf, as he told me the story of the six days.

But success made them reckless. The fifth day was the last of triumph. It was down Battersea way that the last victory was scored, a victory that led to defeat. I would not spoil young Alf's artless story; it must be given in his own words, as he told it to me in that pleasant room behind the bar of the public house off Lambeth Walk. He told it, sitting well forward in his chair, with quick glances this way and that way, and with no turn of the head all the time, his hands between his knees, and his cap bunched in his hands.

'Gettin' well down into Battersea,' said young Alf, 'Billy marked a small shop where there was a ole woman be'ind the counter. So he give me the wheeze, an' says, "You slip in there, cocker". An' presently he pulls up the pony, and I nips back an' goes into the shop. The ole woman was stannin' be'ind the counter.

'"'Arf-a-dozen eggs, missus, an' new laid," I says. "We always keep 'em fresh," says the ole woman. "Well, I want 'em for some-one that's snuffin' it," I told 'er. "Wort you mean?" she chipped in, not 'ankin'. "Well, peggin' out," I eggsplained. So she says, "Dyin', I s'pose you mean", an' 'andin' me the wobblers. Down I planks a two-hog piece, an' she picked it up an' fair screamed. "That's bad," she calls out. "I've 'ad one like it afore today," she says—the old geezer. "Bad, missus!" I says. "I'd like to 'ave a cartload of 'em."

'She didn't say nuffink to that, but she turned round and called out to somebody in the parlour be'ind the shop, an' out comes a bloke wiv a razzo like 'arf a boiled beetroot, or I don't know nuffink about it. Looked as if you wouldn't like to pay for the 'arf of what 'e could lower. Well, ole ruby boko put 'is lamps over me, wiv no error, an' he says, "Why you're the youngster as come in 'ere afore." An' wiv that he picks up the snide. Then I chips in. "Well," I says, "then you can testerfy to my respecterability." 'Cause, you unnerstand, I 'adn't never bin wivin 'arf-a-mile of the shop in me life. "The money's bad," he goes on, runnin' it over 'tween 'is fingers.

'So then I made out as if I was cross, and I says, "What the bleedin' 'ell d'you mean?" I says. "If you finks I've cheated you, or if you finks I've tried to cheat you, then send for the p'lice," I says. Course I see my game, 'cause old ruby boko was 'tween me an' the door. See?'

Young Alf shot a cunning glance at me; and, after a moment's reflection, I saw.

Young Alf leaned well forward in his chair and puffed out his cheeks, whence I inferred an amusing reminiscence. Then he continued his story.

'Wiv that out 'e goes, an' pulls the door of the shop be'ind 'im, so's to cage me while 'e fetches the cops; an' that's a pretty long job, as a general rule. Course that was just what I wanted. In 'arf a mo I was over the counter an' slashin' at the ole woman. Caught 'er one under the chib, an' she give a scream, an' dropped on to the floor like a wet sack. There wasn't no one else in the 'ouse, so I got to work quick, and went froo the till. It wasn't much of a 'aul— nuffink to talk about. I don't fink there was more'n free twoers worf to be nicked. But it was worf more'n bein' pinched, eh? Well, I was out of the shop in a tick, an' there was Billy an' the missus on the pony-barrer, carm and peaceful, jest up by the corner where the road turns off. Course I give Billy the wheeze quick as I could, an' 'e whips up the pony jest as I 'opped up be'ind. An' jest as we drove off there was old ruby boko about a 'undred yards away, running as fast as the cop could keep time to wiv 'is plates o' meat. See?'

But as I have already said, this was the last day of triumph for Billy the Snide, who was pretty well at the end of his tether. There are some things that even the police force cannot overlook, and the doings of Billy were crying to Heaven. Over-production, it seems, was the bane of Billy the Snide. Not content with doing a moderate and comparatively safe retail trade, Billy had made haste to be rich, and had placed a nice little lot of snide money with a pal. There was bad management somewhere, for the pal had been putting it about over the same ground which Billy and young Alf were covering; and the splits were on the look-out.

It was on the following day that the catastrophe came about.

'Never you carry snide coin on your person, 'cept when you want to put it about,' said young Alf, as he told me the story of Billy's downfall. 'An' if you fink you've incurred suspicion, you frow it all away quick as you can. Never mind 'ow much it is. Frow it away. You can 'ford that more'n you can 'ford doing a stretch. An' if they don't find nuffink on your person, why, they can't do nuffink to you. See? You can say it was a mistake, you 'avin' a snide coin at all. See?'

Disregard of this advice, which had been given to him by Billy the Snide, nearly cost young Alf his liberty on that fatal morning. He was coming round as usual to Billy's residence to organize the day's graft, flushed with the pride of success, and carrying in his pocket a quantity of base metal which would have represented about the value of a sovereign had it been honest money. As he was about to turn into Karl Alley he was suddenly aware of a split hanging about. To give Billy the wheeze was to give himself away. Young Alf had decided to go home again and wait upon events, when he found himself rushed before he could turn round. A copper took him off to the police station.

The situation looked desperate, for a pound's worth of snide coin is difficult to explain away; and young Alf felt pretty certain that the game was up.

But his luck did not desert him. When they reached the police station the inspector happened to have stepped out for a few moments, so young Alf was dabbed into a cell to await his return.

This was his opportunity, and he did not neglect it. No sooner was the door closed, than he cleared the snide coin out of his pockets, and pitched it into the most obvious receptacle.

'I knew it was awright then,' said young Alf. 'I jest 'ad time to go froo a bit of a double-shuffle step on the floor of the cell—showin' I wasn't disturbed in me mind, you unnerstand—and then the cop came to take me before the inspector, an' run me froo to see what I 'ad on my person. That's what they say in evidence, y' know.

'Course they didn't find any snide coin on me person, an' as I 'adn't anyfink in the way of good money, it was a case of bein' clean picked. I never see a copper look so seprised in all me born days; looked as if you might 'ave brought 'im down wiv 'arf a brick. The inspector 'e was jest knocked sick, 'e was. Fort they'd got me proper that time, they did. But I reckon if I 'aven't got any sharpness of me own, I got 'old of a little bit of someone else's that time, eh?'

I replied that the incident did him infinite credit.

Young Alf pinched the end of his cigar, and put the stump into his waistcoat pocket.

'So you got off?' I said.

'The inspector told me I could 'ook it,' said young Alf. 'But d' you fink I was going like that? Not me. Not wivout giving 'em some-fink thick in the way of slanging. "What d'yer mean?" I says. "What d'yer mean by interferin' wiv a 'ard-working boy in the performance of 'is employment? I can tell you," I says, "I got my livin' to look after; and now I lost me morning's work jest because a silly swine of a cop don't know a honest boy from a thief. An' I can tell you straight," I says, "I don't get rabbit-pie fair chucked at me, neither."'

That was enough. They bundled him out of the police station by main force. For if you want to make a copper very angry indeed, you have only to mention to him the name of rabbit-pie. It has the same effect on a policeman as an allusion to puppy-pie has on a Thames bargeman. This is one of the many things that young Alf knows.

I inquired the reason of this strange aversion.

'Gives a cop the indigestion,' explained young Alf, 'even if you only talk to 'im about it. But I don't believe anyone that know'd a p'liceman personally would ever think of fool'in 'im wiv such a snack. Rabbit-pie might do for fillin' up odd corners, but if you arst 'im to make a banquet off it, why, 'e wouldn't be takin' any.'

I think there must be some better explanation than that.

But Karl Alley knew Billy the Snide no more. The cops rushed him while young Alf was being run through at the police station.

'Billy the Snide an' 'is missus bofe fell,' said young Alf, as he recounted the melancholy story; 'an' for a week or two it was a case of looking round and about for your 'umble. But I laid low, an' the pair of 'em, 'avin' been before the beak twice on remand froo me bein' wanted to make the party complete, they was sent for trial.'

It was a terrible set-back for young Alf, who was just beginning to get on; the more especially as Billy had taught him only how to pass snide coin, and not how to make it.

Young Alf had pitched away his stock of base money, and had very little of the ordinary kind. Nevertheless, he kept a brave heart, knowing that a boy who had worked with Billy the Snide could not long be out of employment. Meanwhile, he sold newspapers outside Waterloo Station, and kept his eyes skinned for chances.

In the evening papers he read how Billy and the missus came up for trial; how Billy was given an eight years' stretch, while the missus had a twelvemonth that she could call her own, and no one else's; how Billy, undaunted by his fate, made the approved retort —that he could do that little lot on his napper, and was thereafter removed from the sight of men.

Billy the Snide has, as I have said, snuffed out. But he was a good 'un in his time. He gave young Alf his start, taught him many useful wheezes, and was not ungenerous in the division of swag; and young Alf always speaks very nicely about him.

Slang and Phoneticized Words

abart about
accerabat acrobat
acourse of course
agen ⎱ 1 against 2 again
agin ⎰
alwis always
amarnts amounts
'ankin' understanding
anuvver another
anythink anything
'arf a mo half a moment, hold on, take it easy
argufyin' arguing
arsk ⎤
arst ⎬ ask
arx ⎦
arst asked
arter after
at whiles sometimes
auf off
aweer aware
awright alright
awse horse

babby ⎱ baby
bebby ⎰
barrer barrow
barstud bastard

beak magistrate
bilk to cheat or swindle
biz business, any criminal pursuit
bofe both
boko nose
bonnick bonnet
booze to drink
borrer borrow
bosky drunk
bull's-eye 1 a crown piece 2 lantern
bung landlord of a pub

call to order drinks
can 1 barman 2 victim or mug
cawst cost
charing floor-washing
chatter-mag someone who talks a great deal, (a mixture of chatter-box and magpie)
chib mouth
chimbley chimney
chip to chaff, make fun of
chip in to interject or interrupt
chist chest

Chris'mus Christmas
close clothes
clurk clerk
cocker mate or friend
cop hold to seize
cos because
crib, crack a to break into a
   house
curick curate
curtings curtains

daisy roots boots
darn down
dessay daresay
dial face
diptheery diphtheria
doncher don't you
dorg dog
doy die
druv drove, driven

'edn't hadn't
effeck effect
elingphant elephant
enkirridge encourage
'ern her own, hers
'ev have
extry extra
ez as

fake, on the involved in any
   criminal pursuit
farden farthing
fat, to chuck one's f. about
   to talk loudly and
   ignorantly
feer fair
fence receiver of stolen goods
fer
fur } 1 for 2 far
fink think

flush well-off, wealthy
'ford afford
'fore before
fort thought
free three
frippence threepence
froo through
frow throw
furreigners foreigners
fust first

game, to make g. of to tease
garn 'go on!'
git get
gizzard, to fret one's to
   worry oneself
go auf (off) 1 to die 2 to
   miscarry
gorne gone
graft work
green hand green-horn, an
   innocent or non-criminal
   person
guv gave

hap fortune, good luck

impidence impudence
Injer India
inkerridge encourage
'isself himself

kennel gutter
kid to joke or tease
kip 1 home, room or bed
   2 to live or sleep
knoo knew
knowed known, knew

lagged arrested
lamps eyes

lawst last
lifer life imprisonment
linning linen
loy lie

mikin' about mucking about
mindjer mind you
mopy sulky, unhappy
mor'n more than
mouch to creep about
mug 1 face 2 fool
mulatter mulatto
muvver mother

napper head
nark to inform
necking drinking
nick to steal
nipper child
noo new
nyme name

oi I
old dutch wife
'ook it hook it, 1 to run away
 2 'Get away!'
'oo's who is
orful awful
'ow'm oi how am I
oye eye

passel a large number or group
pauped pauperized,
 poverty-stricken
pawse pass
peg out to die
pel pal
perlice police
perlite polite
perlitical political

pertendin' pretending
pianner piano
pinch 1 to steal 2 to
 arrest
pipple people
pisenin' poisoning
plant 1 to pass counterfeit
 money 2 to hide stolen
 goods
plates o' meat feet
plucked plucky, courageous
pork-wine port wine
pull, to get the p. of someone
 to get the better of
purtect protect
purtikler particular,
 particularly
pusson person
put away, to 1 to pawn
 something 2 to be buried
 3 to imprison or be
 imprisoned

quisby ill, out of sorts

rabbit pie exact meaning
 unclear; *rabbit pie shifter*
 was a late-nineteenth-century
 slang term for a policeman
raws bare fists
razzo nose
reckernize recognize
reskid rescued
resky rescue
respeck respect
rinin' raining
rumble to find out, discover
 or realize something

scoot to run away

sech such
seed saw, seen
set-out a to-do or fuss
seving seven
sez says, said
Sheeny Jew
shime shame
shop pawnshop
shutcher shut your
sims seems
skin to rob or fleece
slop policeman
smitch off to run away, abscond
snide counterfeit money
snipe a contemptible person
snuff it/out to die
soigh sigh
somefink ⎱
some'ink ⎰ something
sorft soft
sot drunkard
spank, up the at the pawnbroker's
spiles spoils
split detective
sport to stand treat
s'powse suppose
srimps and creases shrimps and cresses
stannin' standing
stooards stewards
stopt stopped
stow kiddin' stop joking
stretch one year, especially a prison sentence
swag stolen goods
swank 1 to pretend
  2 showy behaviour or speech

symperfy sympathy

tallygraft telegraphed
tallygram telegram
tea-leafing thieving
temp'ry temporary
testerfy testify
thort thought
tike take
tross, sling yer go away, a variant of the more common 'sling your hook'
tumble to understand or perceive something
twoer florin
two-hog two shillings

'ud would
'underd hundred
uvver other

wax up to mess up
wen when
weskit waistcoat
wet drink
wheeze plan or idea
wike wake
winder window
wink, to tip the to warn or signal by winking
wobblers eggs
worf worth
wot what
wrong 'un a dud coin
wuship worship
wuz was

yer(s) you(rs)
yuss yes
yut yet

Bibliographical Note

Arthur Morrison's 'A Street' was first published in *Macmillan's Magazine*, October 1891, and reprinted, with some alterations, as the introduction to *Tales of Mean Streets* (1894); 'Lizerunt' was first published, in part, in the *National Observer*, 22 July 1893, and the complete version in *Tales of Mean Streets*. Rudyard Kipling's 'The Record of Badalia Herodsfoot' was first published in *Harper's Weekly*, 15 and 22 November 1890, and reprinted in *Many Inventions* (1893). George Gissing's 'Lou and Liz' was first published in the *English Illustrated Magazine*, August 1893, and reprinted in *A Victim of Circumstance* (1927). The remainder of the stories in this anthology are taken from the following volumes: Henry Nevinson, 'The St George of Rochester' and 'Sissero's Return' *Neighbours of Ours* (1894); Edwin Pugh, 'The First and Last Meeting of the M.S.H.D.S.' and 'A Small Talk Exchange' *A Street in Suburbia* (1895), 'The Inevitable Thing' *King Circumstance* (1898); Arthur St John Adcock, 'At the Dock Gates' *East End Idylls* (1897); Clarence Rook, 'Young Alf', 'Concerning Hooligans' and 'Billy the Snide' *The Hooligan Nights* (1899).

Suggestions for Further Reading

Fiction

ADCOCK, ARTHUR ST JOHN, *In the Image of God*, 1898.
BESANT, WALTER, *All Sorts and Conditions of Men*, 1882.
GISSING, GEORGE, *The Nether World*, 1889.
MAUGHAM, W. SOMERSET, *Liza of Lambeth*, 1897.

MOORE, GEORGE, *Esther Waters*, 1894.
MORRISON, ARTHUR, *A Child of the Jago*, 1896.
MORRISON, ARTHUR, *To London Town*, 1899.
MORRISON, ARTHUR, *The Hole in the Wall*, 1902.
PUGH, EDWIN, *Mother-Sister*, 1900.
RIDGE, WILLIAM PETT, *Mord Em'ly*, 1898.

Literary and Social Background

BARNETT, HENRIETTA, *Canon Barnett*, 1918.
BESANT, WALTER, *East London*, 1901.
BROME, VINCENT, *Four Realist Novelists*, Writers and Their Work Series, 1965.
EMPSON, WILLIAM, 'Proletarian Literature', *Some Versions of Pastoral*, 1935.
FINDLATER, JANE, 'The Slum Movement in Fiction', *Stones from a Glass House*, 1904.
FRIERSON, W. C., *The English Novel in Transition 1885–1940*, New York, 1965.
INGLIS, K. S., *Churches and the Working Classes in Victorian England*, 1963.
KEATING, P. J., 'Arthur Morrison: A Biographical Study', introduction to *A Child of the Jago*, 1969.
KEATING, P. J., *The Working Classes in Victorian Fiction*, 1971.
LONDON, JACK, *The People of the Abyss*, 1902.
LYND, HELEN, *England in the Eighteen-Eighties*, 1945.
PIMLOTT, J. A. R., *Toynbee Hall*, 1935.
ORWELL, GEORGE, 'Charles Dickens', *Inside the Whale*, 1940.
WEBB, BEATRICE, *My Apprenticeship*, 1926.